EMBRACE the *Fire*

Spring Stevens

CRIMSON ROMANCE

F+W Media, Inc.

This edition published by
Crimson Romance
an imprint of F+W Media, Inc.
10151 Carver Road, Suite 200
Blue Ash, Ohio 45242
www.crimsonromance.com

Copyright © 2013 by Spring Stevens

ISBN 10: 1-4405-6811-1
ISBN 13: 978-1-4405-6811-4
eISBN 10: 1-4405-6812-X
eISBN 13: 978-1-4405-6812-1

Cover art © 123rf.com

Chapter 1

Varick rarely ever dreamed, but as the first rays of the sun peeked over the horizon, images of people he had never known swam to his unconscious mind's eye. Their skin glowed iridescently, transparent right down to their souls. Smoky balls of shadow swirled inside the glow and clawed at their transparent prisons and screamed for release. Their sorrows and pains were magnified by the predominance of unrequited fury and unobtainable justice of their ills.

Dancing and swirling around those unfamiliar faces were black flames and daggers, the same daggers that graced his skin as trademarks of his immortal profession. He was a Destroyer, protector of the One Race and the humans, and bringer of death to the demon spawn of the Underworld. He was one of many but here, in this dream turned nightmare, he was bitterly and utterly alone.

The swirling images settled, the landscape in the mist manifesting under his feet, glowing with the vivid greens and blues of some lost jungle. Swathed in white silk and flowing robes, his form appeared atop a towering mountain minutes before dawn. Known for his unshakable logic and meticulous approach to any situation, he swallowed hard, realizing his insides trembled and his hands shook.

Directly below the peak, hundreds of writhing vampires screamed in agony as the sun rose without mercy, slowly spreading the deadly golden hue. Their dead eyes looked up to him as they tried to claw their way into the ground. And those empty, dead eyes seemed to beg him for deliverance, even if it was at the end of his sword. A quick death by sword was degrees better than suffering the flaming torch of the sun.

And he stood as stone, watching and uncaring.

He twisted violently in his bed of black satin sheets. His mouth opened as if to scream. His long incisors gleamed in the darkness of his chambers as his back arched up from the bed. Still deep in the dream, he watched helplessly as his own skin began to melt and drip from his bleached-white bones. His ashes flew into the four winds and disappeared with the blinding sun's rays.

His eyes flew open, thankful they were looking into the blackness of his chambers. He clutched at his chest, his heart racing wildly.

Jackknifing off of the bed, Varick ran his shaking hands through his long, white hair. He strode across the windowless room, his topaz eyes seeing clearly in the pitch black. He reached for a glass and a bottle of brandy as he tried to collect himself. He swallowed hard, much harder than he had in the dream. Brandy was his preferred drink, blood was his necessary nutrient, and death was but a bittersweet dream.

Laughter rang out as he settled his thoughts. Death? Indeed!

He had experienced it once, and now he wondered when he would experience it again—even immortality had its end. Would his soul ever know peace? Or would Gyth capture it again, as he had so many years ago, when Varick had met his first death?

"Your dreams plague you," a detached voice echoed around his room.

Cursing profusely, Varick spun around, barely managing to keep the glass in his hand. With a soft growl, he bowed slightly as Gyth appeared in the same long, white robes Varick had been wearing in the dreams. Suspicion crept up his spine as the god raised his hand and the overhead lights flooded the concrete and steel dwelling.

This was his sanctuary. It was deep underground and almost out of everyone's radars. All except for Gyth, of course.

"You're shaking," Gyth stated flatly as he turned and inspected the chambers where Varick slept. "Do your dreams often plague you?"

The only time they didn't plague him was when he was blissfully intoxicated. Currently, he was extremely sober, but as soon as Gyth was gone, he was going to remedy that.

Gods, how many years had he been a Destroyer?

Two thousand, almost to the day. He thought back to the time when there had been ten Destroyers, ten who hunted the vampire, the witch, and the werewolf. For over a thousand years, the ten of them had killed without mercy, without pause, and without regret. Humanity had flourished easily with the decline of the demons, their sightings diminishing so much so that the humans had eventually considered the demons myths.

"What do you want?"

"Destroyer," Gyth grunted. "You're not your usual self. I'll forgive you this one insolence, but dare not to make another."

Trying to keep from rolling his eyes, Varick set the glass down. "Alexander is our leader—why come to me? I'm just a Destroyer, and I follow his orders."

"He is only because you refused to accept leadership." Gyth sat on the edge of Varick's bed, looking completely out of place. "Tell me, Varick—being part vampire, does that bother you? Does destroying other vampires plague you?"

A slow burn of bitterness welled up inside his heart. "How do you refuse to answer a god?"

"You don't."

Gritting his teeth, Varick brought the glass to his lips and swallowed. "There's not one day that passes in my long life that I regret slaughtering any of them—not vampire, not werewolf, and not witch. And until I meet my end, I'll continue doing so."

"Why, then, do you have these dreams that make your hands shake? You're a meticulous, calculating Destroyer, eager for battle and eager for the hunt of my enemies, yet when in the confines of your privacy, you have trouble sleeping." Gyth stood, his robes pooling at his feet. "It seems highly illogical."

Biting back his pride, Varick took a deep breath and nodded. "Seems that way."

"I'll leave you with some advice, wanted or not."

Perhaps he had not heard the god correctly, or maybe he was still dreaming.

"Advice?" Varick laughed bitterly. "I don't need your advice!"

"Careful, Destroyer. You threaten to step across a line that will lead you down a paved road to punishment."

"Don't you mean pain? Because that is, after all, what you do when we defy you or threaten your tyranny." Varick stepped toe-to-toe with the white-haired god. "I already kill for you—what else you want? My blood? Oh, wait, you got that already when you let me drain dry before I was reborn. My sworn oath? Oh no, you got that too. Let me guess—my skin hanging in your bedroom?"

A rumble of power echoed around the room as the Destroyer was lifted from his feet and slammed into the concrete and steel wall with unseen hands. Gyth grunted and held him against the wall with his powers.

Releasing him, Gyth announced nonchalantly. "For the next several weeks, perhaps months, you'll find yourself under distress as the Mating Rite lays siege upon your body."

As his backside hit the floor, Varick groaned, letting his head fall back against the wall with a thump. "What? No, I can't go through that."

With a smirk and a quick laugh, Gyth answered. "You already are. Accept it as it is and don't fight it. The more you fight it, the worse it will be."

The Mating Rite was every Destroyer's eventual torture. It was nature's simple way of taking them down a notch or two. The need to mate would overwhelm him, and his control would slowly melt away and leave him depressingly needful of a woman. According to Gyth, the Mating Rite was a necessary evil, the consequence of being reborn.

Must not be his lucky century.

"Why?" he grumbled under his breath. "Why did you come here?"

The god shrugged. "Morbid curiosity."

Slowly, Varick stood. "Curiosity about what?"

Facing the Destroyer, Gyth narrowed his golden eyes. "Why do you not want to be the leader of my Destroyers?"

Destroyers. They were created by Gyth to protect the One Race, a race of people who resided on earth that were descendants of the gods. Members of the One Race were not considered true gods because they had only one parent that was. They were not allowed in the Heavens or in the Underworld. And there was always someone or something trying to eradicate the One Race. The Destroyers eliminated those threats.

Above protecting the One Race, the Destroyers were to obey Gyth, the king of the heavenly gods, in all things, no matter if those orders conflicted with protecting the One Race or not.

Of course, several pointed laws adhered to being a Destroyer. Do not stray into evil. Do not kill humans. Do not reveal your true nature to the humans. Do not rise against Gyth. Follow orders without pause.

"I'm not a leader. I'm a killer now, just as I was when you found me."

An odd expression lingered on the god's face. "Your hatred of your mother's race intrigues me."

"Does it? Then perhaps you should know that my hatred extends far beyond just the vampires. I hate everyone equally."

A muscle ticked in his strong jaw. "It keeps me indifferent and makes me a better killer."

"And this hatred," Gyth whispered. "Is eating at your soul."

Varick turned and spat out, "My soul? I lost my soul when I watched my mother…"

The words stuck in the back of his throat, his eyes burning. He wondered what in the nine hells was wrong with him as memories flooded his mind. Shaking his head, he turned back to the desk where he had set the glass and suddenly needed more of the potent sting of alcohol against the back of his throat.

Gyth, the Great Infallible One—not only was he a god; he was the head god, lord and king of the Heavens and Earth. He was an all-powerful, all-seeing, and all kinds of pain in the backside kind of guy. Yeah, well, the way Varick saw it, if Gyth was so all-powerful and lordly, why couldn't he take out all the demons himself?

He paused in his thoughts as Gyth vanished, blackness closing in, and for a mere breath of a second he wondered why Gyth had come to visit him and why he had announced that the Mating Rite was on his heels.

Who was he to try to understand a god? And why should he care to begin with? It was not in his preordained position to question the whys and how comes. He knew his path. He was a killer—always had been and always would be.

Looking down at his still-shaking hands, he cursed. He was out of his element, out of his usual demeanor, and he damn sure didn't like it. After all, why would a dream and an unusual visit from Gyth affect him this way? It shouldn't have. Yet it did.

Or perhaps it was the Mating Rite closing in? It had nothing to do with his vampire half, nor did it have anything to do with the memories of his long-dead mother. And it sure didn't have a damn thing to do with his past, his present, or his future.

He was what he was. Easy as that.

Agreeing to disagree with himself, he shelved his emotions and forced himself to get a grip. He was a Destroyer, well known for his flawless accuracy and unbending logic and control. He was not going to allow the Mating Rite or anything else to interfere with his life.

Turning on his heel, he grabbed the bottle from the desk and stretched his six-foot-six frame out onto his bed. His rebirth, the day he had become a Destroyer, lay in the back of his thoughts, and that was just where the hell he wanted it to stay. His life before his rebirth was not something he spoke of, nor did he want to rehash those bitter, burning memories.

Closing his eyes, he yawned, his incisors slipping back into their sheaths as sleep once again demanded his attention. The dawn did that to a Destroyer and, unfortunately, it did that to a half-breed vampire as well.

· · ·

The *Book of Creation* lay at the Tree of Life's deeply rooted trunk. The book's silver cover had been inscribed with the eight signs of the true zodiac in a perfect figure eight. The eight symbols depicted the original gods of Creation. Within the book's pages lay ancient knowledge that legions upon legions had fought and died for, that many a soul had given up home, family, and love for.

But the book was just one of many. Many that now needed to be found and brought together with the *Book of Creation*.

The book's caretaker stood on the edge of the small island, his black and silver robe softly fluttering against his long, powerful legs. Shrouded within his robes, his face was hidden, his emotions as unreadable as the wind. His demeanor was indifferent; his stance was that of a seasoned warrior, ever ready, ever deadly. There was but one purpose at all times, to protect and obey the written word of the *Book of Creation* at all costs and protect the Tree of Life.

The book's original owner and creator, an ancient god called Jaiden, was inconceivably missing and thought dead. He alone had protected the sacred words; he alone would have massacred the entire human and god-born races if the book so commanded.

Except now, the books were demanding Charon's attention.

Charon had lived on this island hidden in the translucent waters of the River Styx many years before the book had suddenly appeared. His only true companions were the Tree of Life, the book, and the River Styx. And here he had remained since the downfall of the Olympian gods, waiting, preparing, and watching until recently when he had felt the pull of Jaiden's soul.

The island floated in the invisible river that separated the Heavens, the Earth, and the Underworld; there was no better hiding place. He turned and stared at the silver palace towering above the granite hillside as his mind wandered with thoughts he had never had before. Thoughts that now puzzled him.

The robe covering his face fell away, his red eyes glowing in an ashen, yet beautiful face. With one hand curled around a red-and-black bone scythe, he held out the other and called forth the book. Hundreds of years had passed since he had read from the pages he so precariously protected.

One corner of his lip lifted as the book appeared open in his palm, eager for him to read. He watched the pages turn until midway a page fluttered, its soft glow shimmering as words appeared before his eyes. The translucent waters of the River Styx bubbled and whispered to him, a vortex of water opening at the edge of the island.

The page turned, the words churning in his mind as he slowly closed the book. The fate of the Universe hung in the balance of good and evil, dangled on many single choices, and Charon managed a cold laugh. And now the world's hope lay within the Destroyers' choices, as they had free will if they chose to use it.

He paused before turning to Styx.

Styx bubbled and gurgled around him announcing a visitor. Charon's eyebrow rose. No one had ever visited this place.

With a purple flash and a wisp of smoke, Terror Sky of the Elemental gods appeared before Charon in full dragon glory. Large red scales melted and molded into human flesh. His body contorted and decreased in size until standing before him was a man with long black hair and a single red braid hanging from his temple.

"What brings you to my world?" Charon asked suspiciously.

"As much as I don't want to trust you, Isten informs me that I must do so. He has seen a vision of a new age, insists that you be made aware of the importance of a male known as Varick. His destiny is uncertain, leaving the future uncertain as well."

"Yes, a new age is approaching, and soon these prison walls will crumble around us and the doorways will once again be opened." Charon's face shimmered, leaving behind the bleached white bones of a skull with red eyes. "Soon the tides will be set in motion, and the game shall begin. Only destinies chosen wisely will lead the sun to set on a new era."

"I have kept watch over Varick for many years." Terror Sky ran his hand through his long, dark hair. "He must be protected until the time comes for his decision."

Charon grinned under his hood. "A game of life and death. No doubt you're aware of his former life and what he'll become if the wrong decision is made."

Terror Sky narrowed his swirling eyes. "We must set things right and force the right decisions on these Destroyers if Isten's intended future is to be realized."

The book opened in Charon's hand as Terror Sky said, "Now is the perfect time to push Varick toward the life Isten intended for him."

Pointing a long talon at the words that had appeared in the book, Charon whispered, "This Varick Ta Farg, a half-breed vampire, must rise from his own ashes, choose a destiny that lies before him, and…" He paused as Styx rushed around him, causing small whirlpools to appear chaotically across the island. "And he will pave the road that will lead to salvation or destruction."

Terror Sky replied, "The fate of the world rests on a half-breed vampire's head. Are you prepared for that, Charon?"

Charon laughed. "The book has commanded, and I must obey."

"Someone is changing the words of Jaiden's books. I don't know how or why they do so, but they must be stopped before more harm befalls this universe."

"If the books are to be found, the *Book of Creation* will guide me to them," Charon stated.

Terror Sky paused, listening to the River Styx gurgling and swirling faster around the island. "Varick will have the power to restore the wrongs, but he must choose to do so freely."

Charon shook his head. "Perhaps his death will set things on the proper course."

"With my life, I'll protect him and his power even against the strongest of the gods." The Elemental's voice dropped dangerously low. "Even from that book and from you."

"I will not harm Varick at this time unless the book commands it—you can bet your immortality upon that."

"Or ever. Do we understand each other?" His silent threat hung in the air. "Or do I need to make myself perfectly clear on the subject?"

"Don't threaten me, Terror Sky."

"Harm one single thread of hair on his head, and you'll have no need to worry about your precious book!"

Abruptly the Elemental vanished, his telltale purple flash the only reminder of his presence. Charon laughed. Terror Sky's visit could only mean one thing. Whoever was meddling with Jaiden's books had to be found and stopped.

Styx churned with power as Charon stepped into the vortex of translucent water. Styx swept him up and cradled him as the Tree of Life groaned and settled deeper into the island's core, preparing itself for whatever might come.

Chapter 2

Angelica squirmed around in the uncomfortable leather chair as she waited for the club's manager to come into the dimly lit office. Out of habit, she twined her fingers around her long, black hair as she nervously fidgeted while she tried to get comfortable. She needed a second job, and this seemed to be the only one in the entire city that was available.

Angelica had never worked as a waitress, but hey, she would give it a try; she really needed the extra money, and when desperate times call, desperate measures answer. Well, truth be told, she might actually meet some people here who were not the stuffy bores she was unfortunately getting used to.

During the last six years, she had had a variety of part-time jobs that had not worked out at all, and things kept going from bad to worse every second she had her eyes open. Thankfully, the job at the Museum of Ancient Art had held steady, but even so, her paycheck just didn't cover all the bills she had to pay and to get her car fixed. Not to mention she was beginning to feel as dried up and crusty as the mummies in the Hall of Egypt.

Angelica took a deep breath and relaxed in the chair. She studied her well-shaped, long fingernails as her thoughts turned to home; it seemed so far away now. Gridhorn, Arkansas was probably the smallest town in the U.S, but it was home. "Comfortable and friendly" was what the welcome banner read when you drove into city limits. A chuckle escaped her lips as she fondly remembered the one traffic light in front of the courthouse that always seemed to be on the fritz.

Sure. Comfortable and friendly, but boring as hell.

She desperately missed her big brother. She smiled as his face came to mind. Oddly enough, he had been an adult when she was born.

He was overbearing, pig headed, and way the hell too protective most of the time. When she left home, he had nearly tied her to the ground to keep her from leaving. It was strange that since she had left, she had not once heard from him. A hard jerk from her heart shuddered through her body; even after six years, how could he still be pissed at her for leaving?

She shifted in her chair as the office door opened and a very slender, tall woman walked in. She was amazingly beautiful, almost ethereal. Her hair was a network of blonde highlights twisted in silky, auburn waves, and she had the bluest eyes; she probably wore contacts.

The woman smiled slowly as she studied Angelica's outstretched hand. "I prefer not to be touched. I do hope you won't be offended."

Angelica dropped her hand. "No, no I'm not offended."

"Good. I am Alera. I manage this club, and if you are the one that gets hired, there are a few basic rules you must be aware of."

Well, she was quick to get to the point. "Yeah, okay."

"First, call me Alera. Second, do as I say. Third, don't socialize with the customers unless instructed to do so. Fourth, don't drink while you are working. And, always do as I say. Do you understand?"

Angelica frowned as she stood. "Yes. I sure do understand. I didn't come here to be ordered around like a monkey on a string."

"Good." Alera pointed back to the chair. "Please, sit down. You have spunk and that's what it's going to take to be a waitress at this place."

Angelica squared her shoulders trying to release some of the tension in her neck as Alera sat down behind the old, Victorian-style desk. The woman seemed to fit right into the ancient-looking office. She took an ink pen from the desk drawer and pulled a sheet of paper from a file folder on the desktop. Angelica's gaze was drawn to the necklace around Alera's neck, and she caught her breath as she recognized the symbol on her pendant. Her fingers automatically went to her wrist, which was covered with a wide, silver bracelet.

Now, that was damn odd that this woman would be wearing a symbol Angelica had been born with. A symbol she could not explain.

"Full name?"

Sitting back down in the uncomfortable chair, she answered, "Angelica Dark."

Alera looked up with curiosity etched on her face. "Who was your father?"

Angelica looked away, but answered even though the question seemed ridiculous for an interview. "Feverand Dark." She turned back to Alera and tried to smile. "He died when I was born."

"That's a shame. Birthday?"

"June the twentieth, nineteen seventy."

Alera scribbled on the paper. "Have you ever been a waitress before?"

"No, but I'm willing to learn."

"Do you have another job at present?"

"Yes." Angelica sighed. "But I need a little supplemental income."

"Where else do you work?"

"At the local museum. I give tours and help with the bookkeeping. Is that a problem?"

"No, it's not as long as it doesn't interfere with your job requirements here." Alera paused and pulled out Angelica's application from the stack in her tray. "Pay here is pretty good and most regulars are great tippers. It says here you live at one twenty-two Hillsboro. That's a pretty nice part of the city."

Angelica nodded. "My father left it to me in his will."

"Oh, I see. I'm truly sorry about his death. I'm sure he was a good…" She paused oddly. "…man."

"I never knew him, but my brother says he was a loving father."

Alera smiled. "You have a brother?"

Angelica grinned and laughed. "Yeah."

"And your mother?" One light-colored eyebrow rose as she studied Angelica's features.

"He says she was the most beautiful woman in the world."

Alera grinned. "All men think there is none more beautiful than their mothers."

"Sometimes I wish I had a picture of her."

Alera frowned. "What was her name?"

"Antonia."

For a mere breath of a second, Angelica thought she saw a flicker of curiosity cross Alera's face, but it disappeared so quickly she was not so sure it had been there at all. Angelica patiently waited as Alera read her application.

"To be honest with you, you really don't seem like waitress material." Alera placed the application back in the folder. "There are other applicants better qualified."

Angelica retorted, "And you don't seem like club manager material."

"True enough. Now, do you have any questions?"

"Yeah, I have one." Angelica pointed to Alera's necklace. "Where did you get that and do you know if it stands for anything?"

"My necklace?" Alera ran her fingertips over the pendant. "It was a gift from my father. It is the symbol of my family."

"Why would the symbol for someone's family be on my wrist?" Angelica stood as she shook her head. "You know what? I don't think I am waitress material. Sorry to have wasted your time."

She heard Alera take a sharp intake of breath and watched in amazement as she stood and came around the desk. Her long, white dress swished around her ankles as she reached for Angelica's arm.

"Let me see the birthmark."

Angelica knitted her brows together. "Why?"

Alera grabbed her arm. "Let me see it now!"

Angelica jerked away and pulled her sleeve up, showing the woman her wrist. Alera's eyes widened as Angelica removed her bracelet. A bad feeling began creeping up Angelica's spine as Alera stared at her wrist.

Alera stepped back and pulled her sleeve up, as well. She held her wrist out next to Angelica's, and both women stared in disbelief. In the same spot on their wrists was a light blue triangle with two dots on each side of the top point. Now, how weird was that?

"Does your brother have this mark?"

"Y…yes he does."

"And your mother, did she have it as well?" continued Alera.

Fearful that she might stutter, Angelica whispered, "How the hell am I supposed to know? She died right after I was born."

"What do you know of her?"

The bad feeling she was having turned into an ache behind her eyes. "Why do you ask?"

Angelica watched as Alera nervously rubbed her hands together. She was suddenly very sure she needed some fresh air and a few blocks between this strange woman and herself.

Alera finally answered, "I had a sister that died almost thirty years ago. Her name was Antonia Dark."

"And you think my mother was your sister?" Angelica tried not to laugh, but it was ridiculous. "Look lady, I didn't know my mother. I don't even know what she looked like. All I have is her diary that's written in some kind of messed up language or code."

Alera looked at Angelica and sighed. "May I see the diary?"

Angelica gritted her teeth. Was this woman crazy? Seriously, did she expect her to just hand over the diary like it was yesterday's newspaper?

"I can't just give you her diary." Angelica managed to maintain her composure. "Do you have any idea just how creepy this interview has been?"

Alera slowly nodded. "Forgive me. I just thought that maybe, just maybe I had found one of her children."

Angelica took two steps back. "I don't need this job that bad."

"Wait. If you want the job, you can start tomorrow night. Be here around nine and I'll go over all the finer details of the job description."

Angelica turned to the door and paused. She really did need this job. "What should I wear?"

"Anything presentable."

"Alera…the mark. I've never seen it on anyone else, except for my brother and me. I've always believed it was a birthmark. And that's all it is." She looked over her shoulder at Alera. "I firmly believe that there are things in this world people can't explain, and there are things people shouldn't explain."

"And you think the birthmarks are one of those things?" Alera rolled her eyes. "You have a lot to learn."

"What's that supposed to mean?" Angelica asked as she turned to face Alera.

"My family is very special. And if you are part of that family, there are things you must know." Angelica didn't miss the note of unease in her voice as she continued. "I must make a few calls before I go into any kind of discussion."

Angelica rubbed her wrist, instantly calming herself, and stared at Alera for a minute before saying, "This is totally insane."

Alera took a deep breath. "I understand your position. I would think it was insane if I had never known my mother and some woman I had never met said she was my aunt. Perhaps we should talk about this later."

With a shake of her head, Angelica went to the door. "I'll have to think about this whole situation. It's too hard to believe."

"Please, give me some time. I'm sure we can work this out, but it must wait for now. Go home tonight, and we'll discuss this later."

Walking down the hall, Angelica dropped her head as three leather-clad giants stalked down the corridor. And yes, they were stalking like predators. She stopped, her eyes defying her brain's urge to look elsewhere. Big, muscled walls of steel on a direct approach to where she timidly stood trying not to look like a field mouse.

Edging closer to the wall, she apprehensively took a peek at the three bikers. Leather, leather, and oh, guess what? More leather accessorized with chains and spikes. Yeah, definitely bikers... body-building, bad-boy bikers.

Biting her lip, she swept her hazel eyes farther up from their black biker boots to the leather chaps to the leather trench coats and straight on up to the vaults of heaven that rested on their necks. Okay, so she was female and instantly attracted to the three studs that were getting dangerously closer by the second. It wasn't like she could help herself. All those wide shoulders and tight-fitting leathers; leathers that had apparently been tailor fitted to neatly hug their entire glorious bodies.

God, please don't let me trip and fall on my face!

Straightening her shoulders and forcing herself to stop cowering along the wall, she took a deep breath and stared at the door that now seemed a thousand feet away. From the far recesses of her brain, an odd humming started growing louder, and words that threw her for a loop echoed around her brain like a pinball.

Primal meat! Alpha males to the hundredth power. Sex! Pure, unadulterated testosterone wrapped up in bodies built for sin and erotic indecent, acts of grinding and headboard banging!

Lordy day, could she be any more of a slut? Oh, yeah!

When they passed, she turned to watch them walk away, getting a full view of their backsides. Her face burned as one of the men turned and she met a piercing set of green eyes, snarling lips, a vicious scar, multiple facial piercings, and an impressive set of long, very sharp canine teeth.

"Run, little girl, before I have you for dinner." The exquisite male voice she heard so crystal clear in her mind threatened her sanity. Fear raced through her, she was sure she had not heard him speak out loud.

And so, without further ado, she ran as if her very life depended on it.

Chapter 3

As Angelica closed the door, Alera reached for her phone and dialed a number she had committed to heart. Varick was always just a call away. She waited impatiently as the phone rang.

"Hello, this is Varick."

His voice sent goose bumps up Alera's spine. The velvety crush of his baritone was satin and lace, leather and spice, and pure raw, male magnetism. She reminded herself she was indeed a mated female but could not deny Varick's sex appeal.

"Varick, this is Alera."

There was a long pause before he spoke again. "What's wrong?"

Tears slid down her face. "I have a niece." She paused, waited for a response and received none. "I have found her or…she has found me."

She ran her hand through her hair and pulled out the drawer of her desk. She reached in and lovingly ran her hand across the old, eight-by-ten painting that was covered in plastic. It was an ancient picture of her and her sisters, all six of them, before the Burning had taken place. The Burning—good Heavens, a day she would never forget.

Varick Ta Farg had been chosen to lead one of her sisters through the Burning. She had rejected Varick and had died.

Women seldom made it through the Burning. If it were just a question of physical pain, it would not be a problem, but that was not the case. The Burning was a process of the soul, a transition of blood, and a hellish physical torture. And if that were not bad enough, it was a necessary step in the changing process. Being the descendants of gods and goddesses took a great toll on the body, mind, and spirit.

She closed her eyes. If someone made it through the Burning, they received immortality and a supernatural ability. Even with immortality, people of the One Race could still be slaughtered, as her sister Antonia had been along with Feverand Dark.

"Antonia's daughter?" His voice was barely audible. At her silence, he continued, "Are you sure she is?"

"Yes, and she has Antonia's diary."

Varick took a deep breath. "Alera, does she know?"

"No, I don't think she does, but there is something else you and the others should know."

Seconds passed as she waited, listening to the dead silence on the line. "What?"

"She has a brother."

A long pause followed, and Alera held her breath, hoping Varick hadn't lost his signal. What if Angelica really was Antonia's daughter? Questions and more questions.

"A brother?" A whisper escaped Varick' lips. "Is he here with her?"

"I'm not sure, but Antonia died thirty years ago, and her son just disappeared off the face of the earth." Alera paused. "Varick, do you think maybe it's Eli Dark?"

The Destroyer, Eli Dark, was the son of Feverand Dark, a Destroyer who was one of the first of their kind, one of the first ten. His death had been a severe blow to Gyth and his loyal Destroyers. Feverand had been chosen to take Antonia, Alera's sister, through her Burning. They had bonded their souls and, in the old tradition, they had married. Most Destroyers were unable to bear children, and Eli's birth had been celebrated in Gyth's own palace in the stars.

Alera spoke slowly. "Varick? Do you think that Gyth knows of her? She'll be turning thirty soon. All descendants enter the Burning at that age—all of them."

"If she is to go through the Burning, then Gyth would know. It's conceivable she was born without the mark. Many of the gods' descendants have been."

Alera grinned as she answered, "She has the mark. It's the same as mine."

"I wonder whom Gyth is going to choose. I hope the poor bastard knows what he's getting into."

"Varick, please!"

"Don't take it the wrong way. It's a task I will never take on again."

Alera closed her blue eyes. "You know it wasn't your fault… what happened was…I just don't want you to think I hold it against you."

Varick was silent for a few minutes before speaking. "I would have saved your sister if I could have, but she…"

"You don't have to explain it. It was a long time ago." She heard metal on metal and wondered what he was doing. "Most of us don't make it through the Burning."

Varick growled and hissed. "She didn't want it, Alera. She wanted to die. She wouldn't let me help."

Alera gritted her teeth to keep from trembling and managed to respond, "I know she didn't want to…she didn't want immortality."

Varick was silent, and she continued. "Like I said, it was a long time ago, but I'm worried my niece doesn't know what's going to happen to her body."

"Find out more about her in the next few days, and I will ask Gyth about her. But I'm sure he has chosen for her already. He knows when the Burning is coming."

Alera held the phone to her ear for a long time after he hung up. She looked up at the ceiling and a tear slid down her cheek as she prayed that Angelica made it through the Burning.

●●●

Grace, ethereal and majestic, watched as the scene played out in the office of the club. Her smile stretched across her pale pink lips as a low hum left her mouth. Things were looking brighter every second that passed, whether the darling Angelica knew it or not. She stood, and the cloud she had been floating on disappeared as she waved her hand. It was indeed good to be a goddess.

She glided across the white marble floor to a pedestal of gold and reached down to turn the pages in the silver book that lay awaiting her touch. The *Book of Promises* had long ago belonged to the god known as Jaiden. It was a link between the Heavens and the Earth. Or better yet, it was a link between Grace and the Destroyers Gyth so carefully watched and commanded. And what he didn't know wasn't going to hurt him.

Soft laughter filled the white marble room as she ran her finger down the page to the name of Varick Ta Farg, son of the god Gyth and the vampire Vicery Beth. A brief description of his life before becoming a Destroyer was entered by his name, but the important part was what Grace saw under the description.

Under his name, gold letters appeared, the power of the missing god, Jaiden, evidently still in use. She smiled as she watched the inscription scroll down the page.

"Well, my skilled assassin, it seems our debt will be paid in full in due time. Oh, it does give me such great pleasure to know that a vampire…no…a reborn assassin of your worth will be rewarded so richly."

Smiling with unrefined pleasure, she turned the page and suddenly frowned as she saw another name appear in her book. Damnation! Couldn't a goddess get a break every now and then?

Just because the Destroyers were warriors of the higher powers did not mean they should be emotionally destroyed. Over the years, she had watched their misery and pain surface and explode, but with the help of the *Book of Promises* she had given a few of them a reason to continue. It wasn't that she liked to meddle; she just didn't like Gyth. He was intolerable at best.

She opened her hand, and a small white light appeared as the faces of the Destroyers fluttered in and out of her sight. There were a hundred of them, all as handsome as Gyth himself, all with tortured pasts, and all thinking that they owed Gyth for their making. Unbelievable, but at least they did carry out the main task. They protected the One Race from the spawn of the Underworld and killed as many of the evil creatures as they could.

She sighed. It was a pity Gyth had lost sight of the fact that the Destroyers were a race of unequal endowments. Their beauty and power alone were enough to make her stomach clench hotly. The part that angered her was their pain, each of them suffering in their own way, each of their hearts and souls battered and bruised almost to the point of no repair.

Grace grinned mischievously; she had taken it upon herself to make sure at least some of the Destroyers found happiness, and dear old Gyth was completely unable to do anything about it!

After all, she was the goddess who promoted love and sexuality.

She paused in her thoughts as she turned back to the *Book of Promises*. Varick was going to be in for a life-changing experience. She had already set into motion the events that would lead to his much-earned happiness.

Grace waved her hand and Angelica's face appeared hovering over Varick's name. She was strong but gentle, tough but loving, someone kind but mean as hell when she needed to be. Most of all, Varick would need someone who could make his heart skip two beats just by looking at her. Grace laughed merrily as she manifested a bone pen in her right hand.

She carefully wrote Angelica's name in the *Book of Promises* under Varick's. *Yes, this is the one.*

It was going to take some very careful planning and time, but Grace had all the time in the universe to wait for this. Angelica would be Varick's saving grace. She giggled, saving grace, indeed. What a play on words.

She turned back to the book and hummed into the air. "Amay! Come, join me in my chambers!"

Amay, golden and shining with an unearthly light, appeared before Grace. She bowed slightly and shimmered until she stepped onto the marble floor. Her long, black hair trailed the floor behind her as she glided to Grace's side. Her ocean-blue eyes swirled with the tides of the seas as she smiled. It was a much too refined and practiced smile for Grace's taste.

"Angelica Dark is entering her Burning. Your descendant is quite the picture of loveliness."

"Thank you, Grace." The goddess narrowed her eyes. "It warms my heart that you think of her so kindly."

"Tell me, Amay. Do you think she will love my Varick?"

Amay kept her keen eyes narrowed and looked to the *Book of Promises*. "Grace? What have you done?"

"If it's not her fate to find him, then she won't find him. True?"

Amay bit her lip. "True, but she is to be—"

"A Destroyer? Is that what you think she's going to be, like her brother?"

"Her brother was born a Destroyer and she will be too. It's the way fate works." Amay dropped her eyes and shrugged. "Who am I to question?"

Grace turned on her heel as she spoke. "Gyth is a fool! He has been trying so hard to control the lives of his…" She paused. "… his Destroyers that he has almost destroyed them because he uses them for his own purposes. Is that what you want for Angelica? The one you begged me to hide from Gyth?"

"What are you saying?" Amay's eyes glittered with restrained intelligence. "To go against his wishes is suicide."

Grace delicately touched the book's spine. "Varick can save Angelica from Gyth."

Amay crossed her arms. "What exactly do you want from me?"

"A trade."

Amay scoffed. "What do you have that I might possibly want that I don't have already?"

Grace held out her hand and from the floor of her chamber arose five gold pedestals, each with a silver book resting on its crown. Amay stepped back, and her eyes glowed with anticipation as Grace snapped her fingers. The gigantic chamber doors sealed shut, and the room grew three shades darker. Amay's eyes glittered like diamonds as she beheld the five silver books, books she had longed, ached to see. Grace knew these were the books that, at one time, Amay would have sold her soul to gain possession of.

"Was that really necessary? There's no reason to get all dramatic over this, is there?" Amay bit back her sarcastic attitude as she leveled a cold stare on the other goddess. "Does Gyth know you have these six books in your possession?"

"Of course he doesn't know. Do you really take me for an idiot?" Grace held out her hand, and a small, round pendant appeared in her palm. "I want you to bless this pendant."

"Why?"

"Because, dear Amay, I know the power of calling on Terror Sky lies only within your hands." Grace laughed as Amay's face contorted with hate. "I know he gave you the power to seek his audience."

Amay took a deep breath. "How do you know that?"

Grace smiled softly. "The books tell me everything I need to know.""

Pulling away, Amay turned her back and whispered, "Gyth won't allow me to bless that." She walked circles around the books, trying to keep her wits about her. "If Gyth should find out I aided you in calling Terror Sky forth, he'll have my head."

"And what do you think he's going to do when he finds Angelica?" Grace's eyes glowed dangerously red. "Gyth is a fool. Can you not see that he has overstepped his bounds? Terror Sky must be made aware of what's happening to the world below, what's happening to the Destroyers."

Fear was evident in her voice as her hand fluttered to her throat. "Gyth rules the Heavens! He rules us. If he ever finds out you're conspiring against him, he'll make you regret it."

"Are you afraid of Gyth? Surely you know we're as powerful as he is, and combined, we are stronger." Grace's eyes glittered as she saw the little flicker of hate and betrayal cross Amay's face. "Gyth doesn't rule me, and he doesn't have to rule you, either."

"Don't be a fool, Grace. Gyth controls the godbolts. He could kill us whenever he wants."

"Then I must admit I'm disappointed you won't take an interest in saving your descendant. It seems like a fair trade; you bless this pendant, and I'll change your descendant's fate."

"We cannot change her fate. It's forbidden!" Amay gritted out through clenched teeth. "Gyth is the only one allowed to change anyone's fate."

"Do you honestly think Gyth was meant to decide all the world's fates?"

Grace slid her fingers down the spine of the *Book of Promises*. "Admit it, Amay, he has lost his way." Exasperated, she pointed to the other five books. "We can control Jaiden's words. New inscriptions appear every day, and we have the power to see to it Gyth is stopped."

Watching Amay's reactions, Grace continued, "Terror Sky won't take pity on Gyth or anyone who has broken the Heavenly Laws."

"What do you know of those dictations? You were a mere child, barely able to control the powers of that Olympian bitch Aphrodite, when Gyth became ruler of the Heavens. Under Isten's command, Terror Sky helped Gyth take the throne of the Heavens. What makes you think he'll turn on Gyth when Isten wanted Gyth to have the throne? And do I need to remind you Terror Sky has been dormant since Gyth took over the Heavens?"

Controlling her anger, Grace smiled. "What about Angelica? Do you want her to suffer? Do you want her to die?"

"What are you offering me in return for blessing the pendant?"

Grace went to the five pedestals and picked up one of the silver books, "I'm offering you the *Book of Knowledge*."

Grace handed Amay the book satisfied by the look on her face. "Hope you enjoy Jaiden's cryptic writing." She held the pendant out and waited.

Amay closed her eyes and held out her hand over the pendant. "There, it's done, but I don't want any part of this little plan of yours."

Pouting, Grace asked, "No lights? No fireworks?"

"No, I don't like the dramatics of it," Amay answered dryly as she shimmered and disappeared. "And I'll refuse any knowledge of what you're doing if I'm asked."

"Spoilsport," Grace whispered as she clutched the pendant to her breast. As she looked upon the books, she murmured, "You may have everyone else fooled, but the *books* show me all your secrets. And everyone else's too."

Chapter 4

Varick Ta Farg walked through the crowd at Tortured Souls, the local bar, and gritted his teeth. Humans smelled of sweat, fear, sex, and disease. His white hair hung down his face, covering his left eye. The curse that slid out of his well-formed mouth went unheard as he noticed his black biker jacket was torn at the sleeve and his fingerless leather gloves were covered in gray ashes.

The new jeans on his muscled legs were ripped down the inside of his thigh, and a trace of his own blood peeked through the hole. The wound had healed easily, but Varick's ego had been slapped around pretty hard. It was rare that a vampire ever got a good hit on him. Seemed like these days the bastards were getting smarter and a lot more numerous. The fierce growl that erupted from his throat rumbled through the crowd, parting his way.

The vampires he had slain stank of death and old blood, but then again they always did. Varick laughed viciously as he pulled his jacket off. It would be a cold day in the hottest of the nine hells before he would let a vampire take him out. He had not survived this long as a Destroyer to lose his soul to the damned—or to anyone or anything else, for that matter.

He made his way to the table in the corner of the human-infested club and sat down in the white-cushioned, high-back chair. The others would soon be arriving with news of their encounters. He expected them to advise that the number of enemies was rising, and he frowned at the thought.

Their own numbers were scarce compared to that of the enemy, and if Gyth did not take it upon himself to deliver reinforcements soon, Varick had a feeling things were going to get worse a lot quicker than Alexander had expected.

As Varick turned his thoughts to Alexander, the man himself appeared in the shadows along the wall and sat down in the red-cushioned chair to Varick's left. General Alexander of Greece was a deadly Destroyer, and his accomplishments as a human had never been matched. He was good-tempered and easy to get along with until you pissed him off; then it became a completely different matter.

Varick watched him shift in his chair several times before getting comfortable. His leather pants stretched tight across his thighs as he settled his weight onto the groaning chair. Alexander stretched his foot, clad in a steel-toed, black boot, onto the tabletop and leaned back in his chair.

"How did the night fare?" Alexander's face was void of emotion, detached.

Varick shrugged. "Twelve tonight. Creatures of habit that they are, they were in the same location beside the graveyard in the western part of town. And you?"

Alexander frowned. "Two more covens have risen up. One had ten members, and the other had six. They're getting more and more recruits every day. The humans are being easily led and converted."

"It's the same with the vampires. They're turning humans by the dozens and killing even more." He held Alexander's stare. "It's as you expected, perhaps worse."

Varick growled as he pulled his hair back and tied it into place at the nape of his neck. Alexander turned to the blonde woman who slid up alongside their table.

"What will you have tonight? The usual?" Her voice was deep, and her blue eyes twinkled as she licked her lips.

Alexander smiled a well-rehearsed smile. "Yeah, the usual."

The woman edged closer to Alexander. "You need some company?"

"Maybe later."

"Three. I get off at three," she replied as she leaned closer. "I can meet you at the usual place."

He flatly stated, "Go get our beer."

As she reluctantly pulled away, the third of their companions arrived through the crowd. Kreach paused as the crowd hurriedly got out of his way.

Alexander waited for Kreach to take his seat. "How did you fare?"

Kreach held up his large hands and showed nine fingers. The scars across his knuckles glistened in the strobe lights, drawing Varick's attention to the tattoos across the width of both his wrists. Each symbol told a story and each dot after each symbol represented a number.

Kreach's right wrist depicted a day—his original birth no doubt. His left depicted a day of transition, of a turning of some kind. Varick could only guess that it had something to do with becoming an alpha male. The Destroyer had his secrets, just as he himself did.

Kreach leaned back and pulled the nine canine teeth from his jacket pocket and slid them across the table to Alexander. The lights caught the piercing in his eyebrow, sending hundreds of sparkling lights around Kreach's face.

Varick's frown deepened as he watched Alexander gather the teeth into his hand and place them in the center of the table. With each kill came a token. Werewolves left canine teeth, witches left five pointed star pendants, and vampires left small round orbs.

More vampires, more witches, and more werewolves than ever before meant the tables were turning, and the balance of good and evil had shifted to evil's side. Varick could only hope Payne and Apoc had better news.

Apoc's chair shimmered, and he appeared. First as vapor, then slowly his solid form came into view. Part human and part Fae, Apoc baffled most with his dark beauty. Apoc could have cared less about his looks. And to the Destroyers' good fortune, Apoc was a follower and loyal beyond compare.

Alexander tapped his fingers on the table. "How many?"

Apoc leaned forward. "More than ever before."

Alexander ran a hand through his blond hair and gritted his teeth. "Did you rid this world of all of them?"

"You can bet your sweet ass I did."

"Were they all witches, or were there humans among them?"

"Ten witches and seven humans. And I found two vampires among them. The witches were letting them feed on three of the humans."

Apoc slung ten star pendants and two orbs onto the table. The pendants glowed red as Alexander picked them up.

Witches were heartless and brutally hated men—any men, including the Destroyers—but there was one exception to that rule—their male god, Damon. Why they were now harboring vampires was a damn good question.

"Why would they feed the vampires? It doesn't make sense. They have always been mortal enemies. Every one of us knows witches hate them. So what gives?" Apoc looked at Alexander. "Well, what does Gyth say on it?"

Alexander shrugged. "He's not sure what's going on."

"Oh, just great! The almighty Gyth don't have an answer. Well, we'll just have to kill 'em all and ask questions later. Aye, 'tis a bad omen. If they combine their forces, they could pick us off like flies." Apoc scratched his chin and sighed. "We need more Destroyers. Gyth is going to have to get up off of his arse and give us a hand."

Alexander nodded. "True, we do need more Destroyers but we must make do with what we have for now."

Varick shifted uneasily in his chair as the other Destroyers all looked at him, their eyes narrowing. He wasn't in the mood for the conversation he knew was coming.

"You need to mate soon," Alexander stated a little uneasily. "It's time to let the beast choose a female."

"I will when I'm fucking ready, and you assholes can stay out of it."

He did not need to be reminded of what was happening inside his Destroyer body. He growled in outrage and turned to the blonde woman carrying their beer.

Pathetic human! I would kill such a weakling in my heat. Why in the hell did Alexander always bed such weak woman? Maybe he likes his women timid and inferior. They have to be strong to withstand me.

"Here's your first round. Shifts are changing soon, so make sure you tell the waitress what you like. She's new." The woman smiled and toyed with her hair.

She turned and winked as she skirted to the door in the farthest corner of the bar. As she opened the door, Varick sat up in his chair and turned his head. The scent that wafted out of the door was raw, delicious woman. Vanilla and musk overwhelmed his keen senses.

He had not smelled such a woman in over five hundred years. Good God, he was turned on by the scent alone. He choked his desire down as the door closed behind the blonde.

The curse under his breath went unheard, but when he looked up, Apoc was staring at him with an amused grin on his face.

Bastard! Couldn't a man have a damn secret every once in a while? Fuck, no. Not when you ran around with a bunch of telepathic, empathic assholes.

Varick broke the silence at the table. "Has anyone heard from Eli?"

Apoc shook his head. "I picked up on him a couple days ago, but it was a weak connection. One thing is for sure—he isn't in any mind to stop by for a chat or an explanation."

Alexander ran his fingers through his hair. "Stubborn son of a bitch. What the fuck is the deal with him?"

Apoc nodded and took a long drink from his bottle as he turned to Alexander. "Maybe you should speak to Gyth and find out what his deal is, man—gods know we need him worse now than ever before."

Alexander turned to Varick. "I've already spoken to Gyth about Eli. He informs me he is doing exactly what he wants him to do, and Eli has managed to rid the world of numerous witch covens and dozens of werewolf dens."

"So, now he isn't missing but fighting alone and under no supervision?" Varick grumbled.

Alexander nodded. "Gyth assures me he will soon return to the sanctuary but to keep our questions limited when he does."

"What?" Varick asked. "When the hell have our private lives ever been private? The only secrets we carry are the ones from our pasts. He's part of this damn fraternity, and I'll be damned if I'm going to believe anything else Gyth says."

Varick clenched his jaw, ran his tongue over his fangs, and stared at the bottle in his hand. Fraternity? Yeah, he was definitely going through the Mating Rite, losing control over the emotions he so precariously hid all the damn time.

Varick refused to turn his attention to the door, knowing the female who smelled like the flowers of heaven had entered the large room and was slowly getting closer. The scent of her alone was enough to drive him full force into the Mating Rite. He could feel her gaze on the back of his head, and it took every ounce of his willpower not to turn around. She smelled beautiful, and he could hear her soft footsteps and her steady heartbeat above the hammering guitar and pounding drums.

He could almost read her thoughts as she studied Alexander. His lazy smile did little to hide his pleasure as she categorized him as a rock star. It was almost hilarious. What would the good general say about that?

Varick lit a cigarette and almost choked. Desire-filled thoughts were flooding into his mind and damn, his erection was going full mast. He sucked on the cigarette and grabbed his glass. He swallowed the liquid and nervously shifted in his seat. He had to look at her. She was damn near begging him to take her.

Yeah, I can pour you in a glass and drink you all night long.

He looked up and met her stare. Damn, but she was gorgeous. Skin as smooth and silky as cream and long, curly hair as black as night. Her silk shirt clung to her breasts and was neatly tucked into her jeans. He suddenly had the urge to tear her clothes off and take her on the bar. He looked away as he felt his blood race through his veins. Damn! The Mating Rite was on his heels and gaining ground.

The club got eerily quiet as a large man with long, black hair and a bitter smile stepped through the entrance. His eyes were damn near black, and his steps were those of a predator. If the scene had been a jungle, then he would have surely been the panther.

Varick managed a disgruntled hello as Payne took his seat and nodded at Alexander. He knew Payne would have something to say. The Destroyer rarely ever kept his mouth shut.

"How's our boy holding up to the Mating Rite?"

Varick snarled at Payne, "Don't you worry, my friend. Yours is coming soon!"

Payne laughed and slapped the table. "Well until then I can watch you suffer as your blood starts to boil inside your veins and that little beastie inside of you breaks out and goes on the mad march of lust."

"Enough!" Varick stood, his fists clenching at his sides. "Last time I checked, none of you have permission to be in my business."

His eyes darted to the new waitress as he turned on his heel and strode toward the bar. He ignored the comments from his fellow Destroyers and decided he needed to get a grip on his emotions. Or, better yet, find a willing woman to sate the desires that would slowly drive him insane.

Chapter 5

There were four of them. Unnaturally tall and tongue-a-liciously drip-dragging gorgeous. You know, the kind of man you see in sexy pics on the web. Muscles stood at attention everywhere on their tall bodies and their hair—good grief, they had long, thick, flowing hair. The kind you want to run your fingers through and hope you didn't have a massive orgasm.

Even under the flashing lights of the bar's décor, their finger-licking goodness could be savored. It definitely wasn't a sight a girl got to see every day, so by George, Angelica was going to take advantage of the moment.

The corner table seemed made especially for them. It was rather large and took most of the corner's space. It was set farther from the rest of the bar than the other, less pleasing tables. She carefully eyed the first one sitting closest to the outside. It was extremely dark in that particular corner, but she had uncannily good eyesight.

He looked like a rock star. Black leather pants stretched tight across thick thighs, and his matching black muscle shirt emphasized his wide shoulders. His hair was dark, highlighted with blond streaks, and it made her think he visited an expensive salon on a regular basis. His delicious, long leg was draped across the table's edge, and he was completely at ease.

She forced her smile down as she noticed his biker boots. Tattoos ran up both his arms, and that was kind of hot. The strobe light made it too difficult to decipher the exact lettering of the tats but she was sure it was old Latin. She went to the next man to his right.

Ouch!

Men like the second one just did not exist. He appeared to be tall, maybe six feet, four inches or so. His hair seemed white under the lights and very long. It hung down his broad back in a loose ponytail. He wore black jeans and a black dress shirt. Black cowboy boots completed the outfit. As she continued her appraisal, she watched as he lit a cigarette.

She caught her breath as he shifted in his chair and leaned back. His shoulders were broad and so very defined. If she could just touch him once to see if he was real she would make it worth the effort. Hell, no, she couldn't do that; she might get really turned on then. Oh, but wait—she was already turned on, and the heat threatening to swallow her was barely containable. The muscles in his hard jawline twitched as he looked up and caught her eye. She quickly looked away, but shyly looked up again.

Angelica wanted so badly to run her fingers through his too-white-to-be-natural hair. Visions of all those silken waves surrounding her naked flesh flashed in her mind, and she groaned.

Shaking her head in defiance of her body's reaction, she sighed as she watched the men bring their bottles together in some sort of toast.

She turned her attention to the third one and damnation, he was spectacular. She must be dreaming because he was as perfect as it gets. He was staggeringly beautiful, not in a pretty-boy, handsome way but in a wild, sexually intoxicating way. She bit her lip as she looked closer at him. She could just drink him in with her eyes.

His lips twitched as he rubbed the ring on his little finger. She could almost swear she felt a twinge of heartbreak in him as his eyes softened. But that was a silly notion; she didn't even know him.

White's strong fingers wrapped around his bottle again and brought it to his full lips. Her legs got weak, and she grasped the back of the chair at the bar.

Go ahead, pour me in a glass and drink me up!

How in the hell could she be attracted to a man she hadn't even met? Talk about chemical attraction!

She slid her attention to the fourth man and frowned. She could only see part of the right side of his face, and nothing from the neck down, but he was definitely the one she'd run from a few nights before. She sighed, knowing the rest of him resembled the part of his face she could see. Wow, talk about your handsome nightmares coming to life! *Don't mess with me* was indeed written on this one's rather dark face. She strained her eyes and caught her breath as he turned his head, giving her a perfect view of his profile. Gorgeous but terrifying.

She looked back to the one who had white hair and wiped the sweat from her cheek. He was still better looking than the others, and damn if she wasn't going to fantasize about him in the nearby future. Deep, hot fantasies that were already taking root in her vivid imagination.

"Order up!" The black-headed bartender set the drinks in front of her. "Hey! Order's ready."

Angelica rubbed her neck and frowned. What the hell was wrong with her? "Thanks."

She turned and almost whimpered as she looked back to the table of muscled men. The man with white hair was gone. Damn.

• • •

Alexander tapped his finger on the table impatiently. "How many?"

Payne grunted, "Sixteen."

Payne piled sixteen star-shaped pendants onto the tabletop. They were all bloody as hell, but to the eye of anyone other than a Destroyer, they looked like they were covered in oil. Varick narrowed his eyes as Payne wiped his hands on the napkins lying on the table. He couldn't help but notice and feel the satisfaction pouring from Payne's soul. Payne enjoyed his job far more than any other Destroyer; he liked to kill witches, and he seldom ever killed anything else.

Alexander piled the canine teeth and pendants in the table's center. He turned to Varick. Varick growled and pulled twelve small, white orbs out of his pocket—the slain vampires' tokens.

Witches were the strongest of the demons they destroyed. Werewolves were strong but lacked intelligence, but the strength made them formidable enemies. And the vampires—they were soulless, and their power came from sucking the souls from humans along with their blood. The more they fed, the stronger they became. The more souls they took the more they appeared human, easily blending into human society.

Varick forced down the bile that had risen in his throat. Souls fueled the vampires' black hearts with life, and if one of them ever killed a Destroyer and sucked his soul that vampire would be able to walk among the living completely in human form. Throughout the years there had been a few vampires who had succeeded taking a Destroyer's soul, but Varick could sense any vampire within a few miles.

His hands trembled, and he placed them under the tabletop. He was intimate with the ways and needs of a vampire on more levels than he was willing to admit. As an assassin, his vampiric nature had thrived, had danced in the glory of the kill, had guiltlessly taken souls and blood, lots of blood.

Vampires preyed on members of the One Race as a primary source of souls. Once the vampire had taken a soul from a member, they could walk in the human world during daylight. And that was the best place to be if you were a vampire because Destroyers were confined to night. Except for Eli, he was the only Destroyer who could hunt the vampire down during the day.

For reasons he wasn't sure he wanted to know, Gyth had empowered Varick to be the reaper of those souls. Swallowing the orbs, he could release the souls, relieve the endless torment they suffered as prisoners inside the orbs.

Vampire.

The word stabbed the inside of his skull like daggers trying to penetrate his will. Even though he had been born again as a Destroyer, he still needed that one precious commodity—blood. Human or vampire donors were both acceptable. He bit the inside of his cheek. Better to feed on vampires. Better to eat their black hearts and thrive that way. Yes, better—better because he felt less guilt, less self-loathing that way.

And gods above, he had enough guilt to deal with.

The music grew louder as the air thickened, and a heavy mist filtered around the table, blocking the humans' view. The five Destroyers at the table rose, dropped their gazes to the floor, and crossed their arms over their chests. Gyth stepped out of the mist. His long, straight, white hair fell down his leather-covered chest, and the ends were tinged with red at his waist.

Gyth held out his hand in the center of the table. The five Destroyers each laid their hands palm down on top of his upturned palm. In unison, all spoke the words. "All is one and one is all, for we are the keepers of our brothers," in an ancient language. Gyth sat down, and the Destroyers followed.

All the Destroyers laid their palms up on the table and waited as Gyth spread his hands over the pendants, the black marble-like balls, and the canine teeth. He focused their energies, and from each of his fingertips sparked a purple flame. His fingernails turned black as the energy poured from his fingers and snaked out across the table in five directions.

The purple flames inched their way to each of the Destroyers. Each one closed their eyes as pain shot up their arms. The flames licked their skin, bit down harshly, and disappeared as the fire settled into their veins.

Varick watched as a new dagger, very large and black, appeared on his right arm above the intricate angel-and-demon tattoo. He looked up as the eyes of the smallest snake on Kreach's forearm turned bright red and the scales flared out from its back, twisting around a long golden stake. Payne's skull and bones became encircled with flames.

As if Alexander had willed it, Varick turned to watch as the words "wind of death" etched themselves across Alexander's knuckles in Latin. Apoc flexed his arm as the panther on his shoulder twisted around a long, jagged sword.

Varick looked up to Gyth and frowned as his face shimmered and disappeared. He always left as quickly as he came, never offering any words of wisdom or even so much as a thank you for saving this world one day at a time.

Varick carefully looked around the table. Everyone at the table had at some point crossed the god who had made the Destroyers, all except for Alexander.

In truth, everyone at this particular table owed Gyth something. Varick himself owed the god for a second chance at life, a new beginning. He had freed himself from Grace's assassins, had endured so he could survive only to be murdered by the one female he allowed to get close to him, his mother.

He swallowed hard, fighting the memory down.

Uneasiness drifted up his spine; something was in the air, something dark and menacing. He could smell it, taste it, and the vampire in him longed to listen to the call pulling on his blood. His head snapped up, his topaz eyes shining as bright as the sun. His fangs elongated; his fingers curled and cracked as his claws undulated from his fingertips. The bloodlust of his vampire half hit him squarely in the gut.

Vanishing from the table in the blink of an eye, he swore to himself. Zena, the goddess of the vampires, was calling out her minions, calling the vampire hordes that remained on Earth, unearthing them from their graves. The pull was great, as if she were drawing near. He fought with himself and his nature as he reappeared next to the ocean.

As an assassin for Grace, her powers overrode Zena's, but as a Destroyer, he was susceptible to Zena's call. There was but one way to resist her. His inner demon, the Destroyer that lay so tightly guarded under his skin, had to be released. Falling to his knees, he screamed seconds before his back arched and scales rippled down his spine.

Chapter 6

Careful to control his achy, needy body, Varick waited impatiently for two A.M.. He watched as Angelica cleaned tables as the humans filtered out of Tortured Souls. Occasionally, she would look up with a slight smile as she met his eyes. He was pleased with the fact she wasn't falling all over him like most women.

Her scent was intoxicating. The vampire in him wanted to be at her neck, tasting the sweetness her skin was offering. The Destroyer wanted more, needed more. He could only hope she could withstand those parts of him.

He would have to figure out a way to convince her to trust him. It wouldn't be easy for her. He would have to reveal to her what he truly was; every part of his soul would be laid open before her eyes.

Varick looked around the room, only a few humans remained on the dance floor. There were a couple of them sitting at the bar finishing their last drinks of the night. Soon, the place would be empty and he would approach Angelica.

Guilt hit him in the gut. He knew he couldn't control the Mating Rite, knew he had to have sex with someone but not just anyone. He glanced at Angelica again. His lust rose up and roared in his mind.

If he had a choice, he would walk away forgetting she even existed. The Mating Rite demanded him to stay. He had no idea why the beast inside of him had chosen her. Perhaps, it was her scent, her creamy white skin, or her long wavy black hair.

He swallowed the last drops of vodka in his glass as she came to his table with a tray. Firmly shaking off the urge to sweep her off her feet and kiss her full lips, he shifted toward her, leaning with his elbows on the table.

"It's last call. Do you want another drink?" Her voice sent a shiver of pleasure down his spine.

She reached to take his glass, her fingers brushing his. Electric pulses sparked in his fingers carrying the delicate touch to his brain. He caught the groan before it slipped from his lips.

"No." He grabbed her hand as she turned to leave. "My name is Varick. It would be a pleasure if you would allow me to walk you home tonight." He swallowed hard as she simply stared at him. "It's not safe for a woman to be out this time of night alone."

Her eyes narrowed suspiciously as she pulled her hand from his. "How do you know I walk home?"

He shrugged, leaning back in his chair. "I leave about every night the same time as you do."

"Oh." Her smile was tight. "I'll be fine, but thanks for offering."

"Truth be known." He pushed his chair back and stood, towering over her. "I offered in order to get to know you."

She stepped back looking up at him squarely in the eye. He tried not to smile but he was enjoying her stubbornness. It was not very often that a woman denied him anything.

"Look buddy…"

He interrupted her softly, "My name is Varick, not buddy."

Her hands flew to her hips. "Okay, Varick, if you wanted to get to know me, why didn't you just say so instead of insinuating that you feared for my safety?"

"Can I not fear for your safety just because I don't know you?" He resisted the desire to run his hands through her silky hair. "It's customary for a gentleman to be concerned for a lady's welfare, isn't it?"

She shook her head. "You're definitely not a gentleman."

"No, I suppose I'm not." He reached out to catch a stray lock of her hair neatly tucking it behind her ear. "I find you captivating. You have caught my attention and I merely wish to spend some time with you."

Her shoulders squared harshly, her suspicion evident on her face. "Why?"

Varick blinked his surprise at her question. "Why wouldn't I?"

Her eyebrow rose. "Answering a question with a question is a good way to avoid giving an answer."

He decided he needed to take a different approach. "Would you rather I give you compliments? Tell you that I am very attracted to you? Do you want me to tell you I have waited rather impatiently for an opportunity to speak to you? Or perhaps, you want me to tell you that I have lain in my bed thinking about you as I drift off to sleep?"

For a moment, he thought she would blush or slap him. She surprised him again when she didn't. A groan escaped him as she ran her tongue over her lips and sat the tray down on his table.

"Are you trying to flirt with me?" He was sure she was repressing a smile as she continued, "Because if you are, it's a pretty poor attempt."

He laughed. "Yes, it does seem that I'm out of practice."

Her nose wrinkled. "Yeah, it seems that way. Try harder next time."

Angelica stepped back grabbing the tray, turned on her heel, and walked away.

Without turning to face him, she grumbled under her breath, "I hope you don't think I'm that easy."

Varick stood there, confused.

Her thoughts had poured into his mind, assuring him that she wanted him. He was sure he had caught the scent of her arousal drifting off of her as she had gotten closer to him. She did desire him, he was positive of it. There was no way to mistake that kind of attraction.

Damn it, he hadn't planned on her refusing the simplest of requests. He searched the room until he found her by the bar. She was talking to the bartender as she counted her tips for the night.

She looked up and gave him a blinding smile. His heart lodged in his throat. Shimmers of desire tore throughout his system. He wanted her, in his bed, in his arms.

Stalking to her, hell-bent on getting what he wanted, he trapped her between his body and the bar. He leaned in, real tight, and inhaled her scent. Not wanting to use his vampire pheromones to persuade her to do as he wished, he chose to completely confound her with words. She wanted him to flirt, she would get flirtation.

He turned her to face him. "Very few women have completely stunned me as you have. If you would allow me to walk you home, I'd be honored and pleased beyond words."

Varick heard her sudden intake of air, felt her body stiffen. He hadn't realized he was holding his breath until she relaxed and a slow smile curved her lips.

"That's much better." She placed her hand on his chest. "Although, I wasn't expecting you to try again so soon."

"I'm persistent." He grinned making sure his fangs were neatly tucked away from her sight. "And I took a beautiful woman's advice and tried much harder to get her attention."

Angelica laughed. "She must be a very smart woman."

"Smart? I would say she's very perceptive." He took her hand and placed it on his arm pulling her away from the bar. "She's witty, beautiful, and sexy."

"Attractive." Angelica tilted her head up and looked at him. "Sexy implies sex. And sex isn't the place to start getting to know someone."

He opened the door for her, eager to continue the conversation. She stepped out onto the sidewalk and took his offered arm. He remained silent as they walked, fearful of starting an argument. In the short conversation they had he found she was easily baited.

In a way, he was grateful for her presence. He had served Gyth for so long that his every waking moment was used for the god's purpose. Angelica was a reprieve, a fresh breath of air.

"You're quiet for a man who wanted to get to know someone." She squeezed his arm sending a shudder through his body. "If you're not going to start asking questions, I will. What do you do for a living?"

How was he going to answer that one? *Well, you see, I'm a Destroyer. I kill vampires, werewolves, and witches. Gyth, a god, pays me in gold.* He knew she wasn't ready for that answer.

Varick hated to lie. "I'm self-employed."

She stopped in her tracks and gave him a hard look over. "Self-employed? What do you do? More specifically I mean."

I kill things. She would run from him if he dared to say such a thing.

"I'm a contractor."

"Like a building contractor?"

He skirted around the answer as they began walking again. "More like demolition."

"Oh." Angelica grinned. "It must be a fun job and I'm sure you get to take out all your frustrations on whatever you're destroying."

She had no idea just how much frustration he could take out on vampires, how much anger he could deal out to witches.

"Why are you waitressing at Tortured Souls?"

"I need the money and it's the only part-time job I could find." She looked up at the stars. "Sometimes, I wish I had stayed in Arkansas but I love the house my father left me in his will."

He watched sadness etch across her face. He wanted to wrap his arms around her, comfort her but he refrained. "I'm sorry he passed away."

"It's okay. I never really knew him."

"Still, losing a parent is hard," Varick grunted. "I lost my mother and it still plagues me."

"Tell me about her." Angelica leaned on his arm. "If it's not too hard to do."

"Her name was Vicery Beth. She was the most beautiful woman in the entire universe."

Angelica laughed. "I'm sorry. I wasn't laughing because of your loss. It's just that I have heard other men say the exact same thing about their mother."

"She had the blackest hair. Long and straight. It felt like silk. Her eyes were bluer than the sky." He paused feeling the ache in his heart even after so many years. "She had a very gentle heart and soul. In her eyes, I could do no wrong."

Varick could barely breathe as she ran her fingers down his arm in an attempt to soothe away the pain from talking about his mother. He appreciated her kindness but had no idea how to tell her that. No one had ever tried to soothe him.

All women wanted him for one thing, sex. Not comfort, not as a friend. He tried to tell himself he wanted to get to know this woman before having sex with her, but his eyes were defying the direct command from his brain to stop staring at her lush lips.

His skin tingled in every place she touched him. He could feel desire threatening to claim him as she took his hand into hers. Intertwining his fingers with hers, he failed to recall the last time he had held a woman's hand. Had he ever done so at all?

Varick tried to remember the faces of the women he had been with. He had slept with hundreds of women, had seduced and had let himself be seduced. He realized that not once had he held a woman's hand or talked with her about anything other than sex. Angelica deserved more from him.

Like a reoccurring nightmare, guilt kicked him in the gut again. The Mating Rite caused a lust that could and would not be denied. The beast inside of him would claim the woman he took to his bed; possibly harm her in ways that he didn't dare think about.

Angelica led him across a street to a park. The back of his head tingled as they entered the large wrought-iron gates. Immediately, he went into Destroyer mode, his fangs elongating, his keen senses scanning the area.

He knew his voice was gruff when he stopped and pulled her closer to his chest. "This isn't a safe place to be at night. You shouldn't be walking through this park."

She pushed lightly at his chest and ducked under his arm. "I walk through here every night. It's perfectly safe."

Quickening his steps, he grabbed her hand and hurried across the grass. He heard twigs snapping, a branch falling from a tree, and the crickets stopped chirping. The tingling in the back of his head slammed into his brain, his guts twisting in a knot. Something or someone was watching them.

Angelica skidded to a stop. "I love this place at night." She looked up. "It's the best place in Fether to look at the stars. You can see the entire sky from right here on this little hill."

Varick scanned the area. "Yes but everything in the tree line, the sky, and the surrounding area can see you crystal clear. It would be the perfect spot to surround someone and attack."

Angelica shook her head. "Were you ever a cop?"

"No." He circled her looking into the trees. "Why do you ask?"

"Because you're acting like one." She huffed out a breath of air as if agitated and started walking with her arms crossed.

"How do you know what a cop acts like?" He stopped, glanced over his shoulder one last time, and followed behind her.

"I dated a cop last year. He was always looking over his shoulder, watching people for suspicious behavior, and telling me how dangerous everything and everyone was. According to him, everyone was a suspect and men were all guilty whether they had committed a crime or not."

"He sounds intelligent." His steps landed beside of her as they stepped off of the grass and into gravel. "How long did you date him?"

"Long enough to know I didn't want to be with him for the rest of my life." She purposely bumped into his arm and teased him. "Protectiveness is a nice quality. Over protectiveness can be scary and mistook as controlling."

"Are you implying I'm controlling?"

She walked through another wrought-iron gate and turned to face him. "When the shoe fits…"

"I'm not controlling," He ran his hand through his white hair. "I'm only concerned for your safety."

"Why would you be concerned for someone you don't know?" Angelica waited for his answer, her hands going to her hips.

"A storm is coming."

"Are you avoiding another question?" Her eyes narrowed.

Thunder rumbled over their heads. Angelica looked up as lightning flashed across the sky. Varick took her face in his hands and stepped closer, letting his body touch hers. He wanted to kiss her, wanted to explore every moist spot in her mouth with his tongue.

She grabbed his hands. "What are you doing?"

"Isn't it obvious?" He leaned down, his lips hovering over hers. "I'm going to kiss you."

Heat raced through his blood as she arched pressing her curves into his body. Her lips parted on a sigh, her tongue licking her bottom lip. The dark desire that had been building in his system swam to the surface, begging him to take the kiss she was blatantly offering.

The heat warmed his skin, he felt his body get tight and hard, eager to do more than just kiss her. He knew that one kiss would not be enough. His desire was white hot and blistering in intensity.

Abruptly he let her go. Stepping back, he collected himself and controlled the heat that was screaming to be released.

He forced himself to speak. "Perhaps we should seek shelter before the rain starts."

He watched as her expressions slowly changed. First, her bewitched expression led him to believe she was having a hard time shaking off the same feeling he was having. Second, the fire in her eyes dulled, a frown pulling at the corners of her lips letting him know she was disappointed. Last, she clenched her hands into fists at her sides, her eyes throwing darts at his head.

"What rain?" No sooner than she spoke, the first drops fell.

He couldn't stop the smile that was spreading on his face. "That rain."

He followed as she led the way down the street of white picket fences. At the last house, she stopped. Unlatching the gate, she stepped inside the yard and quickly shut it behind her.

"Thanks for walking me home."

"It was my pleasure." He reached out and tucked a strand of hair behind her ear. "Promise me you will find another route home."

She shook her head. "Controlling."

"No. The park isn't safe." Varick was tempted to use his vampire pheromones to make her agree to find another way. "Just promise me you will."

Biting her lower lip, she shrugged. "Okay. Fine. I'll find another way."

"Goodnight, Angelica."

Varick stood in the rain as she walked down the entrance to her house. He stayed for a long time after she went inside. The longer he stood there, the colder the air got. Pivoting toward the park, a cold wind slapped at his face. The place had a bad vibe, like a curse was hanging over the area. He waited until her lights were turned off and he was sure she was sleeping before he walked across the street and entered the park.

Chapter 7

Into a bowl of ruby blood, Grace dropped three of her silver-blonde hairs. Instantly, the blood shimmered and a face appeared. Zena, deep in the confines of the Underworld, arched a dark brow at her and rolled her black eyes.

"What do you want this time, Grace?" Zena's natural hiss curved around any S sound and made Grace's skin crawl. "Why do you insist on pestering me?"

"It's not what I want—it's what I can offer you."

The shadows of the Underworld passed in front of Zena, and Grace groaned as their miseries downloaded through the connection. "Could you please tell them to go somewhere else for a little while?"

Zena chuckled. "Why? Feeling a little faint-hearted? It's a pity it was not you who was sent down here instead of me."

"Zena, I know you enjoy these conversations, whether you will admit it or not." Grace smiled, a hint of a domineering attitude on her lips. "Like I was saying, I have something you may want."

Zena sneered but sent her minions away. "And what do you want in exchange?"

"Straight to the point. I like that."

"Stop with the small talk or leave me to my own devices," Zena growled. "And this better be good, Grace. You're interrupting my feeding."

"One name. Gyth." Grace chose to ignore the wails echoing in the background.

Zena erupted, her claws slashing at the remains of her latest victim. "How dare you speak that abomination's name!"

"Ummm, I thought perhaps you'd be interested in getting a little revenge but…" Her voice trailed off as Zena hissed yet again.

"But what?"

"Well, I see you would rather hiss at me than strike a deal."

"Striking a deal with you is like poking werewolves with needles." Zena narrowed her eyes.

"There is a certain Destroyer who has entered into his Mating Rite."

"Varick!"

Grace laughed. "Yes, Zena. He is a fine specimen, don't you agree? It's a pity Gyth uses him to destroy your vampires." Carelessly looking at her fingernails, Grace continued. "Ironic really."

"Gyth blocks him from my summons," Zena growled. "But you knew that already. Get to the point."

Grace smiled, her eyes glittering like diamonds on black velvet. "Gyth has plans, high hopes for Varick. He plans on using him to destroy you." It was not above her to lie to get what she wanted. "That was never his intended fate and fate is screaming for retribution."

"I could care less what the fates are screaming. I personally like the sound of screams."

"I know a way to get you to earth and now would be perfect timing. During the Mating Rite, Varick will be susceptible to your summons." Grace waited patiently as Zena digested the information.

"Impossible!" Zena shook her head. "The Underworld was sealed off from the River Styx when the Olympians fell."

"I'll tell you how to get to earth. All you have to do in return is use Varick against Gyth."

"How am I supposed to do that?" Zena huffed.

"I'm sure you will find a way." Grace rolled her eyes as Zena laughed. "It shouldn't be very hard, Varick already hates him and you'll be able to control him."

Zena nodded. "Seems we have a deal."

"Good." Grace leaned closer to Zena's image. "There are hidden portals in the Underworld that open into the River Styx that Charon once used. Find one and use it."

"You may think me a fool, but I know you're up to something, Grace." Zena rolled her head, pivoted it around her neck. "If Damon finds out I have found a way to Earth, he'll dismember me."

"Damon? Why would you worry yourself over Damon?" Grace clicked her tongue. "Now, you wouldn't find a portal and not tell the Lord of the Underworld. Would you?"

"You wouldn't strike a bargain with one of the very goddesses Gyth confined to the Underworld. Would you?"

Grace shrugged. "Let's just say that the fight between them doesn't concern me and you."

Zena's laughter bubbled up her throat causing Grace to shudder. "Damon is lord here as Gyth is lord there. If we're going to conspire against them in any form, we should expect consequences."

The seriousness in her voice almost made Grace laugh. Consequences? If Zena could manage to control Varick just long enough to knock Gyth off the throne, there would be no consequences. All the cards had to be in place and according to the *Book of Promises*; it could happen if the events unfurled as needed.

"I'll deal with the consequences on this side." Grace leaned closer to Zena's image. "Just make sure you keep your end of the bargain."

"Or what?" Zena arched a black brow.

"I will summon Damon and tell him how you conspired against him."

"Bitch." Zena curled her hands into fists. "You're as self-righteous as Gyth."

• • •

As Zena closed the connection with Grace, she rose into the air, her body turning to mist. Traveling along the ceiling, she made her way to her private chambers.

Manifesting her body in the center of the room, a violent shudder racked her body. She scowled as she let it pass through her. Varick! That bastard half-breed was denying her call yet again! He was the one vampire that eluded her beck and call, the second in her lifetime that had ever been able to resist her.

She so wanted a piece of him. Literally. She had desired his blood for over a thousand years, had wanted to rake her fangs along his neck and drink his blood until he begged her to punish him for being such a bad boy. And she would—she would feed from him daily, let him feed from her, and she would make absolutely sure he never denied her again.

She hissed in outrage as she thought of the other who denied her calls—Vicery Beth. She had been Zena's greatest accomplishment. Twenty-two hundred years ago, from her own womb, she had taken an egg and merged it with the sperm of a human. Encasing it in the flesh of mutilated vampires, she had fed it from her own vein. The fetus had grown for nine months in the fleshy cocoon. She had even snuck into the chambers of the abysses and pulled out a condemned female soul to give the fetus.

She snapped her jaws shut, her teeth grinding together, and her claws scraping against the wall. Bargaining with Grace, she'd had the soul purged, cleansed of its past. Once the fetus had accepted the soul, Vicery Beth had been born. She was born a vampire with a soul, Zena's child, fed from her body.

Her chest seized as the memories of her child flooded through her. That bitch Grace had betrayed Zena, had told Gyth what she had done. On Vicery's thirtieth birthday, Gyth had appeared and taken her, disappeared from the Underworld with the one thing Zena loved, the one thing that had made her feel complete.

Time had not diminished the pain nor had it weakened the bitter taste of betrayal.

The bitch would pay. So would Gyth. And this Varick, this Destroyer who dared to deny her call, he was somehow linked to Grace and Gyth. Cold hatred welled up in her heart. Varick would pay as well. He would beg on his knees like the dog he was; he would bow down before her, his queen, and praise her as he spat on the faces of Grace and Gyth.

All she needed to do was find one of the portals that led to the ground above. Entering her chambers, she called to her minions. They slithered out of the shadows by the dozens, their dead eyes glowing with admiration of their queen.

"Search the Underworld—look in every corner and crevice. I want to know where the portals are, and I want to know yesterday. Go, and don't return without answers."

In unison, they answered. "Yes, our queen, your wish is our command."

Chapter 8

As her shift started, Angelica couldn't stop her gaze from traveling to the far back corner of the bar. Varick was there with his friends as usual. The crowd tonight was thin, probably because of the well-known band that was playing at the bar across town. But still, there was a mesh of female bodies on the dance floor, most of which were eyeing the same table in the back that she had been.

Well, a woman just couldn't help it. And good lord, she was woman! So much so that at this point she was beginning to think she should have a one-nighter to ease the pain that throbbed between her legs. She groaned at the thought of a stranger groping at her. Nope, not going to happen.

The bartender frowned as he slid the tray to Angelica's waiting hands. "Table in the back corner."

Oh, shit! But I was just staring a hole through those guys!

"Hey?"

"Yeah, what ya need?" A soft smile met Angelica's eyes.

"You know those guys?"

The bartender lost the smile. "Yeah, they're regulars. They come in 'bout every night around this time."

"Are Varick's friends bikers or body builders?"

He laughed and rolled his eyes. "Don't think so. They're friends of the boss lady."

She paused. "They don't seem to be the type Alera would hang out with."

He paused and cracked his knuckles. "If they ask you to join them, just do it. Boss's orders."

She eyed him. "I'm a waitress not an escort."

"Don't worry; they rarely ever ask for company and besides, you dress like an old maid."

She stuck her tongue out at the bartender and grabbed the tray of beer. "Yeah, well, you dress like a mobster."

She was proud of the way she dressed. A black, long-sleeved silk shirt and jeans were perfectly normal wear for someone her age. Well, that wasn't exactly true, to be honest. But she wasn't here to impress anyone.

She walked through the crowd and edged to the table. She kept her eyes on the tabletop as she set the beer down on the little black napkins, carefully working her way around one of their boots. She counted five men now, but she could have sworn there had been only four, or maybe the strobe lights had been playing tricks on her.

"Can I get you boys anything else from the bar?" She wasn't going to be nervous—hell, she had a brother back home.

"My name is Alexander." The one she had referred to as a rock star stated. "Just keep the beer coming. We're a thirsty lot."

She looked up and smiled, but her smile faded as she looked into the most vivid blue eyes she had ever seen. "Y-yes, I'll do that."

Varick spoke up. "What exactly do you drink, Angelica?"

Angelica turned to him and grabbed the table top. Since the night he had almost kissed her, she had been avoiding him. "Me?" *Could I sound more like a mouse?*

"Yes, you. What is your preferred drink?"

"Uhh, I guess it's scotch."

"Good. Bring a bottle and two glasses."

Angelica turned and hurried back to the bar. Damnation, Varick had a voice that could bring angels out of heaven and turn demons into fairies. If you believed in that sort of nonsense.

"I need a bottle of scotch and two glasses."

"Order up." The bartender said as he set the scotch on the bar.

Angelica returned to the table and sat the scotch and glasses in front of Varick. "Just wave at me if you need anything else."

As she turned to leave, Varick spoke. "Angelica." His voice wrapped around her, sliced through her skin. "Come join us. We are in need of a woman's company."

"I…have work to do."

Varick shoved his chair back and stood. "I insist you join us! Sit down."

He towered over her, his eyes searching her face intently. But she wasn't here to be bossed around by an overbearing controlling man.

Angelica laid the tray on the table and eased around Alexander to Varick' side. "Look, I have to work to pay my bills, and we already had the discussion about how controlling you are."

Varick gritted his teeth. "Sit down."

Angelica narrowed her eyes, intent on putting him in his place. "I don't like being told what to do. And apparently, whatever interest you had in me disappeared a week ago in front of my house."

"Just sit down Angelica," Alexander urged. "Varick isn't used to getting denied the pleasure of a woman's company."

"Well, he just got denied! There are thirty women in this place that would love to sit next to him, but I don't!" *Take that!*

Varick pulled his chair behind her, took her arm, and pushed her backwards. She fell into the enormous chair, and he shoved it to the table's edge. "I won't take no for an answer."

"You arrogant, egotistical jerk!"

Varick slid another chair next to hers, sat down, and wrapped his arm around her shoulders as if it was his every right. Angelica shivered as his whispers flooded into her ear. His voice was entrancing, and she was grateful she was sitting, because she was sure she would have collapsed at his words.

"I'm hungry for you. I have dreamt of the kiss we have not shared and with each passing day, I want it more and more. My desire for you is slowly driving me insane." She shivered as he paused and ran his fingers down the side of her neck. "Your skin is delicate, like the satin blooms of the Tacca chantieri."

"The what?"

"Tacca chantieri. The bat flower." His voice was a whisper in her ear, a direct line running to her core.

Angelica took a deep breath and tried not to visualize his hands on her body. And why the hell did she feel so damn drunk? She had not taken even a sip tonight. But that smell—it was darkly seductive, a blend of brandy, male flesh, and honeysuckle. Heaven could not have smelled better. Lord, could it be that amazing scent that was coming from him? It was potent, an instant aphrodisiac.

Oh, good God, am I that hard up? Am I going to let this guy? Hey wait a minute. What the hell is he doing?

Angelica grabbed his hand as it made a beeline to her leg. "Oh, no you don't!"

"It's what I want," he whispered as his tongue flickered out and caressed her earlobe. "I would touch you now, taste you."

"Ummm…" *Did I just moan? Am I nuts? He's a virtual stranger!*

"Stop it!" She had meant for it to be a little more demanding, but he continued to draw her closer to his rigid and—oh, crap—hard body. "You're acting damned odd. Are you drunk?"

"No," He replied softly. "But I have hungered for you in ways that have been unbearable."

"Varick! Not here."

Thank God for Alexander.

She looked down and groaned. His hand was still in hers, and damn if she wasn't enjoying the way his thumb was caressing the inside of her palm. If he could create all these sensations just by touching her hand, then dear lord, what else could he do with those hands? Angelica groaned again as heat filtered out from her loins and rose up her chest. Her mouth went utterly dry and her face went red with heat. She was sure her body temperature had just risen twenty degrees.

"Next order of business?" Alexander asked as he looked to each of his comrades and dropped his leg from the table. "We're being split up. Gyth advised that Apoc and I are to go to Las Vegas tomorrow night."

Apoc leaned up out of the shadows and braced his arms on the tabletop. "And the job we are to do?"

Angelica caught her breath at his dark expression. His eyes were as black as longest night, his long, bluish-black hair hung down in soft waves, and, of all things, he had a tattoo on his face. She wondered where else he was tattooed and noticed the one under his left eye was a very detailed, small, black Celtic knot.

That's kind of odd. But hey, they all were kind of odd in their own way. Absolutely gorgeous but odd and scary.

Alexander dropped his head, he looked tired. "The Hellic Coven is hosting a masquerade party, and they have invited some of our soulless friends to stop by for a snack."

Apoc grinned as the light in his eyes brightened. "How many?"

"At least twenty. I seriously expect more to show up."

Apoc threw his head back, and deep laughter filled the space of the table. "It's going to be a hell of a ride."

Alexander looked to the fifth of the group. "Payne, there's a special assignment that needs your attention."

Angelica caught her breath as she looked across the table at the man Alexander was speaking to. He appeared angry, the lines in his face running deep.

Payne grunted as he made eye contact with Alexander. His lip twitched as Alexander dropped his eyes.

"Well, go ahead with it, Alexander. Where are you sending me?"

Alexander ran his fingers through his blond hair and looked disgusted. "To Kentucky."

"You're kidding me!" Payne scratched his jaw. "Why?"

"Gyth wants you to…"

"To what?" Payne leaned back and closed his eyes. "Just tell me it has something to do with a good fight."

"No, Payne, my friend, Gyth has chosen you to escort a woman through her Burning."

Payne's eyes narrowed into tiny slits. "I'll be damned if I will!"

Alexander stood and towered over the table. "You will! Her name is Chanta Timbers and she is but a year from the Burning. It's a great honor to be chosen."

Payne stood, slamming his chair into the wall. "Fuck you and Gyth, I won't do it! You take the bitch through her change."

Alexander growled, "It's an order!"

Payne turned on his heel and walked away, shoving people out of his way. "Fuck you, Alexander. I don't need this shit!"

Angelica tried to pull away from Varick but he held firm. She had heard just about all she wanted to hear for one night. Not that she could make any sense out of what Alexander was saying.

"I hope Gyth knows what he's doing where Payne is concerned." Alexander took a deep breath, sat back down, and looked at Varick. "You'll be staying here."

Varick took a long drink from his bottle and nodded as he looked at Angelica. Her cheeks were burning. She looked away suddenly nervous under his stare and wondered what was going on between these men.

"Varick, you and Kreach keep a watch over the city." Alexander stated roughly as he looked over his shoulder at a blond and smiled.

"As always, Alexander, it will be done as ordered," Varick replied.

Kreach stood. He was at least six feet and a good six inches or better and weighed in at around three hundred pounds. Angelica cowered in her chair as the words from a night several weeks before made the hair on the back of her neck stand to attention.

"Run, little girl, before I have you for dinner!"

Oh, dear God, she wanted to run, wanted to hide and cower from him. As if sensing her fear, Varick cradled her under his arm, gently running his hand through her hair.

She summoned her courage and looked at Kreach's arms. Both were covered in twisted snake tattoos. His head was shaved, and the same snake tattoo pattern on his hands ran from his forehead to the base of his neck. He stared at Alexander with his intense green eyes for a few seconds and then bowed stiffly.

When he bowed, Angelica saw the wide, jagged scar. Damn, he was one scary S.O.B.! The biker boots, black leather pants, spiked gloves, spiked collar, and long black leather jacket did not help matters much. Several piercings graced his would-have-been handsome features, but the sneer on his face easily extinguished any thoughts of actually sidling up to the guy. Angelica's eyes widened in fascination and then turned to horror as she looked closer and saw several deeply etched scars in his jaw line that resembled dog bites, only bigger—much, much bigger.

Yeah, he'd most certainly eat me alive!

Without so much as a word, Kreach left the table and disappeared into the crowd. Angelica frowned as Varick and Alexander toasted each other. What was she doing? She was sitting and listening to three complete strangers talking about God knows what, because it sure as hell made no sense to her. Sweat beaded her forehead as Varick's hand sent delightful goose bumps up her arm. Good lord, she needed a stiff drink.

By two in the morning, Angelica was well on her way to being plastered. The closer Varick got and the more he whispered in her ear, the more she drank. The more she drank, the more she was willing to take him up on the licking-her-all-over offer. She was vaguely aware of being pulled to her feet and led across the empty barroom. She held the hand that refused to let go of hers and followed blindly behind.

She took a deep breath as doors closed behind her. It tasted like rain and felt good in her lungs. She giggled and tripped. The hand that caught her before she fell pushed her up against the brick wall.

"You're going with me to my place. Say it."

"You're going with me to my place. Say it," she repeated with a slight slur.

"Say it right."

"It right." Angelica giggled as he ran his hand down her face.

"I want you tonight, and you are coming of your free will. Say it."

"Coming?" *What a delicious idea!*

"Say it," he growled.

"Ask me nicely and I might." She grinned as the muscles in his jaws twitched. "Beg me and I will."

His nostrils flared. "I don't beg!"

"That's a pity. I kinda like a man who begs." *Just where the hell did that come from? I'm flirting with him. Ah, hell, I want him!*

"Dogs beg. I do not." His voice deepened. "You are coming of your free will."

"Not unless you beg first." Angelica giggled in delight as he ran his hand across her breasts. "You'll have to work to get what you're asking of me."

Varick growled. The sound was pleasure wrapped in satin and dipped in chocolate.

Angelica wrapped her arms around his waist and sagged forward. "I'm really drunk. Can you take me home?"

Varick growled again as he ran his fingers up her spine and grabbed her hair. She moaned softly as his lips touched her neck. She had to feel his chest. The buttons miraculously came undone under her fingers, and she slid her hands inside. Her knees buckled as her hands contacted his skin. He was hot and chiseled like a statue, and Angelica was not about to refuse what she wanted to come next.

Her fingers tingled as she explored his raw flesh. She smiled when she heard his gasp as she lightly pulled on both of his nipples. Alcohol induced fantasies sizzled through her brain.

She wondered how she could possibly convince him to strip right here in the alley. Her hands dipped lower, running down over his six pack, inching lower following the line under his navel. She moaned as her fingers contacted the hard, silky skin of his manhood.

She tilted her head up, parted her lips, and waited for the first man she had ever touched so provocatively to kiss her.

Yep, that was Angelica Dark.

A thirty-year-old single woman living and breathing in the sinful city of Fether, California. She was in a dark alley in the middle of a rain shower with a man she barely knew. She was now working for an odd woman who thought Angelica was her niece. And she was totally on board with the fantasy she was having about Varick.

Well, at least Varick had a fine ass and a beautiful head of hair and muscles and hot skin and was as close to perfection as it gets. And his arrogance—it rolled off of him in tidal waves. What a way to end one of the strangest weeks she had ever had! That was the last thing she thought as she slipped into the numbing whirlpool of alcohol and honeysuckle.

Chapter 9

Varick caught Angelica as she stumbled. He rolled his eyes and chuckled as she moaned against his chest. Just his luck to find a woman who turned him on and bam, she passes out. He picked her up and drifted down the street, staying in the shadows and keeping a watchful eye over his shoulder. As he rounded the corner, he stepped back and narrowed his eyes.

The hair on his neck stood up as a vampire strolled out of the alley in front of him. Damn! Angelica cuddled closer to his chest as he eased back along the wall of the building. A cold rush of air went up his spine, and he pressed his back against the wall. Double damn! Another blood-sucking bastard strolled out of the alley he had just passed.

He closed his eyes and shimmered. He didn't like running from a fight, but he couldn't take the chance on leaving Angelica here in a drunken stupor. She was entirely too tempting a morsel to leave unguarded.

He looked down, and Angelica smiled groggily. "Key…uncer pot."

Varick laughed as he looked at the porch. A large pot with a dead plant sat next to the front door. Well, she sure didn't have a green thumb. He walked to the porch and eased her against the door as he slid the pot over with his foot. Sure enough, the key was there, and he picked it up.

Angelica leaned against his chest as he unlocked the door. She giggled as she fell backwards. Varick caught her as her butt hit the floor. A big, black cat jumped out from behind the door and hissed as Varick stepped in.

"Easy, friend. I'm just bringing her home. Seems she had a little too much to drink tonight."

The cat growled and turned away as Varick picked Angelica up. "Well, cat, lead the way to her room."

The cat strolled through the house and down a hallway. He stopped in front of the first door and rubbed up against the doorframe. Varick went in and laid Angelica across the bed. He grinned as he slid her sandals off of her feet. He looked around at the cat and laughed.

"Don't worry, friend, I won't hurt her."

As he walked out of her bedroom door, the cat hissed and stalked to the front door. He laughed as the cat glared at him. He locked the door and replaced the key under the pot. It was nearly sunrise, and he needed to get back home; being extra crispy bacon didn't appeal to him in the slightest.

Tomorrow was another day, and it was not like he didn't have all the time in the world; time was as easily found as it was lost. And as for Angelica, she was definitely going to cross his path again.

As he stepped off the last step, his form misted, swirled, and disappeared. The air was heavy and thick, and it reminded him of when he had been on Grace's pay role as an assassin, reminded him of times best left forgotten. But he couldn't forget, he would never forget or forgive himself for what he had done.

• • •

Two thousand and two years before present time, Grace had a group of assassins under her control. Among the wingless dragons, one male stood out.

He was known as Varick, and he was the only human-looking male among the lot. Fear was a rare quality to be found among the assassins, but it was the one feeling that he evoked from them all.

He was neither intimidated nor wary of the large assassins that surrounded the campfire. To look upon him, he seemed eerily out of place, but he was by far superior to any of the other assassins. When he spoke they listened. When he killed they cheered. When he slept they watched him with a wary eye.

Varick gritted his teeth as the others fed from the harvest pot. Kills had been many, and far too much meat had been wasted. The assassin clan had become gluttonous and annoyingly fearful since Grace's last visit. It would be justified if the others knew what the goddess had told him or, better yet, what she had ordered him to do.

He watched in silence as the assassins nervously kept their distance, chewing on bits of deer bones. Their long, sharp fangs scraped against the bones and crunched loudly as the twenty-four others settled in for the night.

Twenty-six assassins who knew not what was coming.

Twenty-six black-scaled, horned demons that walked as men, talked as men, and killed for a small payment from Grace.

For the first time in his life, Varick felt disgust roll through his body, clenching at the pit of his stomach.

Varick grinned slowly; Grace had offered him more than her usual token to fulfill her wish. He looked at the deerskin tent that stood a hundred paces to the east of the camp. His mother, a female vampire condemned by her own kind for being a handmaiden to the god Gyth, had been resting now for over an hour thanks to the aid of the sandalwood root he had slipped into her nightly goblet of blood that came from his own wrist.

His gaze traveled farther to the cave at the bottom of the mountain that was barred and the guard who was sleeping at his post. Twenty-seven assassins who took female humans as mates and kept them caged like animals until they died of disease, famine, or brutal torture were waiting.

Among the females, ten were bearing offspring. Thirty-seven assassins. And along the walls of the cave, hissing and huddled together, were twenty young assassins. Forty-seven assassins lay waiting, and they all would soon be exterminated.

A loud, crisp roar drew his attention to the night sky. Terror Sky cried out as he flew over the campsite. Varick grinned as his lifelong companion—what had the humans called him? Ah yes, a dragon—sliced through the air and landed on top of the cliffs. He waited eagerly as Varick turned his attention back to his next kill, his last assignment.

When he stood with swords drawn and a smile on his lips, Grace's words flooded his mind. "The assassins have dishonored me. They no longer justify the means, and they have become inferior to the other gods' creations. I want them eliminated, all of them. Do not leave a single survivor. Kill the human females and rip their organs from their bodies. If there is any offspring in their wombs, burn them. The young that huddle in the caves are to die as well. Search every hillside, every mound of rotting Earth until you destroy every last one of them. The exact number is four thousand four hundred and forty-four. Count them, Varick, and do as I command. In exchange for your services, I free you from servitude. And as a token of my appreciation I will give you a gift if the deed is fulfilled. The gift is mine to give at whatever time I choose. Do we have an understanding?"

He swirled and danced as one with his blades, and the assassins began to fall. Varick's reign of death lasted well into the early hours of morn.

As the last assassin fell, Terror Sky landed in front of him, heavy, sulfuric smoke billowing out of his great nostrils. Varick stepped back, his swords dropping to the ground. The great dragon rarely ever made such contact. He stayed off in the distance but close enough Varick could always see him.

He watched in awe as the giant lifted his neck and spewed a mountain of flames across the sky. His front legs lifted and his great wings stretched wide. Red mist filtered out of his skin as the dragon grew smaller and smaller. Varick fell to his knees as a man's form appeared where the great dragon had been. Dressed in black robes, the man raised one red-tinged black eyebrow and hunched down in front of him.

"I am Terror Sky. I am an Elemental." His sudden smile radiated menace. "Tell me why you have killed these assassins. They raised you, fed you, and trained you. Did they not deserve some respect from you?"

Varick fell forward, his body suddenly entirely too heavy for his bones. "The goddess I serve, Grace, ordered it of me."

"Oh, really? Did she order it or did you make a bargain with her? Can you not think for yourself?" Rage dripped from his voice. "You are pathetically ignorant, Varick. Why do you follow her orders?"

"She is a goddess. She controls everything here. You don't decline to accept a bargain with a goddess." His voice trembled as it had never done before.

The man—no, the god—snorted. "She controls you because you let her. You could have refused the deal. You could have at least listened to your soul before you took the lives of these assassins."

"I have no soul."

He laughed, a deep pacifying melody. "Of course you do."

"My mother is a vampire. Vampires don't have souls."

Again, the god laughed. "You and your mother are two of a kind. Vampires with souls."

Varick stood on shaking legs as the image before him warped back into dragon form. He reached out; he had to feel the scales to convince himself this was not a dream. His fingers slid over smooth scales, his sharp fingernails retracting as his hand dropped.

The dragon lifted, his great wings expanding. "You made a bargain with Grace and it's just the beginning of your destiny."

"What do you know of my destiny?" Varick stood. "I will make my own destiny."

"Is that what you want, to rise above what you were born to be?" Terror Sky circled above him, his voice booming across the mountains. "Accept what you are, learn how to control yourself, and be wary of the treachery of the gods above and below. Then, maybe, you'll be able to control your own destiny."

Varick shrugged. "That's not an obstacle. It can be easily done."

"Not if you're dead."

Varick stepped back, bent to retrieve his swords, and hissed. "Is that why you show yourself? Do you plan to be my assassin?"

The dragon god circled in the air above him, his fire-filled breath scorching the land around his feet. "You have two years, Varick, son of Vicery Beth, two years to enjoy the rest of this life. Then you will die."

Varick laughed with vicious ire. "I'm not afraid of death. It beckons me with such a sweet voice."

"No," Terror Sky roared. "That's not death that beckons you, it's the goddess Zena, the queen of the vampires."

Chapter 10

Angelica took a deep breath and knocked on the ancient-looking door that opened into Alera's office. The door creaked open, and Angelica walked in like a schoolgirl with her tail tucked between her legs. Guilt had a way of doing that to a girl, even if she was thirty years old.

She looked up and frowned as Alera rose from her chair and waved toward the chair in front of her desk. A strange shiver went up her spine as she heard the door close softly behind her. Just who the hell had opened it if Alera had been behind the desk? And furthermore, who the hell had just closed it?

"There's something I would like to speak to you about." Alera raised one eyebrow in curiosity as Angelica looked over her shoulder at the door. "Is something wrong?"

"How did that door just close?"

Alera shrugged, "The wind?" She pointed to the chair in front of her desk. "Please, sit down."

Angelica sat down. "We're inside, there isn't any wind."

Alera grimaced. "Perhaps the door is off centered. Look, we need to talk about your mother."

"Why? I already told you, I never met her." Angelica vaguely wondered why the woman's eyes were so bloodshot. "Alera, I think I might quit."

Alera leaned back in her chair and frowned. "I see. Is there anything I can offer you to get you to stay? I know you work a lot at the museum and on weekends here. We could change your hours, make sure you have a day off."

Angelica knitted her eyebrows together and stared at Alera. "Not really. I think you were right, I'm not waitress material."

"I'm aware of what happened." Alera smiled, a pained look washing over her face. "The security camera caught you and Varick in an embrace right outside the club. Is he the reason you want to quit?"

"No." Angelica rubbed her temples and crossed her legs. "The bartender told me that if they asked me to join them, you said to do it. I resent that you used me like some kind of escort for your friends."

"Do you regret it? Spending the night with him?"

Angelica's face turned three shades of red. "Well, uh, you see, it's just. Yeah. Oh, good lord, that's none of your business."

"I guess it isn't." Alera's eyes dulled. She rose from her chair and came around the desk and stood in front of Angelica. "Give me your hand."

She took Angelica's hand and pressed a cold metal charm into her palm. Angelica looked at the two-sided charm. On one side there was a dove in front of a sunrise and on the other was a dragon in front of a full moon. Angelica took a deep breath as a wave of heat hit her in the stomach.

Alera spoke quietly as Angelica ran her fingers over its surface. "I want you to have this. It's very old and the only one of its kind. If you believe in magic, then you may appreciate that this little object is said to contain the force of our creator's hand."

"Why are you giving this to me?"

Alera smiled weakly. "I think you may find you will need it more than I ever will. Grace, an old family friend, gave it to me. She told me that if you ever needed something bad enough, all you have to do is rub it and your need would be granted."

"Sounds like a fairy tale."

Angelica slipped the charm into her pocket and pulled out the diary she had hidden there. The book in her hand was old and the cover was discolored, but the name Antonia was written across the front. She clutched the book to her chest as Alera eyed it. Angelica's heart burned with ache as she assured herself it would be kept safe.

Angelica handed the book she was so carefully protecting to Alera. "This is my mother's diary. The language is close to Old Latin, but no one at the museum seems to be able to translate it. They all think it was some sort of joke because of the Egyptian hieroglyphs mixed in with the other characters."

Alera delicately took the book as Angelica handed it to her.

Alera stared mutely at the first page as her sister's words burned into her mind:

Today, I spoke with Grace. She had wonderful news. I am pregnant. I have decided to keep this journal in hopes that someday it will serve as a path to the past, our past, our love, and our journey to the future.

Forcing her tears aside, she cleared her throat before speaking. "Only a few people can decipher this particular written language."

"That's a little too far-fetched to believe." She bit her lower lip. "Only a few people in the entire world? I know I shouldn't even bother to ask but who?" Angelica leaned forward.

"I'm one of those few. It's the written language of my people."

Angelica frowned. "Will you read it to me? Or at least teach me how to read it? I have wondered about her for so long, and it would mean a great deal to me and my brother if we could at least know what's in those pages."

"Perhaps I should speak with Gyth about this. There are things in this world he may or may not want you to know."

Irritation ran through Angelica. "Who is Gyth? And why would I have to have his permission? That diary was my mother's, and I don't understand why its contents should be anyone else's business."

"In time, I think you'll understand, but for now I'll begin to translate it. If Gyth advises me to allow you to learn the language, then I'll teach you, but until then I can only say that it begins with her pregnancy with your brother."

Angelica frowned but nodded her head. "Okay, I'll leave the diary here. If I have family somewhere else on this planet—aunts, uncles, or cousins—will you at least let me know about them and if they're mentioned in her diary?"

"Let me speak to Gyth first and we'll see."

Angelica stood, trying not to show how much leaving the diary behind was bothering her. It had become a part of her somehow. Turning to the door, she rubbed the charm. "It's a beautiful charm. I guess I could continue to work weekends for now but I won't be used like an escort again."

Alera nodded. "Thank you, Angelica."

•••

Alera frowned as Angelica closed the door behind her. Grace had placed the charm on her desk barely an hour ago and had instructed her to make sure it was placed in Angelica's hand. Well, she had done as ordered. She wondered if the girl knew what was coming, and for a split second she wished her niece the best of luck. If she could defy Gyth for Angelica she would, but she couldn't. No one defied Gyth and lived to tell the tale. If she kept the diary from him, she was dooming herself.

She shuddered as her thoughts turned to Varick. He had entered the first stages of the Mating Rite. She could smell it lingering on his skin like battery acid. Rubbing her aching eyes, she caught her breath as she realized Angelica might very well get caught up in the trap of servicing Varick. And, sweet merciful Heavens above, Angelica was thirty and the Burning was coming! Alera damn near fainted at the thought.

She had witnessed a Destroyer's Mating Rite first hand, and she was in no way eager to experience it again. Her face froze, her eyes becoming darker as she thought of her mate.

Alera shifted in her chair, tears welling in her eyes, and tried to remember what Grace had told her. It was not like her to be forgetful. And why was she suddenly overwhelmed with ill feelings towards her mate? Forcing her mate from her thoughts, she took a deep breath and refused to allow the last thousand years to catch up to her heart.

She was Alera, owner of Tortured Souls, and she was no sniveling little princess who cried over spilled milk or lost her senses because she suddenly no longer wanted her mate. She tried to keep things in order—all things must go as planned, and no outside interference was allowed in the sanctuary of the Destroyers.

Angelica was still human—that in itself was going to be a problem. Varick would be brutal, and he would not hold back. She slammed her fist down onto the desk. Angelica would die. If the terror of his beast didn't kill her, the Destroyer in him would. An odd thought occurred to her as she fumed; she wondered what Varick looked like in his beastly form. Would he be a monster? A demon? An angel? What form would he take to finish the Mating Rite?

Choking back her tears, she dialed Varick' cell. When he answered with his usual quick banter, her heart lodged into her throat.

"I have Antonia's diary." Her voice cracked, and she heard his rumble of curses. "Her daughter wishes for me to translate it."

"Is it in Atlantian?" A distinct, bone-crunching sound echoed in her ear as she heard metal contact metal.

"Yes." She sucked in a harsh breath as she heard a shrill cry and then utter silence.

His voice was deep, twisted. "Translate it for her, but if it mentions anything about the gods, call me first."

Chapter 11

Angelica groaned as she found the schedule that had been hidden by the monstrous piles of papers on her mahogany desk. The day had progressed slowly, her back and legs aching. Rubbing her neck, she stared at the schedule as if it would magically change. Twelve tours, three new Egyptian admissions, and a mandatory meeting were all scheduled in three days. The museum seemed to just get busier and busier every day. Seemed like she never got to enjoy it anymore.

She wanted something to enjoy. The urge to call her brother struck her heart strings. She missed him, his jokes, his selfish ego, and his big stubborn eyes. Not once had he answered her calls. And she had called hundreds of times. Not one letter. His last words to her when she had gotten into her car were 'I can't make you stay here, but you're making a mistake.'

With her eyes closed, she leaned her head back against the soft leather of her chair and took a deep breath. Varick came to mind as she plowed through her thoughts. He was the sexiest man she had ever met in her entire life. She wanted to just sit here and enjoy the fantasies that were spilling out of her mind.

Another groan eased from her lips. If her body didn't quit aching, she probably wouldn't be enjoying much of anything. Her door opening brought her head up, her eyes open. Theo, her boss, smiled and closed the door behind him.

"Hey, lady. Just got this in a little over two months ago." He held up an old, tattered book. "It's been warranted as a fake, and since the museum owners didn't want it, I bought it. Thought you might want to take a look at it."

Angelica stood, watched him rake his fingers through his short graying blond hair, and took the book. "Thanks. What is it?"

"It came over with the shipment from Nigeria. It's the oddest damn thing." He mumbled under his breath, shrugged. "It puzzles me."

"What do you mean?" she asked as she gently opened the ragged, tattered front cover.

"Well, at first I thought it might be some kind of spin-off of the book of the dead, but once I looked at it closer—well, you'll see."

Angelica caught her breath. "These are the same symbols as in my mother's diary!"

"Yeah. I figured you'd like to have it even if it's a fake." His wide smile melted Angelica's heart. "And besides it makes the perfect gift."

Blinking in surprise, she laughed as he pulled out a birthday card. "Happy birthday. Everyone here has signed it."

"Thanks Theo. I love the book and the card." He laid the card on her desk. "It's nice to know someone remembered my birthday."

He grinned. "You're welcome."

She examined the cover, and her eyes widened as she ran her fingertips over the four corners. Underneath her fingers were finely etched dragons and doves, the same as on the charm Alera had given her. Her mind raced and tumbled around as Theo left.

Returning to the book, she drew closer noticing that underneath the hand written symbols there was faint silver lettering. Softly scratching at the ink, she uncovered one word. Rjurazmi. In Sanskrit, it meant resurrection.

She jumped as the intercom on her desk chimed and the receptionist spoke. "Angelica, you have a call on line two."

Laughing at herself, she reached for the phone. "Hello, this is Angelica."

"Angelica. This is Varick." She shuddered, his voice sending goose bumps along her skin. "I must apologize for the other night. I was under the influence and not acting like myself."

"And you think I will forgive you just because you called?" She leaned back, stretching her legs. God, her muscles ached and her back felt like a twisted towel. "Today is my birthday. Take me out, then I will consider forgiving you."

"As you wish."

"Where are we going?" she asked as she gently placed the book in her desk drawer. An intricate sequence of pictures ran through her mind. Like an old movie player, images of Varick in different poses flipped in front of her eyelids.

"Dinner and then to a club, and please wear a dress. I've never seen you in anything other than slacks."

The pain in her back tightened, pelted down her spine. She twisted to the right, then to the left hoping the pain would lessen. But it didn't.

"If you'd give me a massage, I'd be tempted to wear leaves and vines," she mumbled as she searched her top drawer for back pain medicine.

"Now, that's a picture I would enjoy looking at," Varick responded seductively. "Of course, I would prefer the privacy of your place or mine for such an occasion."

Angelica smiled as she locked the book safely out of sight. "Seriously though, can you not be so controlling? I mean, I like the way I dress."

He sighed softly. "I know you do. I will pick you up at nine."

As an afterthought, she said, "Varick, I wasn't serious about the vines and leaves thing and this doesn't mean I'm going to climb into bed with you."

"Don't stomp on a man's dreams, darling. It's not good for my ego."

"Believe me, you have enough ego to spare a few heartbreaks."

"You know, if you would just give me a fair chance, I could prove I'm a man of exquisite talents."

"A fair chance?" Angelica grinned. "I've given you a chance. And do those talents all lead to the bedroom? Or are you going to leave me hanging like you did the night you walked me home?"

"You're downright insufferable, to say the least. A wisp of a woman pointing out my mistakes and then demanding an apology from me, unbelievable." He laughed. "It was a poor decision on my part. Truly, I am sorry I didn't. I wish I had of kissed you."

"I don't know what it is about you Varick, but I like bantering with you." She glanced at the clock on the wall. The day couldn't be going any slower. "You're controlling, demanding, you have this huge ego to contend with, and you're too good-looking for your own good."

"Don't forget the best part, I'm persistent." She could see him running his hand through his hair, a smile on his lips. "I promise to make that kiss up to you."

Angelica slowly sat down, leaned back in her chair, and closed her eyes. She wasn't going to let a little backache ruin her night. "Nine, and if you are a minute late, I won't go."

"I'll see you then."

"Remember, don't be late." She twisted the top off the medicine bottle. "And I'm not wearing a dress."

"The leaves and vines, perhaps?" His chuckle echoed in her head, made her smile.

"You're not getting that lucky."

"I look forward to our…" He paused. "Date."

"So do I. Goodbye Varick."

"Goodbye." The phone clicked, dead silence on the other send.

Angelica returned the phone to the base, put the pills in her mouth, and swallowed. Visions of Varick swam in her mind, creating a drugging fantasy. His hands, his mouth, and his body all over hers, in hers. She groaned, shook off the fantasy.

Varick was a head or two above all the other men she had ever met—hell, he was the icing and the cake. He was the pot of gold at the end of the rainbow, and all other men were like greedy little leprechauns that wanted what he had.

Laughing, she had to admit she sure as hell wanted what he had. Now that she thought about it, she guessed that made her greedy, too, because she wanted to have her cake and eat it while sitting on top of that beautiful, big pot of gold.

Chapter 12

Zena toyed with the hair of the fledgling vampire that sat at her feet. The male behind her hummed as his long, ashen fingers worked through her hair, undoing the black braid. A female stood in front of her holding a triangular mirror, its reflection staring back at the vampire goddess relentlessly.

Vanity was such a cruel term. Zena hissed, letting her double-edged fangs extend. She leaned back, her clawed fingertips curling into her slave's hair.

Without her minions, without their precious blood, she would age, or at least her skin would. And that was not something she would allow.

Carefully, she tried to choose one of the minions to feed upon. In the Underworld, they were her cattle, so to speak, and did not need sustenance. The ones that had been on Earth when the portals were closed had not been so lucky. They had to feed from humans to retain their health and youth. She grunted and spat on the black floor. Human blood was so unsatisfying. She needed the blood of her minions. It was why they had been created. Her black eyes narrowed into tiny slits.

The war between Damon and Gyth had caused so much misery. Relentless hatred welled up in her throat for both of them. Their stupid war had led to Gyth imprisoning Damon to the Underworld and any who had followed him, including herself. Here, in this dark hole, she had adapted, found that to nourish herself she could feed from the vampires. Above nourishing herself, she found that she enjoyed it far more than eating the ambrosia in the Heavens.

"Mistress?" One of her nameless minions came slithering to her throne. "We have found something of interest."

She abruptly stood. "Where?"

He bowed his head as her horns came rushing out of her skull and twisted down the sides of her head. "I will take you, mistress."

Zena followed, her heart thudding desperately in her chest. They followed corridors, deeper and deeper into the labyrinth that was the Underworld. Minutes seemed like hours as she slithered behind the minion.

At the end of a long tunnel, the male stopped and smiled, showing his jagged yellow teeth. They were slimy and glistened. "Here, mistress, feel the wall."

She pushed him out of her way and gently laid her palm against the root-covered wall. She gasped and jerked back as a bolt of electricity raced through her veins. "Tear it down, shred the roots, and reveal to me what lies beyond!"

Anxiety filled her as she watched as the roots give way, soft green light filtering out of the many slits and tears. Her heart stopped as the doorway revealed itself.

The soft green glow led into a wide chamber. Dust had settled over every nook and crevice of the gigantic room. In the center stood a large, blacked-out mirror, its frame glistening and glowing. A soft lull lilted through the air as she slowly made her way to it.

Reaching out, she touched the mirror, its cold black surface instantly turning to lukewarm ripples of sand. Her hand began to shake as she attentively stepped through the warmth. She kept her eyes closed as her body was propelled through. Voices surrounded her, begged her to stop and speak to them. Ripples of unseen water touched her arms with the barest flutter of butterfly wings. And for the first time in her long life, she felt a sort of peace.

Unable to control herself, she opened her eyes and gasped. She was surrounded by translucent water, but at the same time she breathed. Her body was not wet, yet she felt like she was submerged, pliant with the gentle pulls of nature. The water churned, bubbling softly all around her. She laughed as she popped bubbles like a child, giggled like she had found a new lover, and splashed the clear water as if she were a water nymph.

A scream ripped from her throat as hands as cold as Gyth's black heart wound around her and dragged her down into the churning bubbles. A voice, one so soul-shatteringly beautiful and full of sorrow that she nearly wished herself dead, roared and whipped through her body, sending her headlong into desperation and regret.

Through her bloody tears, she cried, "This is the River Styx! I have found the portal!"

Laughter filled her ears as she was thrown into a vortex of purples and blues, sparks of purple-black flames licking at her skin and stripping her of sanity. When at last she knew she would give in to the overwhelming misery, she fell to her knees in cool, gritty sand.

Urging her body to listen to her impulses, she looked up and laughed with absolute satisfaction. She stood on shaky legs and stared at the small ball of transparent water before her. Willing her hand to reach out, she lightly touched it with her fingertips. Instantly, her body slipped back into the vortex. This was the answers to her prayers—Varick would be hers very, very soon.

• • •

Charon stood on the edge of the Isle of the Blessed and Condemned. He felt the pull of Jaiden's books, felt their power humming in the air. His robes fluttered in the breeze as Terror Sky appeared beside of him.

"I have located several of the books. Two have crossed Angelica's hands," Charon stated. "Several of them are in the Heavens above. Varick's destiny is being tampered with as we speak and so is Angelica's for that matter."

Terror Sky nodded, his expression blank. "Travel to Earth and find those books. It's time we intervene before more damage is done."

"What of Gyth? He'll not be so welcoming once he learns who I am and what I'm after." Charon lifted the hood of his robes revealing his face. "He will fear the worst if he suspects I am after Varick."

"Let him fear whatever he will." Terror Sky turned to walk away. "Someone needs to put some fear into him."

Charon narrowed his eyes. "Do I have free reign?"

Terror Sky stopped in his tracks. "Do what you must. Varick must make the choice, regardless of what the gods above or below have planned for him. Gyth has changed so much of his true destiny it's uncertain if we can even correct his path."

"And Angelica? Is she to be protected or is she disposable?" Charon laughed as Terror Sky dropped his head. "Disposable then."

"Her destiny is of little importance. In truth, she was never meant to be born. She is a consequence of Gyth's actions. Pity that she must pay the price for Gyth's lust to create the perfect Destroyer."

"Is she not as her brother is? Will she not be a Destroyer after she goes through the Burning?" Charon's question hung in the utter silence.

"Isten doesn't see her future. Women were never to be Destroyers. Her destiny is a blank page. Varick is to be the focus of your attention." Terror Sky turned slightly, shadows of secrets in his swirling eyes. "If Angelica becomes a problem, kill her."

"Will that be necessary?"

"I wouldn't order her death if it wasn't." Terror Sky's jaw tightened. "Go. Do what must be done."

Charon waved his hand and a vortex appeared. The River Styx gurgled, swirled, and waited. As he stepped into the vortex, an odd sight was displayed before him. Zena's image appeared in the bubbles, swirled in different directions, and slowly disappeared.

She thought to use the portals without paying the ferryman? Charon grinned. She would pay; all paid the ferryman in one form or another. It had been too long since he bartered with someone for using Styx and he looked forward to the collecting. And he was eager to see exactly what the beautiful vampire goddess had to trade.

Chapter 13

Alera waited patiently in front of the museum for Angelica to come out. Running her hands over the steering wheel of her Jaguar XKR, she tried to convince herself she was doing the right thing. Angelica needed to know to the truth, needed to know what was going to happen over the next few days.

Her hands trembled as she looked down at her arms. Turning, she grabbed a light jacket from the back seat and shrugged it on. Her mate had returned home briefly and had left his calling card all over her. As quickly as tears slid down her cheeks, she wiped them away. She wasn't going to feel sorry for herself, but the shame would always be there, lingering in the depths of her heart.

Lost in her thoughts, Alera jumped when a horn beeped. Squaring her shoulders, she watched as Angelica walked down the steps in front of the museum. She shut her eyes, counted to five, and stepped out of the Jaguar.

"Angelica?" Alera smiled when Angelica waved. "Do you need a ride?"

Angelica hurried across the parking lot. "Sure."

Once they were both seated, Alera started the car. "You know, it's not real safe to be walking alone around here."

"I don't have much a choice. My car is broke down and can't afford to get it fixed anytime soon. Besides, God gave me two legs and two feet, might as well use them." Angelica looked out her window. "I don't see any danger in walking. It's not like someone is going to jump out and grab me in broad daylight."

"Still, you should consider getting your car fixed." Alera tapped on the steering wheel nervously. "There's all kind of things that could happen, especially to someone like you."

Angelica laughed. "Someone like me?"

Alera thought of her sisters. Women who were descendants of the gods above needed to be protected at all times. So few of them lived through the Burning.

She knew it was time to explain things to Angelica whether she wanted to hear it or not.

"Yes, someone like you. There's something I need to explain about that birthmark." Alera glanced at Angelica; saw the sudden peak of interest in her eyes. "Just promise to listen to everything I need to tell you."

Angelica slowly nodded, biting her lower lip. "Okay."

Pulling up to a red light, Alera reached over and squeezed Angelica's hand. "Some of the things I'm going to say are going to be hard to believe."

"You act like there's going to be skeletons falling out of the closet." She pulled her hand away. "I'll listen just because I'm curious about my mother."

The light turned green as Alera cleared her tight throat. "We're descendants of the goddess Amay, the last descendants."

"Stop the car." Angelica grabbed the door handle. "Stop the car, Alera!"

Alera swerved to the curb, the front tire hitting the concrete. She grabbed Angelica's arm. "You said you would listen."

"You need professional help." Angelica jerked her arm away. "I'm not going to listen to this garbage."

"You're going to enter the Burning." Alera slammed the car into park. "Things are going to start happening to you. Your hormones are going to go into over-drive. The first signs are dizziness, confusion, an overwhelming need to have sex, and…"

Angelica jumped out of the car, slamming the door behind her. Alera cursed under her breath and slammed her palms onto the steering wheel. She had to get Angelica to listen even if she didn't believe any of it.

Turning the key off and getting out of the car, Alera followed Angelica, sped up to catch her. "And there's a chance you won't make it out of the transition alive."

Angelica stopped. "Do you have an idea just how crazy you sound?"

Alera glanced down the sidewalk, noticed how quiet and empty the row of houses looked. They were all the same; white picket fences in neat little rows, same structure, and same color. The wind wasn't blowing; the air was dead and empty, stale. She felt like she was standing in the center of a movie prop or a ghost town.

She shook off the eerie feeling and nodded. "Yes, I know it sounds crazy." She held out her arm, pointing to the birthmark. "This isn't just a birthmark. It's a sign, a warning for those of us who have to go through the transition."

Angelica looked at her wrist. "What transition?"

"Descendants born on Earth mature in a human form until they reach thirty years of age. That's when the Burning starts." Alera took Angelica's hands into hers. "The dormant DNA in your body will surface, change your cell structure. It's painful and terrifying. If you survive, the power of the One Race will flow through your veins."

"If I believed anything you're saying, which I don't. My first question would be; why would descendants have to go through pain? Why wouldn't they just be born with power?"

"Members of the One Race are only part god or goddess. The laws of the Heavens decree anyone born with human DNA isn't allowed to dwell in the Heavens. Those same laws say that for us to have power, immortality, or any kind of distinction, we must endure the Burning." Alera released Angelica's hands. "You must allow someone to take you through it."

Without a word, Angelica pushed past Alera and walked away. Alera stood there, praying to Gyth for Angelica's safe journey. Her niece had no idea just what she was going to experience, the pain, the fear, the maddening drive to mark the one who took her through the transition.

She looked up to the clear sky and closed her eyes. "Gyth. Angelica Dark, my neice, descendant of Amay, has no idea of what is to come. Please, pick a worthy, gentle Destroyer to help her survive this."

Lightning danced across the sky, thunder rumbling in the distance. When she opened her eyes, clouds had appeared. Quickly getting back to her Jaguar, she trembled as she slid under the wheel. Her car started of its own accord, the radio blasting in her ears.

The sky rumbled and hail fell from the Heavens.

• • •

Gyth glided down the hall of One Race Legacy, his pristine robes swirling about his bare feet. On both sides of the hall, scrolls lined the shelves. Within the pages, every member of the One Race was listed. Their birthdate, names, and their date of death inscribing as the events unfolded.

Stopping, he reached out and took one from the shelf.

Amay's name was etched into the seal and he slid his fingers over each letter. The letters began to glow and the scroll opened. He ran his finger down the length of names, dates, and genders until he found two that were not deceased. Gyth stared at one of the names, his eyes swirling with golden fire.

Angelica Dark's name stared back at him. Gyth read the small passage under her name, his anger flushing his cheeks. Someone had taken very careful steps to hide her from him but thanks to Alera, he now knew of her existence.

He spoke and the walls shook, the floor groaned, and dust fell from the ceiling. "Daughter of Feverand and Antonia Dark, the only female born from one of my Destroyers."

Slamming the book shut, he turned on his heel. No doubt, Amay and Grace were behind this incident. They continuously conspired with one another, creating drama and needless chaos. He had overlooked most of their childish antics; this time however, he would not be so forgiving.

"Lord Gyth?" The female voice was low, childish. "I would speak with you."

"Yes." Gyth narrowed his eyes as one of the bookkeepers appeared in front of him. "What is it?"

"Charon is awaiting you in the throne room. He insists he must speak to you at once."

"Charon?" Gyth handed the small goddess the book. "Charon the ferryman?"

She nodded, her blond curls bouncing around her angelic face. He watched her float up and replace the scroll. His jaw flexed as he leaned against one of the shelves.

True, he was lord of the Heavens, but he wasn't all-seeing or all-knowing. That didn't mean he didn't have eyes and ears everywhere.

"Who else comes to visit this place?"

She turned, still hovering by the shelf. "Most of the other gods and goddesses have been here."

"Do any of them look at these scrolls?"

"They stand and stare at most of them, but only open their own." She shrugged as she floated to his side, "A few have tried to open other books but no one ever succeeds. The books only open to you and to the bloodline of which it's inscribed."

"Amay and Grace?"

"They have stood where you stand now. Thirty human years ago, Amay opened the same one as you." She looked down the hall, her blue irises swirling. "Charon grows impatient."

Gyth could barely remember the old god's face, hadn't seen him since the Olympians had been defeated. And he didn't really care if Charon was growing impatient or not. Under the circumstance, he had bigger issues to deal with.

Angelica Dark's Burning. What were the odds she would be like her brother? What were the odds she would make it through the transition alive?

"If anyone comes to this place again, inform me immediately." He straightened himself and glided back up the hall.

She bowed her small head, "Of course, my lord."

Chapter 14

Varick stood in front of Angelica's door. Nervously pulling at the collar and tie of his black dress shirt. He considered turning to mist and taking his ass back home to change into jeans and a T-shirt. A quick glance at his Dodge Viper changed his mind. How would he explain his disappearance if she saw the car before he returned?

He was a proverbial train wreck, derailed and useless. He readjusted his collar and ditched the tie. Trying to convince himself he could make it through the night without appearing to be crazed, he cracked the muscles in his neck and regained some of his calm.

The dark purple roses in his hand slipped from his grasp and he caught them an inch before they hit the porch floor. Inspecting them carefully, he wished he had gotten the red ones. Or the yellow ones.

He ran his free hand over his hair making sure it was neatly pulled back and secured at the nape of his neck. He could do this. Romancing a woman was easy. A few right words and a few well-placed touches and she would be more than ready for him. She would be begging.

He had this under control.

Gods above, who am I kidding? He was completely hot-wired, a remote controlled time bomb waiting to explode and Angelica was holding the detonator.

Said detonator holder opened the door and he forgot how to breathe as he took her appearance in. She was flat out gorgeous.

A black, tight leather skirt hung from her hips like a second skin. Her black hair was pulled back with ringlets of hair hanging down her shoulders. Onyx earrings dangled from her ears and she wore a matching ring on her forefinger. He silently wished he was her black, silk sleeveless blouse so he could wrap around her body the same way it did.

She smiled, her eyes dropping to the skirt. "It's not a dress."

Varick handed her the roses rather clumsily trying to find his voice. Angelica stepped back, invited him in.

"I like it. You look good in black."

"I love the color black, always have." He went to the living room as she spoke over her shoulder. "I'll just put these in some water and I'll be ready to go."

He looked at the door, was tempted to haul his ass right back out of it. But he couldn't do that. His beast needed to be sated. He turned and watched Angelica. He liked her, she was spunky and charming. The best inside his mind roared with agreement.

The way she was standing and moving reminded him of a moth. Delicate. Soft. He liked moths. They were graceful and beautiful. And creatures of the night, just like him.

He shook his head. What the hell was he thinking? Once he was through with her, he would go back to his normal life of hunting and destroying. She would be just a memory and he would never look at another moth the same.

Angelica set the flowers on her table and walked toward him. "Ready?"

He nodded. Letting her take his arm, he led her out the door and waited as she locked up. Her scent danced around him making him to want to bury his face in her hair, in her neck.

She stepped off the porch and looked over her shoulder. "Is something wrong?"

"No." He tried to smile. His face felt like it was made of stone. "It's been a long day."

"We can cancel, if you want to." He sensed her disappointment. "I've had a long day too."

He went to his Viper, opened the door for her. "Absolutely not going to cancel. We have a date and it's a special day. Happy birthday, Angelica."

Her face lit up. "Okay. Where we going?"

"I made reservations at Raven's." She slid into the car giving him a questioning look. "Raven's is down by the beach on Third and Main. Members only."

"Oh." She relaxed into the leather seat as he closed the door and sprinted around to the driver's side.

He slid into his seat and started the engine. He heard her laugh. Glancing over at her, he put the Viper in reverse. "Is something funny?"

"A demolition man?" She ran her hand over the dash of the car. "Very nice car."

He drew his eyebrows together. Nodded his head. Realization dawned on him, he had driven one of the most expensive cars he owned and was taking her to the most expensive place in Fether.

"Destroying things pays damn good."

"Apparently, it does." She smiled. His heart hammered. "Maybe I should go into that line of business."

Varick laughed. "It's dangerous and dirty. Lots of smoke, fire, and flying debris." He backed out of her driveway and pulled up to the first stop light. "Long hours and huge messes to clean up."

They rode in silence through the city, the occasional street light flickering. When he pulled into the parking lot at Raven's, he took her hand and kissed her knuckles before getting out of the car.

If he were smart, he'd take her back home. Just forget the whole thing and deal with the beast on his own. He opened her door and knew he couldn't. As she stepped out and slid next to him, his heart seized and his beast rattled his brain cells.

• • •

In the park across from Angelica's house, a slack jawed woman stood. Her empty eyes followed the black Dodge Viper as it drove down the street. Through her eyes, Damon watched. As he closed the connection, the woman fell forward, dead before she hit the ground.

Damon turned from the cauldron in his room and paced the floor. He had been keeping an eye on Varick for some time now and knew the Destroyer couldn't sense witches as he did vampires. It was disgustingly easy to spy on him.

This woman Varick had become attached to intrigued Damon. And the street she lived on was interesting as well. The witch could not cross the street which meant someone was protecting the woman. Someone was hiding her.

He turned as the snake at his feet coiled and prepared to strike. He felt the presence before he appeared. Narrowing his eyes, he waited for Charon to appear. In his usual fashion, Charon's footsteps sounded first. The crunch of dead leaves bounced around the room and the ferryman appeared.

"Damon. How do you fare?" Charon's face switched from man to skeleton. "Are you enjoying your rule of the Underworld?"

Damon smiled. "I'm enjoying it rather well. Tell me, what brings you back? We had our bargain long ago."

Charon's scythe appeared in his right hand. "Indeed we did." Charon looked across the room at the mirror that stood beside of Damon's bed. "I see you have achieved most of what you desired."

Damon held out his hands. "I'm the king of the Underworld. I control everything and everyone in this place. I can sit on my throne and watch as Gyth's precious Destroyers are tormented and tortured. I watch as members of the One Race die. What more could I possibly want?"

"You'll want more." Charon's eyes glowed red. "More power. More death. More revenge."

Damon had no regrets. His bargain with Charon had ensured him the throne of the Underworld. He was exactly where he needed to be to make sure Gyth never rested and was always reminded of Damon.

"I need something from you." Charon stepped forward, the snake at Damon's feet striking at him. With a swing of his scythe, the snake's head rolled past Damon's feet. "I'm willing to bargain with you to get it. So, tell me, Damon. What is it you want most?"

A fine layer of sweat broke out across Damon's forehead. What did he want? He wanted Gyth's head.

"That I can't give you." Charon barked a laugh. "Even after two thousand years, you still hate Gyth with an undying passion."

"Tell me what you need from me and then I'll figure out what payment I want in return."

Charon's face twisted back to man. "You will spare the life of Angelica Dark."

Damon threw his head back and laughed. "Spare her? Why would I do that when I could kill her and make Varick Ta Farg more miserable than he already is? Or convert her?"

"Because Damon. Either you'll make this bargain with me or you'll lose this war between you and Gyth tonight." Charon grinned. "At no time will you attempt to kill her."

Damon cracked his neck. He knew Charon was powerful. He was one of the few remaining old gods. And it was better to have him on your side than against you.

Pacing the floor, an odd thought occurred to him. He stopped and looked at Charon. "I'll spare her for a little information."

"The deal is set."

A silver chain appeared in Charon's hand. He lifted the hood and pulled out a single black hair. With his scythe, he sliced his palm. He wrapped the hair around the chain and let his blood fall onto the hair.

"Body, flesh of mine. Blood, power of mine. Soul, power of the gods. I give you my word." He held out the chain. "If you break your word and she dies, your soul will belong to me."

Damon nodded. "And if you tell me an untruth, your soul will belong to me."

Damon went to Charon and took the chain. It wrapped around his hand and melted into his flesh.

"What information do you seek?"

"What is Gyth's weakness?" Damon grinned.

In a burst of smoke, Charon disappeared as he spoke two words. "His son."

Chapter 15

Angelica groaned as Varick pulled up in the parking lot next to Tortured Souls. They had just had a wonderful meal at Raven's even though he seemed a little detached and stiff. She had wanted to get him in a more private setting; a little club not to crowded would have been nice. She definitely hadn't expected him to bring her here. Of all the clubs on the coast, why had he chosen this place?

Anywhere, please, anywhere but here. In her mind, the perfect night with Varick did not include coming to the place where she worked. What was he going to do, show her off to his friends?

He grinned like a schoolboy as he got out of and came to her side. He opened the door and took her hand. She silently hoped no one would recognize her as she waited for Varick to lock the car. Suddenly, she didn't think she could do this, was she ready to take things farther with him?

"You're absolutely stunning." His voice was low, sexy.

Angelica smiled, though she wanted to groan. "Thanks. Look, maybe this wasn't such a good idea."

He ran his hand through his hair and sighed. "I have to check in with my friends to make sure I haven't missed a job. This shouldn't take long."

"Seriously?" She rubbed her temple, suddenly getting an ache behind her eyes. "We're on a date and you're worried about a job?"

He looked at the door of the club, seemed to be trying to make a decision.

Angelica looked down at the asphalt, "If you're job is that important to you that you need to break away from our date, just take me home."

Varick with his big, gold, heavy-lashed eyes smiled and brought her into his arms for a sweet embrace. "You're not getting away that easily. If I have to spend the entire night wooing and coaxing you, I will. I'll walk on glass and eat fire just to steal a kiss from your lips."

Oh, man! He was so saying the right words.

Stepping back, she managed to smile at him. "All that for just a kiss?"

His large hands cupped her face. "Yeah, all that just for a taste of your lips. One taste."

He leaned in closer, his chest pressing against her breasts. She swallowed hard as her stomach tightened in anticipation.

She shivered, surely from the brisk breeze.

"Varick," she managed as his fingers slid to her neck, caressing, rubbing at her pulse. "Stop taking your slow time and kiss me already."

He didn't crack a smile, not even a laugh. He simply stared into her eyes for a long minute, his lips pressed into a thin line. Angelica reached up, slid her hands around his neck and gently pulled his head toward hers.

If he needed a little help, she would give it to him.

For a split second, she didn't think he was going to kiss her. Then his lips were on hers, his tongue in her mouth. Heat enveloped her, his scent driving her hormones into overdrive. He broke the kiss and she groaned.

His voice was in her ear, whispering, wanting more. "I want you, Angelica. Gods above, I want you like a dehydrated man wants water."

Her body jerked as he pressed against her. He was rock hard from head to toe, especially the bulge rubbing against her stomach. Pushing hard at his chest, she stepped back.

"Then what are you waiting for?" Her voice was a hoarse whisper. "My place is just a few minutes away."

Her heart skipped a beat when he opened the car door and nodded. She slid into the seat and waited as he fumbled in his pocket for the keys, getting in awkwardly as if he had forgotten how to control his limbs. Glancing his way, she noticed his hands were shaking as he started the car.

"There's no reason to be nervous." She smiled as she took his hand, entwining their fingers. "I won't bite."

"I might." Releasing her hand, he put the car in gear and pulled out of the car lot. "But I don't want to hurt you."

Well, that just gave me a whole new set of fantasies.

"I might like it." She tried to lighten his mood. "Leaves, vines, and lots of biting. A girl could work with that. A kinky nature scene amid flowers and running water."

He barked a laugh. "All we'd be missing is the trees and the pale moon light."

"There's always the park." Her body relaxed as he turned his head and gave her a blinding smile.

"Are you sure about this?" Varick stopped, glanced up at the red light at the corner of the street she lived on.

She had never been so sure of anything in her life. "Yes."

He nodded, went down her street, and parked the car in front of her house. And just sat there, his lips were thinned into that straight line again. Angelica opened her door, frustration bouncing around her brain as she went to his side of the car and pecked on his window.

Slowly, he opened the door and uncurled his large frame from the car. His scent, that intoxicating aroma of honeysuckle invaded her, brought back the heat she had felt earlier.

No sooner than she had the door unlocked and they were inside, he had her in his arms. She vaguely heard the soft clap of the door closing and the lock sliding into place.

Tilting her head back with one large hand on the nape of her neck, he took her lips in a soft kiss. His lips curved over hers, his tongue sliding over her lips. She parted her lips, gasping as his tongue darted between her teeth and caressed the roof of her mouth.

Yeah, he could kiss. And yeah, she was going to let him keep doing that just because she was more than curious, she was needful, aching. She slid her tongue next to his and suppressed a laugh as he groaned into her mouth. His hand fisted in her hair, pulled her closer as his other hand slid from her shoulder to her waist. She leaned into him, purely because she wanted to know if that bulge was back. Oh, yeah, it was, and glory day, it was hard as a rock.

His hand slid down her thigh and cupped her butt. She pushed at his chest, breaking the kiss. His hand stayed in place as he ran his fingers down her jaw, and his thumb rubbed her bottom lip.

"I liked that." His breath whispered over her forehead. "Makes me want more."

She pulled out of his arms, a whimper lodging in her throat from the loss of contact. "I'm offering more."

Looking up, she caught her breath. Heat flooded her, her pulse banging like snare drums in her ears. The way he was looking at her reminded her of a starved, caged animal that had been taunted with sticks.

It should have had her running, but she wanted to get closer to that animal. Breathing hard, she knew even skin-to-skin wasn't going to be close enough.

Varick put his hand on the small of her back and led her to the living room. Angelica knew he was whispering something, but she failed to hear him as thoughts of him running his hands up her legs forced their way into her mind. If he didn't hurry this along, she was going to implode.

His voice was strained, almost too controlled. "Perhaps we should slow things down a bit."

Slow? Was he serious? "If we go any slower, I'm going to burn up from the inside out. Do you want to do this or not? You act like you want me but you're holding back."

He stood there in silence, not a muscle moving, his eyes unblinking. Man, she was tired of this game.

"I'm pretty sure I've given you every indication I want this. Take off your clothes and come get me already." She pointed to the door. "That's your way out of this. Off with your clothes or out the door."

• • •

Varick was utterly speechless.

He watched in astonishment as she pulled her shirt over her head. The black lace of her bra strained against her tight nipples as she reached up and let her hair down. Her hands went to her waist, pushing the skirt down to her thighs. Her matching underwear sent a shiver of appreciation down his spine.

He knew he needed to leave, to get away from her before he succumbed to the lust. She deserved to know what she was getting into, she deserved better than what she would get. He had no idea how bad things would be, didn't know if he could control the beast, didn't know if he would hurt her.

His mouth watered, his fangs threatening to elongate. Gods above, he wanted to get inside her. Taste her. Lick her. If it wasn't for the Mating Rite, he would've already been at her throat, between her delicious legs.

"Varick." His name was almost a whimper as she came to him, reaching for his chest.

He let her hands slide under his shirt, a groan of pleasure slipping from his lips. Varick dropped his head to the hollow of her neck. His fangs slowly elongated as she ran her fingers over his nipples. He knew he was getting caught up in the desire, but he was helpless to stop himself.

Kissing her neck, his hands went to the clasp on her bra. With no control of his own, he turned her around, pressed his body to her back and cupped her breasts with both hands. She leaned back, her hands covering his urging him on. Her head tilted to the side, her pulse tempting him even further.

He needed to taste her, just one taste. He dropped his head back to her neck, ran his tongue from her collar to her jaw. Angelica moved his hand down, urged him to follow the trail she was leading. He didn't resist.

Varick slid his hand between her legs, felt the wet heat of her arousal. She was ready for him, hot, wet, and beautiful. His erection pounded, demanded he take her right where they stood. One finger, then two he invaded her. She was wet satin, hot and sweet.

Something in his head snapped, made him come to his senses. His fangs were poised, ready to strike. He didn't know if he could stop once he tasted her. She was a drug, potent and intoxicating.

Varick heard her labored breathing. She turned around, her face was flushed. There was determination in her eyes as she stepped right up to him pressing her hand on his erection. He was incapable of stopping her as her other hand went to the button on his jeans. He stood there and let her push his jeans down, watched in fascination as she curled her delicate fingers around his cock.

He groaned as she looked up, stared straight into his eyes. "I need you inside of me now."

Before he realized what he was doing, he had her on the couch, spreading her legs. He went to his knees and kissed the inside of her thighs. Running his tongue along her skin, he made a direct path to her center.

His mouth was on her, sucking and licking at her arousal. Her hands were in his hair, holding him closer as she arched, needing his tongue to go deeper. Varick growled his approval as she arched again and whispered his name.

He was coming undone at the seams, his fangs scraping her delicate flesh but he couldn't stop, didn't want to stop. When she came, he roared. Not giving her time to come down from the sexual high, he slipped his finger inside her.

She screamed his name as she came again. His fangs ached with need as he struck. He buried them into the skin on the upper inside of her thigh and sucked hard.

Varick felt her jerk, but he kept pushing her over the edge of pleasure with his hand. Closing his eyes, he put a mental damper on the Mating Rite. Careful not to take too much blood, he retracted his fangs and licked the wound.

Tonight, he was going to satisfy her, give her what she deserved. He kept working at her, controlling his lust and his hunger. He concentrated hard, focused solely on her pleasure, not his.

"I need you now." She whimpered as she arched again. "Varick, please."

He leaned over her, kissed her deep and long until she was breathless. Her heartbeat thundered in his ears, her face aglow with the pleasure she was feeling. She came again, her body relaxing, her eyelids closing.

A satisfied smile formed on her lips and slowly disappeared. "You're here, but yet you aren't."

"I'm right here." He pressed his lips to her forehead, settled his body beside of hers as she turned onto her side.

She sighed. "You know what I mean. You didn't even get undressed."

"I…" He choked. Didn't know what to say.

"Don't worry about it." She yawned. "We'll talk about it in the morning."

"I can't stay," Varick muttered. Morning meant sun, sun meant fried Varick.

"Why?"

"I have to meet Alexander." He cursed under his breath. He didn't want to lie nor did he want to tell her the truth. "For work."

"Yeah, okay." He felt her stiffen as he wrapped his arm around her. "Lock the door on your way out."

"I can stay a little longer if you'd like me to."

She sat up, shielding her breasts with her hands as she stood. "I have to work in the morning too. You might as well go now so we both can get a few hours of sleep."

"Angelica?" Varick eased himself up from the couch. "You're angry."

She grabbed her shirt and skirt from the floor, shielding her breasts once again. "No, I'm not angry." With jerky movements, she clothed herself. "Did you even want to have sex with me?"

"Yes." He grabbed her hands, bringing them to his lips. "I just didn't want to hurt you."

"Then why did you bite me? And why did it feel a little one-sided?" She pulled her hands away and walked towards the door. He followed her, the silence deafening in the few steps it took to get there. "I may have enjoyed it, but you didn't."

Varick suddenly didn't want to use her to relieve the Mating Rite. It wasn't fair, wasn't right. If he hurt her, he would never forgive himself. And he knew he would. The beast inside of him was pure menace, a vicious killer.

He knew the destruction the beast was capable of, had unleashed him upon hordes of vampires. There was no controlling him once he was out. The thought of unleashing that menace on Angelica sent a cold wave of pain through his gut. No way in hell was he going to let the beast get to her.

Running the tips of his fingers down her cheek, he inhaled her scent. It was better that she be angry at him then harmed.

"Sleep well, Angelica."

"Yeah, you too." She opened the door, stepped back and wouldn't meet his eyes as he stepped outside. "Goodnight, Varick."

Chapter 16

The music pounded, and the lights flashed like mad. Varick forced a smile as he watched Angelica walk towards the bar with her tray in her hand. He shrugged nonchalantly as the bartender grinned and raised his hand to her.

She was having a busy Friday night. The place was packed, teaming with humans. She worked the tables tirelessly even though Varick knew she had worked at the museum earlier that day. It had been almost twenty-four hours since they went on their date and he wanted to talk to her, needed to hear her voice.

Hell, he didn't even care if she was still angry at him or not, as long as she talked to him. Okay, maybe he cared. Maybe he wanted to apologize and make things right with her. He growled. Seemed like he had apologized a lot lately.

"Varick?" Alexander's voice brought his thoughts back to the table. "You okay?"

Varick nodded, grabbed his bottle, and swallowed the remainder of its contents. "I'm good as gold. Right as rain."

Alexander shook his head. "Really?"

"Yeah, really."

From the corner of his eye, Varick saw a man grab Angelica's elbow. She was nodding, listening to the man. She laughed as he stood and walked back to the bar with her. It was obvious the man was flirting with her, hinting at things only Varick had the right to.

Only, he didn't have the right.

The bottle in his hand shattered. He looked down at the broken glass on the table knowing Alexander was staring at him.

"Varick, get a grip on yourself. There are too many humans here tonight for you to display…"

Varick cut him off. "Shut it, Alexander."

He heard Alexander's voice, but the words weren't registering as he watched the man put his arm around Angelica's shoulders. She shrugged him off and shook her head. The man wrote something on a napkin and urged her to take it.

Every sane thought left his mind as Varick stared at the napkin. Utter menace flowed through his muscles, gripping his insides with fury as he watched the man touch her again. Ripping both his arms out of their sockets would not be enough—no, but ripping and slashing and gouging out his eyes just might do it.

He tightened his control, harnessed his anger, and reminded himself he was a Destroyer. He was to protect humans, not shred them like cheese.

But he desired just to take a good piece of the man's skin and stretch it across the Sahara desert, drain every last drop of his blood, and throw his entrails to the vultures.

He clenched his teeth, his jaw twitching and his neck popping. He looked at her as his thoughts tumbled insanely around his skull, kicking and bucking wildly against his control. When he stood to make good on the silent threats roaring through his mind, Gyth appeared out of nowhere.

"Sit down." Gyth ordered. "We have business to discuss."

Varick grimaced as the toe of Alexander's boot contacted his shin. Glancing at Alexander, Varick sat down, kept his mouth shut, and turned his attention to Gyth.

• • •

A chill tingled up Angelica's spine, bringing her head twisting around to stare at the table in the far back corner. Varick's friends had gathered, he among them. Other than Varick, another caught her eye and held it. He too had long white hair, although it was tinged with red at the ends that fell to his ripped waist. And chains. And leather. Very gothic. She tried to look away, but he held her gaze.

Her feet moved in his direction, her hip bumping into an empty chair. Her body got warm, not sexually warm but fever warm. Sweat trickled down her nose. The closer she got, the closer she wanted to be.

A soft smile spread across his full lips. He was archaically beautiful, graceful and either rich or powerful or maybe both. Every slight move he made was so controlled. She shuddered as he ran his gaze over her face and down her throat, and then she was overwhelmed with sadness—not her own but sadness for this beautiful man that she had never met. His gold eyes held a past she dared not know, dared not to endure. And then, as if he had been a dream, his outline shimmered with gold and silver, and he dissolved into thin air.

Angelica's heart stopped dead in its tracks. He disappeared!

She slowly realized she was standing in front of the table where Varick was sitting. Her eyes made contact with his and she stepped away from the table.

"I'm sorry; I think I need to leave." Her entire body jerked, as if she had stuck her finger into an electric outlet. "Like now, right now."

"You'll stay," Varick stood, his chair scraping backwards. "We need to talk."

Angelica swallowed hard as she looked into his eyes. Her knees trembled under his fierce angry stare. He reached across the table and took the napkin out of her shirt pocket.

"Why did you allow that man to give you his number?"

Still a little dazed and confused, she grabbed the napkin. "He's a damn good tipper."

Varick came around the table and took Angelica's hand.

Without hesitation or invitation, Varick pulled her into his arms and kissed her like a man bent on proving that she belonged to him. Angelica leaned forward, losing herself in his raw heat. He felt like silk melted over hard marble. Hot, hard, tall, sexy marble. Roman sculptures had nothing on this man.

Her lips parted as he pushed into her mouth and skillfully sucked on her tongue. Sweet torment. She groaned as he released her lips. Her brain fired, sent a thousand electrical impulses along her body.

"We need to talk, right now."

She didn't want to talk. She didn't want to think. All she could see was Varick naked and ready, ready for her.

Gathering her wits, she spoke up even though it was barely above a whisper. "My place or yours?"

"We do this here, now."

"Here?" Apparently, he wasn't thinking what she had in mind.

Angelica's body jerked again, her thoughts scattering. Her limbs felt like jello, her brain sluggish. Tilting her head, she marveled at Varick's beauty. She noticed a thin, red line running down his neck. Before thinking, she reached up and ran her finger down the line. It was dried blood.

"Varick, you're bleeding."

Varick grinned. "It's not my blood."

She stepped back. "Whose blood is it?"

"No one important."

"How?" She glanced over at Alexander who was grinning like a fool. Her thoughts gathered, collected, jumped back on the track they had derailed. "How did you get someone else's blood on your neck?"

"It isn't important. Just come with me. There are a few things I need to explain to you." He pulled on her hand, tried to coax her his way.

"It is important." She turned to Alexander. "Why the hell are you grinning like that? Is there something funny about him having someone else's blood on his neck?"

Alexander didn't answer. He stood, bowed slightly, and left without a word. She turned to Varick. She wanted answers.

"Who was the man with white hair? He was standing at your table a few minutes ago." *And then he vanished into thin air.*

"His name is Gyth. He brings us our jobs."

"I'm beginning to think you're hiding something from me." She pointed at his chest. "Where was your last job?"

"It doesn't matter."

"Doesn't matter?" Her temper sky-rocketed. "The hell it don't. Tell me where your last job was at?"

"The park, okay?" Varick looked up at the ceiling as if he was praying. "I destroy things for a living. Gyth is more like my boss."

"You said you were self-employed." Her nose twitched. "I walk through the park every day and there hasn't been a blade of grass moved out of place." She leaned in, got real close, and whispered. "You're lying to me."

"You promised not to walk through there anymore." He smoothed a stray strand of her silky hair out of her eyes. "Please, Angelica, don't argue with me. Not now when I need you so badly."

She snorted. "Are you begging?"

"I don't beg," he answered as she turned on her heel only to be jerked back around to face him.

In a voice as sweet as sugar, as heart-breaking as a dove's lonely cry, he whispered into her ear, "Can't you see you're all I need? Tonight, at this moment, I'm lost without you."

Angelica closed her eyes as the music disappeared and time itself seemed to stop. Leaning closer to the infuriating man, she slid her arms up to his neck and held on as tightly as she could. His heartbeat thumped in her ear as he kissed her forehead and ran his hands up her spine. It felt so right, so perfect. It was like finding that single strand of sunlight on a cloudy day.

Varick stood up and took her arm. She tried to pull away as he dragged her through the crowd. She looked to the bartender, but he turned his head as a man sat down at the bar. Varick pulled her through the door at the back of the bar and slammed it behind her.

"What the hell do you think you're doing?" she spat out as the door closed and he dragged her down the hallway to the door next to Alera's office.

"We need to talk," he gritted out as he pulled her inside the dark room and made her sit on the couch.

"Could you turn on a light or something?" she whispered. She heard a distinct locking sound.

She tried to see him in the dark room and jumped when he ran his fingers down her arm. "I like the dark."

"What do you want from me?" she whispered as he crouched in front of her and took her hands in his.

He worked her thumb into his mouth, sucking on it as she groaned. "I'm about to go through something called the Mating Rite."

Angelica's heart pounded in her head as he kissed her wrists. "What does that have to do with me?"

"I need your help. Will you aid me in this, Angel?"

Even in the dark, his gold eyes were bright as diamonds as he ran his hands up her legs, pulled the hem of her dress up to her thighs, and kissed her knees.

"I wish I had found you before the Mating Rite started boiling in my blood."

Angelica knitted her brows together as she spoke. "This is the twenty-first century—why not turn on some lights?"

He stood and a heartbeat later light flooded the room. Her head spun, she blinked her burning eyes. Placing a hand over her mouth, she felt her stomach lurch.

"I don't feel well." She swallowed hard, her stomach calming.

Varick kneeled in front of her, ran his fingers over her forehead. "You don't seem to have a fever. Perhaps, I'm making you nervous?"

Her stomach flipped, twisted. "I think you're making me sick." She slowly breathed in and out. "Every time you get close to me, I feel worse."

His eyes lowered, showing only the slightest hint of gold through his white lashes. Her stomach calmed as he ran his hands along her arms. "I haven't meant to do this to you."

"The Mating Rite? What kind of aid do you want?"

"I would have loved to continue our romance. But now there is no time, and I must have you soon." His voice was as gentle as light rain as he continued. "I won't lie to you, nor will I beg you to have me. I am as I am." He paused as he ran his hands up her legs. "I can feel how much you want me." Something that sounded like a hiss spread his breath across her exposed thighs. "I can smell your arousal."

His groan shattered her defenses. He leaned into her thighs, his face liquid fire to her skin. "I need you."

Angelica ran her fingers through his hair, trying to comfort the pain he seemed to be in. "Then tell me, what it is you need me to do."

She knew she couldn't resist the devil who was so manipulating her senses. Lord, she could feel desire rising up her throat, and she'd be damned if she wasn't going to give in to it. And for the life of her, she didn't know why, but she wanted him like she had never wanted anyone before.

His breathing became harsh. "There is this thing inside of me, a terrible beast that wants you."

Angelica pulled away and stood up. Stepping away from Varick, she crossed the room and was instantly surrounded by his shadow. She hugged herself and turned to face him. He towered over her. But it wasn't fear that made her hands tremble—it was the sheer desire for him running through her body. Desire that only he seemed able to inspire.

"The beast in me is strong. He will surface soon, not because I want him to, because I have no other choice." Truth that it was, it was all the explanation he had.

Angelica reached into her pocket and rubbed the surface of the medallion Alera had given her. Varick crossed the room in a blur and pulled her into his arms. His arms were hot, and his breath scorched her as he bent to kiss her lips. She met his lips and melted into his arms. His sweat dripped on her skin as his kiss deepened. God, this felt so right.

She moaned in his mouth as his tongue caressed hers. Sensation after blissful sensation coursed through her as he ravaged her mouth and ran his fingers up and down her back. Her hands went to his face and traced his jaw line to his temple as he lifted her from the floor. His face was hot as fire, and sweat ran into her mouth as he kissed her.

His sweat was sweet and hot on her tongue. He tasted like hot honey, and her body screamed to have more. He released her lips and left a trail of kisses down her chin to her neck as he moved to the couch. The heat that was left on her skin burned blissfully as he sat down, putting her in his lap. She sat astride his legs as he cupped her breasts and licked her neck. She fell forward and groaned as his hands pulled her dress up and over her head.

This is what I want. This is what I need.

Angelica threw her head back as a gasp of delight escaped her mouth. His tongue danced across her nipples, and surges of need burst from her loins and sent heat up her chest, making her mouth go completely dry. A smile formed on her mouth as sweat beaded her forehead and her eyes hazed.

"You feel so good under me!" she breathed as he tongued her tight nipple.

The world was spinning, and it was better than any high she had ever gotten with alcohol. She grabbed his head and pulled him back as she took his lips and bit his tongue. She rubbed her core against his crotch and dug her fingernails into the tender flesh of his shoulders. He arched upwards and growled with pleasure as she bit his lower lip.

Angelica licked her lips, savoring the iron and sugar in his blood. Her skin felt alive, her head spun, and her heart seemed to swell in her chest. She wanted to taste his skin, his hair, his very being as she ran her tongue down his chin and neck. Varick caught her hair as she bit into his neck and ran her tongue over the bite marks. The muscles under his skin rippled against her bare flesh, creating sparks of fire inside of her.

Heat consumed her, molded her body to his. The only thought in her mind was him, how much she wanted him.

"Take me!" She screamed as a shudder wracked her body. "Now!"

• • •

Varick strained to keep his beast under control, but Angelica was lost in her passion, and he loved every second of it. When she bit down on his neck again, he caught his breath and held her head to his neck as she licked and sucked on his skin. He could hear her thoughts pounding in his mind as she gave in to the lust taking control of her body.

Honey. Sweet nectar. I want him. Now! For the love of God, please take me now!

Varick stood and set her on her feet. With one clawed finger, he ripped her panties and threw them aside. She grabbed his shirt, popping the buttons as he slid his fingers up her back. As she ran her fingers up his chest, a blast of raw heat rolled off her body.

Varick caught her as her eyes fluttered shut. She went limp in his arms, and he stared down at her in complete disbelief. What the hell had happened? Had he hurt her? He ran his hands over every inch of her body and found no broken bones, no wounds, and sensed no pain coming from her.

Her unconscious thoughts drifted in and out of his mind as he carried her to the couch. He gritted his teeth and, for the second time, he walked away from her with a massive hard-on. He couldn't take it much longer. He needed her, and his blood was begging for hers.

"Damn!" he spat as he took another look at her.

The grin on his lips spread as he went back to her and picked her up. They shimmered and disappeared as she curled closer to his chest. When they reappeared, he was standing in front of a very large, very old bed.

He kissed her forehead and laid her across the white satin bedspread. Realizing exactly what he had just done, he cursed. Would she consider this kidnapping? There had to be a few possible ways he could convince her he had driven her here.

Jackknifing off the bed, he cursed again, not that it helped. He knew he had to tell her the truth, all of the truth. No holding back.

Varick bared his fangs as Gyth's voice filled his head. *"Come to Tortured Souls. There is much to discuss."*

He rubbed his temple as he went to his closet. Gyth had always found the worst of times to summon the Destroyers but he didn't do it very often, which could only mean one thing: shit had hit the fan.

Chapter 17

Eighty-seven Destroyers were gathered around the table when Varick appeared out of the mist he had created. The usual banter and non-stop arguments were in full swing as he took his place to the right of Gyth's head seat. Kreach sat to his immediate right and nodded his hello.

Varick peered down the table, and a sudden laugh escaped him. What would Angelica say about this? Would she think they looked like a motorcycle convention or a gothic gathering? Or both? What would her quick tongue say? He could hear it now.

She would slap that pretty hand of hers on her hip and narrow her hazel eyes and say, "You boys trying to express your true feelings or just offend the world with all that dead animal skin?"

Twenty floors beneath Tortured Souls, the god who commanded the Destroyers appeared at the head of the ancient wooden table and raised his hands to quiet his warriors. "All is one, one is all, for we are the keepers of our brothers."

The Destroyers all bowed in unison. "We are our brothers' keepers."

Gyth stood tall and strong, an unbendable oak tree with centuries of pain in his golden eyes. "Feverand's son, Eli, will be joining us once more."

Varick sat up, and his jaw twitched as Eli Dark appeared in front of the chair that had been empty for thirty years. Eli's short black hair, square jaw, aristocratic nose, and dark, dauntless eyes reminded Varick of Feverand; the resemblance was uncanny.

Eli bowed and took his seat. The hint of defiance was smoldering in his eyes as he exchanged an odd glare with Gyth. Something was amiss; Varick could feel it in his bones.

Gyth narrowed his eyes. "The time draws near when we will need to stand as one against the demon hordes once more. This sanctuary will be manned at all times, the streets combed every night. The vampires have tripled their numbers as have the witches and werewolves."

A chill went down Varick's spine as Gyth stared him in the eyes. "They have begun to congregate together, drawing more and more humans into their clutches. Members of the One Race are now at an all-time high risk. They must be protected at all costs."

A few grunts and growls erupted from the table. Varick stood, looked down the table at the Destroyers. "A few nights ago, I found a small group of vampires huddled in the park on Hillsboro Avenue. They had captured a member of the One Race, before his Burning. He was dead when I got there.

"That park is close to one of many sanctuaries that my father built after I was born. I don't know how they found it but they have. Everyone who lives there is a member of the One Race." Eli leaned on his elbows. "One Race sanctuaries all over the world are being targeted. They are picking members of the One Race off like flies while they're still human."

They had fought the demons for centuries—that would never change—but why would their enemies change tactics now?

Alexander stood as Gyth vanished. He and several of the other Destroyers gathered at the head of the table. Each one of them were like Alexander, they gave a motley little crew their orders.

Many of the Destroyers dematerialized, not a word spoken from them. Varick stood, following Eli and Apoc into another room. Legs that felt like rubber carried him to a chair to the left. Memories danced in and out of his mind. A shaky hand ran down his face, a little reminder of the beast under his skin.

Varick stared at the flames in the fireplace. Eli laughed and joked as Apoc retold the many stories of the last thirty years. Several of the Destroyers filled the room with their broad shoulders and deep voices. Their black trench coats were slung over the backs of the chairs and they appeared perfectly at ease as they talked with Eli. As if he had never really been gone. Three decades had passed, and yet it seemed like only yesterday.

"Kreach reached over his head and swung his axe with the gusto of a god, and the handle slipped and came flinging backwards at Alexander. The blade sliced the sapling next to Alexander in half. I lost it. Gods, I laughed so hard I fell to my knees, earning a nice punch to my brain from the blasted beast in front of me. The werewolves that had us surrounded were confused as hell by our loud laughter." Apoc grinned as he told the story.

"What the hell did poor old Kreach do?" Eli chuckled as he ran his hand over his chest. "I would have loved to have seen the look on his face."

Apoc slapped his leg and made a long "O" shape with his mouth. "It was hilarious. Kreach looked like he had been slapped in the face."

Eli grinned. "Damn, I've missed this shit."

"It's good to see you, Eli. It's high time you came back home." Varick grimaced as pain twisted his insides.

"I won't be staying." Eli stared at Varick. "That beast of yours is wanting out."

"He is none of your concern. And don't go getting into my shit, my brother, or I'll slit your damn throat."

"Go to hell, Varick Ta Farg."

Varick grinned, trying not to reveal the pain coursing through his body. "I've already been there. Great place to visit." He stood, took a set toward Eli. "Where the hell have you been?"

Eli tossed a black orb to Varick. Varick caught it and gritted his teeth; the sweet stench of vampire filled his nostrils. He stared at the orb, his insides jerking as a slow burn developed in the pit of his stomach.

The vampire token pulsed, a low, steady beat. Inside the orb sparks of light swirled, dimmed, and swirled again. This token contained a soul.

Varick grabbed the back of a chair, suddenly unsteady on his feet. "Is it the one who…"

Eli answered, "Yes."

"Are you sure it's the one?" Varick asked as he rolled the orb around in his palm.

A snarl appeared on Eli's face. "That's the one who killed my mother. The other one, the one that killed my father escaped. I hunted for years and have never found him. Not one goddamn trace of the bastard."

Varick bowed his head, feeling Eli's pain. There was only one way to release a soul from the token of a vampire, and Varick was all too well aware of what it entailed.

Damn, sometimes he hated his job. Varick swallowed hard as he placed the orb in his pocket. He knew he wasn't strong enough in his present condition to release her soul, at least not without releasing the beast.

Varick shook his head and reached for his jacket. "She has waited for thirty years. A few more days isn't going to hurt."

Menace swirled around Eli. "Damn it, Varick. She was my mother. She died in my arms with my sister still in her womb."

Varick's eyes flamed. "A few more days!"

"Sister? What sister?" Apoc grabbed Eli's shoulder.

"Every day that passes she suffers. Free her," Eli pleaded as he grabbed Varick's arm. "Free her soul. Let my mother have the peace she deserves."

Varick's hands trembled as the beast inside clawed at his skin. His back twisted, and pain shot up through the muscles in his neck. Eli and Apoc stepped back as black flames burst from Varick's arm.

Varick bared his fangs as his legs grew weak. Apoc rushed to his side and grabbed his other arm. Varick jerked away, and the flame went up to his shoulder as he fell to his knees.

The voice he heard as he spoke was dark, twisted, not his own. "Don't touch me."

The Destroyers watched as the black flame engulfed his body. His scream split into their minds like hot needles. They all groaned as the weight of Varick's predicament slammed into their chests.

Varick forced the beast to be calm, and the flame slowly died. Steam rolled from his body as he pulled himself to his feet. He was losing control, and he was well aware of it. He turned to Apoc and fell forward, his body heavy and his limbs refusing to acknowledge orders from his brain.

• • •

Apoc caught him as Varick fell. He knew Varick was stubborn as hell, but this was going too far. He picked the brute up and slung him over his shoulder grunting under his weight. If Varick didn't mate soon, he would go insane as the beast within him consumed his soul.

"Stubborn son of a bitch!" Apoc turned to Eli. "Pray he lives through this!"

Eli glared at Varick. "If he lives through this, I'll take his head if he doesn't release my mother."

Apoc's face twisted into a battle-ready grin. "Know that you must face me as well if you want him dead."

Eli stepped forward. "It'll be a pleasure to put you bastards in your places. You've been around so long; you've begun to think you're indestructible."

Apoc's laughter filled the room. "Feverand's son is as bold as he was. Put your balls of steel back in your pants before someone melts them."

Eli grabbed his jacket and headed for the door as Varick twisted in agony. Eli placed his hand on Apoc's shoulder. "Has he chosen someone?"

Apoc shook his head. "I'm not sure. He's been seeing a woman at Tortured Souls. A waitress."

"Then maybe you should have a talk with her and let her know what's going on," Eli offered.

"Varick wouldn't want it that way."

Eli opened the door and replied, "By the look of him, he's going to need an angel."

"Aye, 'tis true," Apoc whispered as Eli shut the door behind him. "'Tis true."

Chapter 18

Varick felt like someone had put a double barreled shotgun to his head and had squeezed the trigger. Sitting up on the leather couch, he groaned as someone entered the room and slammed the door. The sound sent splinters through his head.

Cracking his lids open, he watched Alexander prowl around the room. Apoc stood in the far corner, his face unreadable. They both kept looking over at him, waiting for him to speak. They wanted an explanation. Varick wasn't sure if they were angry, worried, or fearful of his current state of mind. He would guess all three.

"I want you to take care of this problem. Immediately." Alexander's voice boomed around the room. "We've got enough shit to deal with without you being stubborn and out of commission."

Solved that question, Alexander was angry. He paced back and forth in front of Varick like a great lion waiting to pounce on its prey.

"I'm fine." The lie fell from his lips as he broke out in a cold sweat.

"Yeah," Alexander replied. "As fine as two Mac trucks colliding at a hundred miles an hour. Look at yourself."

Varick looked down, smoothed his black shirt down with shaky fingers. "I've got it covered."

"You call this covered?" Alexander sat in the chair across from the couch. His face was tight, hard angles jutting out his chin. "What's going to happen when that beast comes rampaging out and you're surrounded by innocent people?"

"That's not going to happen." Varick stood. "I won't let it."

Varick went over to the fireplace, grabbed the bottle of 10 Cane and a glass from the mantle. It wasn't his favorite but he poured himself a double shot of the rum and swallowed hard.

Alexander stood, took the bottle and slammed it into the fireplace. Glass shattered, tiny bits flying across Varick's boots. The Destroyer grabbed Varick by the lapels of his shirt, got up close and personal.

"Back off, Alexander." Varick held his ground. "What's going on with me isn't your business. How I handle the Mating Rite is no concern of yours or anyone else's."

"You do what you need to do or I'll take you off duty." Alexander shoved Varick backwards, menace flowing from his body. "I don't want to be the one that has to hunt you down if that beast isn't put on a leash but damn you, I will."

"My beast would devour you." Varick looked down into the empty glass, wished he had more rum or vodka. If he wasn't killing something, alcohol kept the edge off, kept his beast calm. "You want a piece of me? There's no sense in waiting, come get it."

"Stop this," Apoc roared as he stepped between Alexander and Varick. "Save this fight for our enemies."

With a roar, Varick turned to mist.

He went to his chambers, materializing in front of his bed. Angelica was sleeping, her face relaxed. His muscles loosened, the ache in his head slowly disappearing as he stood there and watched her breathe.

•••

Charon appeared in Zena's chambers as she slumbered in her bed of black silk. His black robes swirled at his feet as he stepped over the minions littered on the black marble floor. When he lifted the hood from his face, the skeletal bones filled with blood, veins wrapping around tendons as flesh filled the contours. His curled lip twitched as he stood over her bed, and his red eyes glowed with fury.

This one, this Zena, was the one who had dared to use the River Styx. He gripped his scythe and ran his knuckles along her cheek. Closing his eyes, he searched for her weaknesses. Grinning, he opened his eyes and wrapped his fingers around her throat.

Zena came awake gasping for breath and staring into a set of glowing red eyes. She grabbed at the hand at her throat and struggled wildly against his hold. As she felt her brain shutting down from lack of oxygen, she ran her hand under her pillows and pulled out the dagger she kept within her reach. Blindly, she stabbed at his chest, the blade embedding deep within his body.

"Fear plays mind games with you." He released her throat.

Strangling her wouldn't kill her, but he enjoyed catching her off guard. Enjoyed it in the sense of how cats enjoyed tantalizing mice.

He laughed and shoved his robes aside to look down at the useless piece of metal protruding from his stomach. "You can't kill what is dead already."

He released her throat and pulled the dagger out, flinging it across the room. It sank into the marble wall up to the hilt. She scrambled up the bed and hissed fearfully as he reached for her ankle. She jerked her legs up and gasped as a bony hand dragged her back down the bed and into his clutches.

He laughed, his face going transparent and his skull gleaming in the purple glow. "You owe me for using the River Styx, and I have come to collect."

She tried to call out to her minions, and again he laughed. "As long as you are indebted to me, I can take your soul."

"Impossible. No god can do such a thing." She tried to jerk away. "The only god that can is…" She swallowed. "Charon."

He watched her face drain of color.

"I want your soul or your payment." He bowed slightly as she tried to use her powers. Her muttered curse added to his pleasure.

"I owe no ferry. I don't know what you're talking about!" She whispered it because she couldn't scream.

"No?" His face filled with flesh, and his lip curled. "You traveled through Styx. And I always collect what is owed to me."

As his hands wrapped around her wrists and pulled her to her feet, she jerked away. "What do you want from me?"

Her eyes narrowed as he vanished into thin air. She gasped as he appeared behind her with one arm wrapped around her waist. His other hand appeared on her shoulder, a long, silver chain dangling from his fingers.

"If you want to use the River Styx again, I have a bargain for you." He smelled her hair, memorizing her scent. "Upon this chain, from your body, you'll bind one hair, one tear, and one given word."

Fury clawed at her. "I will not do any such thing!"

Charon's face twisted, his eyes turning black and empty. "You will." Grabbing her hair, he hauled her to her feet and slammed her into the wall. "Body, flesh of yours. Blood, power of yours. Soul, power of the gods."

With his scythe at her throat, she hissed and tried to sidestep him. The blade cut into her flesh, and she roared with pain.

"I know all your secrets, Zena. I know you're still very much the virgin even though you had a child." He laughed as her eyes widened. "I know you covet your virginity. The reason you have never lain with a man is because part of your powers will be transferred from you to the one who takes that precious virginity."

Tears of blood streaked her cheeks as he leaned closer and kissed her lips. "You'll give your virginity to whomever I choose, or I'll take something far more precious from you."

"I have nothing else that I hold dear." She turned her face away as he slid his fingers down her arms and pulled the robes from her body.

"Oh, but you do, little innocent Zena. One day you'll hold him so close to your heart that his happiness will be the blood that pumps through your veins. He is his father made over. Unfortunately"—he gazed at her ample flesh—"he did not take after his mother in looks, or his grandmother, for that matter."

She shook with rage as his hands moved over her stomach and curled around her untouched breasts. "Stop it!"

"One hair, one tear." Charon's hands drifted up her chest and cupped her face, bringing her eyes to look into his. "Your given word. Or I shall take your soul and his too."

He released her slowly and stepped back as she reached for her robes and pulled them over her body. He let the chain hang from his fingers, dangling in front of her face.

"Your soul or your given word. Your choice." His mouth opened, a dark spinning vortex opening behind him. The screams of lost souls echoing in the emptiness the vortex contained.

She slid down the wall, her fear widening her eyes. "Why have you come back after all this time?"

His laughter echoed around her chambers. "I had a wake up call."

Slowly, she plucked a hair, ran it through her tears, and reached out to the chain. With shaking fingers, she laid the hair over the chain. "I give you my word."

"All these years, that wonderful body has been untouched. Such a pity." His laughter echoed in her mind as he vanished.

Chapter 19

Angelica awoke abruptly and sat up. She was completely surrounded in darkness. Clutching at the sheet in her hand, she brought it to her chest. Disorientation flooded her, fear grasping at her mind.

Her heart stopped as her hand came into contact with warm, hard skin. Maybe he had passed out; after all, he had been drinking. His arm twitched, and he rolled over. She jerked her hand away and slowly eased her body off the left side of the bed.

Frantically, she recalled how she had reacted to his touch. She could make her escape while he slept if she could find the door in the dark. She stood and put her hands out in front of her. She took a step and realized she was standing on the softest carpet she had ever walked on. Taking another step, she grabbed her mouth as her toe came into contact with a very hard, unforgiving surface.

As she hobbled on one foot with the other curled around her leg, a soft light came on and shed some light on her foe. A Victorian chair sat next to the bed, and clothes were neatly folded and lying in it. She reached for the clothes and stopped. Where was that light coming from?

Overhead, small lights lined the ceiling. As she stepped backwards, another came on. Stepping to the left, she watched as another came on.

Her eyes widened as she looked upon Varick. His arm was draped over his eyes, and his hair flowed down the pillows and fanned out from his body. Shirtless and breathtakingly gorgeous, he was the most entrancing male she had ever laid her eyes on.

And if she had been in a better situation, she would have let herself enjoy the landscape.

Damn it, she had to keep looking. He was like a drug dragging her eyes back to the addiction. She groaned in pleasure as his arm dropped to his side and he took a deep breath.

His abs were a perfect six pack, and his slow breath tightened his muscles and pushed at his broad chest. The tingle in the pit of her stomach from the night before returned, and her knees grew weaker the longer she stared at him. Male perfection!

A tattoo ran down his left arm from his shoulder to his fingers. It was a beautiful picture of angels and demons. Fire leapt from the angel's hands, and ice poured from the mouths of the demons. She had noticed the tattoo before but now she paid attention to the intricate detail of the work.

Each angel held a sword, and each demon held a long staff. They were all surrounded by dozens of red and gold daggers. Across his knuckles, the words "soul reaper" were etched in Latin.

She slowly moved about the room and took a deep breath. Angelica was amazed to find that the walls were deep purple, almost black, and there were no windows. A large fireplace sat directly in front of the bed twenty feet away. Above the mantel, a large painting hung. Ten warriors from days long ago rode across the Valley of Kings on horseback. The Egyptian attire was carefully painted and stood out against the night scene. The faces of the riders were hidden in shadows.

She turned to the furnishings in the room. Everything looked like it had just stepped out of a Victorian magazine, right down to the bedspread. There was one exception. The door was a solid hunk of metal, and there was not a doorknob in sight. She stood and ventured to the door and inspected the four-by-four-inch button panel. So much for making an escape.

She turned to Varick and slowly returned to his bed. Why did he have to be such a gorgeous man? She reached for a book lying on the nightstand. *Poetry From the Greatest Minds* lay like an invitation. She loved poetry.

She looked at Varick, pushing her wanton thoughts aside, and picked up the worn book. She made her way back to the chair and curled up as she placed the book in her lap.

Angelica flipped through the book and shook her head. Everything in its pages was related to death, disease, murder, demons, and lust. She stood and returned the book to the nightstand. As she turned, her head snapped up as Varick's hand wrapped around her wrist.

"Did you find what you were looking for?" His voice was husky, sexy-deep, and his eyes were still closed.

Angelica jerked her arm away and glared down at him. "If you are referring to those poems, then no, I did not!"

Varick chuckled. "They weren't to your liking?"

"From what I read, no, they were not!" She turned and crossed the room, afraid she would leap upon him like a madwoman.

"Life is not all butterflies and spices." He grinned as she frowned. "Most good poems are about death and fear."

"You're wrong. They are about life's trials and the heart's adventures."

"Fantasies that lead to heartbreak." Varick sat up and swung his long, powerful legs off the bed. "Come here."

She did not like being told what to do. She shook her head and stared at the painting above the fireplace.

"I said to come here, woman!" His voice dropped an octave, his hand held out for her to take it. "Come here."

Her right hand dropped to her side, and she jutted out her charming chin. "I want to go home now."

Varick stood, and Angelica turned to face him. He was completely naked, and his erection bobbed up and down as he cleared the space between them. She swallowed hard as she held her head up and prayed she would not give in.

"The door won't open for another twenty-two hours. Until then, you are stuck here with me. We might as well enjoy ourselves."

Angelica looked at the door. "Open the door and let me out."

Varick grinned. "It's set to a timer. Now, come closer."

Angelica clenched her fists. "This is kidnapping. And who in their right mind would set their door to a timer?"

"Twenty-two hours and you're free to go. However, until then, you belong to me."

"I don't belong to anyone. You are insane." She stepped back as he came at her. "Don't you dare touch me!"

Varick grabbed her waist and jerked her against his chest. "I didn't bring you here to argue." His voice turned to gravel. "Stop being afraid of me."

His anger and nerve were intolerable. "What were you expecting? Did you honestly think I was going to be all over you? Get your hands off me."

She stiffened as the all too familiar stoic expression filled his face. "You weren't complaining about my hands being on you yesterday."

"That was yesterday, before you kidnapped me." She shuddered in spite of the heat that had enveloped her.

Varick spun her around and wrapped his arms around her shoulders, running his fingers over them. Angelica stiffened as her body betrayed her mind. She leaned back, pressed into his chest, and closed her eyes. His arms felt so good wrapped around her body. She could smell him and feel his heartbeat against her shoulder. When he slid his hands down her arms, she caught her breath and relaxed. He was driving her out of her mind, and she wanted more of him.

His fingers grabbed the hem of her shirt and pulled it over her head. Her skin burned, and flames spread through her body as he pressed against her back. When he slid his hand across her stomach and ribcage, she held her breath. His touch was maddening. She melted against him and moaned as he cupped her breast and slid his thumb across her nipple, wickedly teasing her desires.

Sanity pushed into her mind. "Varick?"

He kissed her shoulder, dragging his tongue in small circles over her skin. "Yes?"

"I know Alera is a friend of yours." She paused as he gently nipped her shoulder. "And she's a little eccentric, but do you think she's crazy?"

"No." His answer was a whisper as he pushed her skirt to her knees. "She's one of the sanest women I've ever known."

"Are you sure about that? She thinks my mother was her sister." Angelica couldn't suppress the rumble of desire that escaped her throat. "She told me I was a descendant of a goddess."

• • •

Varick smiled as Angelica raised her free hand and reached up to his shoulder, giving him complete access to her breast. He nipped her shoulder again and squeezed her breast. With his other hand, he unfastened the bra and slipped it from her shoulders. She moaned, and he turned her to face him. She closed her eyes and let her head fall back as he leaned down and captured her nipple in his mouth. He licked, sucked, and then gently bit down. Her hands flew to his head and pulled him closer.

And then it hit him, hard.

Descendant.

Mother.

He shoved her away and turned on his heel. No, he wouldn't believe it; he couldn't believe it. He turned to look at her again and grimaced at the hurt look on her perfect, angelic face. She didn't look like Antonia.

Angelica had jet-black hair and dark sultry eyes. Her nose was straight and set above her lips like a blessed dais of sultry moonlight. The women from Atlantis were all blonde, all six feet tall or taller, all blue-eyed, all slender, and all of them were small-breasted.

He walked around her five-foot-eight-inch frame and shuddered with appreciation. She was well rounded, curvy, and female in all the right places. She was not like Antonia, didn't look like Alera, and didn't resemble any of Amay's descendants.

"Why are you looking at me like that?" Her voice was high, a squeak of tension easing out in her words.

"Alera cannot be your aunt. You look nothing like Amay's descendants." The words scolded his tongue, and he hissed in rage. "You're not a member of the One Race."

Angelica's face twisted with fear. "Varick? Of course I'm not. Gods and goddesses don't exist. They're nothing but fairy tales."

Did he dare ask? Did he want the truth? "Who was your mother?"

She eased out of his arm's reach. "What's wrong with you? Why are so angry at me?"

"I'm not angry." Yet he knew he was roaring and could not find the calm he needed. "Tell me her name!"

"Stop it, stop screaming at me!" She jerked away as he reached for her arm. "Let me out. Let me go, Varick, you're scaring me."

She backed up as he pushed her back into the wall, slamming his hands beside her head. "Scaring you? Babe, you haven't seen anything yet. Surely you know I'm raging beast, a menace to this world."

She looked up, and their eyes met in a storming clash of wills. "Don't call me babe."

"By the end of the night, I'll devour you and you'll like it, you'll beg for more. You'll hurt in places you didn't know you had and you'll still want me." His smile was toxic, venom on his lips as he licked them and crushed his body into hers. "Isn't this what you feared? That I would like it rough?"

Angelica forced her tears back. "What now? You plan on raping me?"

He hissed in her ear, grabbed her hands, and jerked them over her head, arching her back in the process. "I won't rape you because you want me. You want me inside you. I can smell your arousal, the sweet scent of wetness between your legs. Even as you stand here fearing me, you still want to get in my pants, use me to pleasure yourself." He ran his tongue across her lips. "Your flesh burns for mine."

Her eyes narrowed and grew two shades darker. "You arrogant bastard."

He laughed. "Yeah, get mad, get pissed, and fight me."

A tear slipped free of her control and slid down her cheek. He caught it with his tongue and closed his eyes, savoring the stormy ocean taste of it. She bucked against him, her teeth grinding and her fingernails sinking into his palm.

"Let me go! Let me go!" she screamed. "You bastard. I should have taken that man's offer at Tortured Souls and called him. I would've been with him instead of you tonight."

Something nasty snagged his chest, brought his heart to an abrupt halt. He saw red as he remembered that night with vicious clarity. The way the human wanted her, put his hands on her body, and fucked her with his eyes sent him into a private hell where he was the devil and the human was the bastard he carved into slivers with his bare hands. Never had he wanted a human's blood like this before. His fangs pushed out, and he hissed above her head

She continued to buck against him, and he pulled back as he tried to control the red haze overtaking his vision.

Not yet, not now. Need more time. Calm. Peace. More time!

He released her, and she crumpled to the floor at his feet. She kicked his shins and punched him in the gut. Her heated rantings were of little importance as she tried to scoot past his legs. He knelt down with his red eyes shut tightly and pulled her into his arms.

She clawed at his shoulders and chest. The pain from her nails strangely calmed him, easing his beast for a precious second. It was what he needed to regain control. She stilled and cried against his chest.

He didn't know how long they sat there, but her sobs subsided and she finally spoke. "I think I hate you now."

He nodded and opened his eyes, the red haze still present but waning. He hated himself for scaring her, for wanting her, for needing her.

She pulled back and looked up at him before he realized what she was doing. Her gasp was more than enough to make him curse.

She scooted backwards, ending up with her back against the wall. "Oh, God. What sick game are you playing with me?"

He swallowed hard and wished his fangs would retract. They didn't even though he was willing them to. He knew what she was seeing.

"I am…"

She held her hand up and shook her head. "Shut up! I won't listen to this."

He was a Destroyer, a half breed vampire. He knew pain beyond what Angelica ever needed to know. And yet he wanted her to know on some level, needed to share his life with someone. Not for pity—no, there was some deeper instinct trying to force itself to the surface, and he dared not let it. Closing his eyes, he fought against himself.

•••

Charon appeared in the middle of Angelica's office. Holding out his hand, he summoned the book he knew was hidden in the room. As it appeared in his hand, its silver inscription began to glow.

Angelica Dark and her boss had no idea what they had found. Theo had been close to correct when he had thought it was a spin-off of the Egyptian Book of the Dead. In fact, the Egyptians had used this text as the basis for theirs.

The book had remained unattached to anyone, therefore, the book could be taken without the owner's consent. His eyes glowed bright. The other book in her possession was attached to her. The game would have to be controlled if her consent to give it to him would be delivered.

The *Book of Resurrection* pulsed in his hand, eager to be near its master. "Soon, soon we will bring all the books together!"

Laughter echoed and Charon disappeared as thunder rumbled in the distance.

Chapter 20

Angelica stared, refusing to even blink. He had fangs—two very long pointed fangs that hung just over the edge of his bottom lip. Fangs! This was insane. She was trapped in this room with a drop-dead gorgeous, leather-wearing, bleached-white–haired, wannabe vampire psycho. Heaven help her.

Hot tears coursed down her cheeks. It was not fair!

"Angel, I know what you're thinking, and I can offer you no consolation." He leaned back on his heels and ran his hand over his face.

"You." She took a deep breath. "You are insane."

"Maybe." His grin revealed more fang, and she shrieked like a mouse caught in a trap.

"Oh, God, don't do that! Don't smile!" She shoved at his chest, sending him crashing backwards onto his ass. "Open the goddamned door and let me out right now!"

He laughed as he stared up at the ceiling. Who would have ever thought he would end up on his ass? He laughed again as she kicked his leg and scrambled past him on her hands and knees.

He turned his head and groaned as he watched her butt wiggle away from him. She had to have the finest ass in all history. Round and very eatable. He raised an eyebrow as he caught sight of her glistening core. His cock jerked maddeningly; it demanding he fill her up. But first he wanted to taste her again, lick her core until he drowned in her release.

He rolled over and pushed himself up onto all fours. Eager to sate the fantasy in his mind, he crawled after her. Feeling like the predator he was, he growled low, the sound a rumbling vibration growing louder in the back of his throat.

She glanced at him over her shoulder and scrambled to her feet. "Oh, hell no! Don't even think about it. I don't want any part of your sick little game."

Varick knew he was an animal, an animal on all fours staring at her like he wanted to eat her whole, with extreme amounts of chewing and licking involved. He felt anger blast through her arousal, heard her thoughts as she ran to the door. She was angry at herself for being attracted to him, angry at him for kidnapping her, and even more angry at the fact all these things should have quenched her attraction but seemed instead to be adding to it.

She banged on the door with her fists and screamed with fury, "Let me out!"

Varick stood as she dropped her fists and turned to snarl at him. "You plan on keeping me prisoner, don't you?"

He nodded—no sense in lying to her at this point.

She made a beeline to him and tilted her chin up to stare straight into his red eyes. "I should punch the crap right out of you! I won't be a willing prisoner! And I will absolutely not have sex with you!"

He stared down from his towering height and sighed. Her fear was gone, replaced by the sulfuric smell of irritation. Her hand rested on her hip, her breasts on delicious display.

"But I'm not going to punch you. You're going to answer my questions, aren't you?" He remained silent. "Aren't you, vamp boy?"

His mouth gaped. Vamp boy? Honestly, where did she come up with those phrases of hers?

"Don't open that mouth unless you're taking those fangs out." Her finger punched into his chest. "Nod your head."

He nodded, trying to bite back his smile. She was amazing. No, she was beyond amazing. She was worthy.

"Don't smile, either. I can see them when you smile." He chuckled as she stepped back and glared at him. "This isn't funny. I won't be kept prisoner!"

"Twenty-two hours." He was honestly trying not to grin as she bit her bottom lip and her gaze traveled down his naked chest. "Mine for twenty-two hours."

"That's not acceptable." Stepping back, she eyed him warily. "Why the hell do you want to act like a"—she shuddered—"a vampire? I mean, I know people role play all the time but this is—this is crazy. You're freaking crazy! People go to jail for kidnapping."

He grunted. "I'm not human, Angelica. I won't go to jail, and I'm not crazy. Not in the way you mean, anyway."

She slapped his hand as he reached for her. "You forgot the part where you say, 'I'm not a vampire and this is just a game to me.' Say it!"

"I am a vampire." For added effect, he opened his mouth as his fangs came gracefully to their full length. He hissed as he let his eyes go completely ruby. "I. Am. A. Vampire."

Before he could blink, she was beating at his chest and screaming, "I told you not to do that anymore."

He captured her waist and brought her flush against his naked skin, letting her continue her abuse. "I want to make love to you, Angelica. I burn with need for you."

"Why me?"

He held her gently, his arms not restraining her, yet she stayed. He could not answer her question. For the life of him, he didn't know the answer. He was acting on instinct, wasn't he? It was the Mating Rite, wasn't it? He knew he wanted her, that the beast wanted her.

Her hands worked up his chest and went to his shoulders. "I'm not going to have sex with you. I'm not."

He nodded and grinned as her leg lifted and rubbed along his thigh. "Of course you're not going to." Her arousal was a kaleidoscope of scents—musk and ocean storms, passion and need, fire and ice. "I need you right now, right here."

He groaned as her hands worked into his hair and she tilted her head back, her eyes half-mast and her pink tongue running across her lips. It was the perfect invitation. He dropped his head to take full possession of those lips and taste that wicked little tongue of hers.

And then his cell rang. The blare of Metallica's "Sandman" made him groan. The sound echoed in the room, and she jumped. Dazed, she jerked out of his arms and practically ran across the room. "Don't you think you'd better get that?"

Growling with the pain of his erection, he went to the bed and grabbed the offending piece of metal and plastic, plastering it to his ear. "What?"

Alexander's voice sent hot coals over his ears. "Get to the damn park. There's too many of them. I've counted at least forty."

Angelica kept her distance throwing daggers at him with her eyes. Varick growled under his breath as he turned to stare at her. Listening to the voice on the cell, he narrowed his eyes. Angelica frowned, and he almost laughed as the thought occurred to her to flip him off but she knew that was ridiculous. Childish as it was, she did it anyway.

He raised one eyebrow and grinned. Bowing slightly, he murmured, "Your wish is my command."

"Shut up!" She pointed to his cell. "Don't you have something better to do than annoy me?"

He grunted, said, "I don't have time for this right now."

"Make time. Vampires are your forte, not mine." Gunshots echoed in the background. "Gods above, they're everywhere."

Watching Angelica as she paced the floor, he tried to breathe steady. The beast roared in his mind, slamming against his brain demanding to be released. He shut his eyes, tried to ignore the pulse in his fangs.

A vicious roar vibrated through his cell. "Put your dick on hold. You're a Destroyer, act like one."

"Screw you, Alexander. You wanted me to take care of my little problem. I could if you'd leave me the hell alone."

"The sooner you get here, the sooner you can take care of your shit."

Varick wanted to scream. He turned to Angelica, closed the cell, and tossed it on the bed. "We'll have to postpone our current engagement. I have work to do."

• • •

Angelica shut her eyes, covered her breasts and huffed as she heard clothing rustling. When she opened her eyes to unleash her tongue on him again, he was gone.

She cursed rather loudly. Just how the hell had he gotten through that damn door?

Chapter 21

Angelica was lost in complete surrender as he lifted her from the floor and carried her to the bed. He eased her down onto her back and placed his knee between her legs. The soft hair on his leg stimulated her desire, making her arch her back. She cried out as he ran his hand down her stomach and bit her nipple. His hand ventured farther down, and he growled as he ran his fingertips into her core. She was hot as liquid fire, his body smooth as silk as he worked her core.

"Angel. I cannot wait any longer. I must have you." His words were deep and soft as he lowered himself on top of her body. "Come for me, Angelica, come for me."

His fingers were creating a sublime heat from her toes to the top of her head. She groaned and caught his hair, bringing it to her nose. He smelled feral, a wild animal needing to be petted. Oh, and she so wanted to pet him, touch him, run her hands over each delectable inch of his utterly perfect body.

He settled between her thighs, his weight pushing down onto her, into her. She growled with pleasure as his palms cupped her breasts. Wrapping her legs around his hips, she locked her ankles and arched under him.

"Tell me, Angel, tell me you want this." He licked her bottom lip and sucked on it as his fingertips rolled across her nipples. "Tell me you want me."

As he rocked against her, she screamed, "Yes, I want you!"

He reared back, his fangs gleaming, red eyes glowing, and roared as he plunged into her body. It was heaven, the perfect bliss. There was nothing to compare to the way his hot body felt against hers. It was almost more bliss than she could bear.

Angelica surfaced from the dream and jackknifed from the bed like it was ablaze. She was alone, the room lighting as she moved. She tried to steady her erratic breathing and focused on the flicker of the flames in the fireplace.

Minutes, maybe hours passed as she calmed, as she forced the dream from her mind. She turned on her heel and inspected the room warily.

Where the hell was he? Right, he'd gotten a phone call and, when she had turned around, he was gone.

And why the hell was she so desperate to see him again? She wasn't supposed to feel this way. She was supposed to hate the man who was keeping her imprisoned. Hate him, she told herself.

Yeah, right, like she could hate a man who made her insides melt. He might just be crazy and a freak, but her body sure didn't have a problem with that. Vampire? He wasn't a vampire. He was just a loon, a gorgeous loon.

"He's not a vampire. He does not suck blood." She said it out loud so she could hear it. "He's not a vampire. Vampires don't exist."

She whirled around as a cold breeze slid up her spine. "Yes, I am and yes, I do."

Varick stood inches in front of her. "How did…Where did…"

"I am a vampire, Angelica." He spoke again, the tips of his fangs gleaming in the light. "Part vampire, anyway."

She shook her head. "No, you aren't. You're sick in the head. You need professional help, buddy boy, and I strongly suggest you go find some real soon."

He barked a laugh and turned to the fireplace. "It's drawing closer. I don't know how much longer I can deny the beast inside of me."

She slapped his shoulder and glared at his back. "Stop it. You're not scaring me, so just freaking stop it already."

He shrugged and smiled at her over his shoulder.

"Don't grin, don't smile, and don't you dare speak. As a matter of fact, don't do anything with your mouth until the fangs are gone." Her tone was even, unshakable.

He was still smiling as she sat down in the same chair that she had stubbed her toe on. "I'm hungry. Please tell me you aren't going to starve me as well as keep me prisoner."

His smile broadened, his shoulders shaking with laughter.

"Well?" She crossed her arms over her chest. "Are you?"

He shook his head, leaned down, and pulled her onto her feet and into his arms. "Tell me what you want to eat, and I will scour the darkest and most dangerous corners of the world to get it."

"I told you not to open your mouth." She sighed. "I want you to let me go."

He frowned. "I can't do that."

Her stomach rumbled. "Fine. I need food, sometime today, if you don't mind."

"I will return shortly."

Yet, he stayed. His arms still held her to his chest. His fingers were doing the most awesome things to her shoulders and back. She wanted to melt into his arms, give as well as receive, but instead she made her body stiffen, resisting the urges that seemed so natural.

Hoping he would listen, she whispered, "Listen, I really am hungry."

Pulling away, Varick granted her a delicious, devilish smile. He bowed and vanished. Angelica dropped to her knees, her hand covering the scream that had risen to the back of her throat. It was a trick, an illusion! It had to be.

With wide eyes, she leaned forward, running her hand through the air where he had been standing. Nothing. Just empty space.

Scrambling to her feet, she searched the room frantically. No mirrors, no hidden doors, no frigging stairs. What the hell was this room, a damn coffin? Her knees shook violently under her weight.

"Oh, hell, no!" She made her way to the chair by his bed and slowly sat down, letting her body slump into the curved back. "Come on, there is no freaking way this is real. I'm dreaming."

Angelica stood, scanning the room again. No refrigerator, no cabinets, no stove, no necessities of life other than the bed and the bathroom. Frowning, she went to the center of the room and took a deep breath. True, the bed had a purpose. But the room itself was cold and empty. Lifeless.

She looked down at her bare feet and signed. At least the carpet was plush, soft as kitten fur. And warm? She leaned down and ran her fingers through its thickness. Yes, it was warm, almost like heat was rising upwards. She stood and shook her head. It didn't make sense that the floor was so utterly warm and the air just above it was cold.

She shivered. What the hell had she gotten into?

The fact Varick had fangs, his room was cold and lifeless, and his little vanishing act were all scaring her. And he thought he was a freaking vampire. And he had literally kidnapped her, holding her hostage. And there was no way she was going to believe he was some cold, undead creature that stalked the night looking for people to feed on.

Instantly, she crumpled to the floor and screamed. Since she had taken the waitress job, she had become surrounded by insane people. Why, of all the men on Earth that were nuts, did he have to be?

Forcing herself to stand, she went to the bed and sat down. Aimlessly, she tried to open the drawer of the night stand. It was locked. Her anger spiked. Shoving with all her might, the stand tipped over, the lock broke and the drawer slid out. Varick's book landed face down.

Feeling like a fool, she went to her knees and reached for the book. The glint of metal caught her eyes and she reached into the drawer. A black combat knife and a Smith & Wesson 952 were inside.

Angelica squared her shoulders and wiped away her tears. Did he expect to come back and find his little helpless victim scared and utterly at his will? She looked at the gun and laughed. Well, if that was what he was expecting, he was so very wrong.

• • •

Varick glided down to the ground, stepping lightly onto the awaiting asphalt. His body hummed, his bones vibrating. His only thought, Angelica needed food. She needed him to get her food. Even though her need for him was by his own doing, she still needed him, had asked for his assistance in obtaining it.

He ran his fingers through his hair. He had kidnapped her. He had scared the crap out of her. And he had laughed at her in her distress. Three strikes usually meant you were out, didn't it? Well, perhaps he could make it up to her by bringing back something good to eat.

He looked down the street and idly wondered what she would like to eat. He had never considered it before, hadn't asked. She had ordered a grilled chicken salad on their date. Would she like to have another one or something different? Did she eat the same thing every day? In all his years as a Destroyer, he had never taken the time to find out such frivolous things about humans. Suddenly, it didn't seem so frivolous. She was hungry.

Stopping in front of a restaurant, he glanced into the window and watched a trio of women eat. They each had something different, a salad, a baked potato, and a bowl of stew.

He shrugged and entered the restaurant. He heard several gasps and breathless *ohs* as he made his way to the counter. The older, robust female behind the counter smiled.

"How can I help you?"

He frowned as he looked up at the list of what they offered. He decided there were too many choices. "Would you prefer salads or cheeseburgers? French fries or baked potatoes?"

"Excuse me?" The woman smiled again, her eyes growing two shades darker as she devoured his appearance. "Salads and baked potatoes. A girl has to watch her figure."

His frown deepened. "Angelica has a perfect figure and needs not watch it. She is hungry, and I need to know what to buy her."

The woman, whose nametag read *Mabel*, shrugged. "Lucky girl."

Varick strummed the counter with his fingers. Cursing under his breath, trying not to hear the women's thoughts, he muttered, "I need some vodka."

Mable laughed. "Well, honey, you're in the wrong place for vodka."

A flush brightened his cheeks. "Give me one of everything you have."

Mable's eyes widened. "One of everything?"

"Yes, and make it quick." He pointed to the chocolate cake at the end of the counter. "And some of that too."

As Mabel gave the order to the man behind the small window, she looked over her shoulder. "So, this lucky girl having cravings?"

Varick leaned against the counter. "What do you mean?"

As the woman mumbled and talked on, Varick stepped back and growled low in his throat. The pull on his blood was suddenly strong, stronger than it had ever been. He fished out his wallet and threw a hundred-dollar bill on the counter. He could feel Zena's presence and she was close and he sure didn't mean Underworld close.

Varick went to the door, his blood pounding in his veins. "I will be back shortly. Please have everything ready to go."

Mable turned and before she could say anything, he was out the door in a dead run.

He misted into the night, Zena's presence closing in around him tighter and more accurately than ever before. He followed the pull to the far side of Fether, along the shoreline to a hidden part of the beach.

Chapter 22

Varick hit the beach, his combat boots skidding to a stop. Zena's stench was everywhere. It was the smell of death, and it hung heavy in the air as he pulled his trench coat off and slung it across a *Keep Out* sign.

"Varick." The charm of her voice was intoxicating, demanding. "I have waited for this day."

He turned on his heel, searching the beach. Dozens of vampires crawled along the sand, hiding in the shadows. It was unusual for them not to attack. Her voice filtered into his mind, mesmerizing.

"You cannot resist me. Come to me. Come to me, Varick."

He turned, fighting the heavy compulsion in her voice, fighting the beast under his skin. "Zena. What brings your nasty ass to the surface?"

She laughed. "Why, you, of course."

He chuckled as his swords appeared in his hands. "Tired of me taking your minions out of existence?"

The wind howled furiously around him as she spoke with rage. "You're part vampire! How can you destroy that which you are?"

His fangs punched out. "How can I not?"

"I am your mistress. You will no longer defy me."

He bowed slightly. "Sorry to burst your little bubble, Zena, but I faithfully follow Gyth." His eyes gleamed with the taunt.

Sand blasted against his back as she misted to her human form. He struggled not to fall to his knees. She was beautiful, a goddess of the Underworld, and she reminded him strangely of his mother.

"Don't you dare speak that name to me." Her fangs were long, sharp, and perfect. "His name is not worthy of my ears."

He circled her. "Now, Zena, why would you call out to a Destroyer? That's not a smart move on your part. Then again, Gyth has warned us the gods and the goddesses of the Underworld are not as intelligent as the heavenly ones."

He watched as her anger rose to a volatile level—just what he wanted. "But then again, there is the possibility that Gyth is biased."

"Gyth is an idiot, a selfish dog that needs to be neutered and skinned alive." She watched him out of her black eyes and hissed as he laughed at her comment. "Make no mistake, Varick, he'll get what is coming to him."

Varick listened as she ranted and raved about Gyth. All the while, he assessed her little horde. They had worked themselves closer, compelled by her voice. They writhed on the sand and groaned with each word that poured out of her ruby red lips.

He gripped his swords as he stopped and turned to her. Gritting his teeth, he refrained from giving in to that melodious voice, that soft, urgent, underlying message that beckoned to him like a flame to a moth. Promises of sweet surrender and insurmountable pleasures rushed him like a ragged blade. Even as his body stepped toward hers against his will, he reminded himself death was but a bittersweet dream that had always escaped him.

"That's it. Come to me." Her lithe, agile body swayed to unheard music, her fingers dancing in the air as if she commanded the orchestra of his mind. "I am your queen, your mistress."

Varick roared to the Heavens as he fell to his knees and stared into the fathomless black pits of her eyes. "No!"

"Yes, I am your queen. I'll have my revenge. I will have you, Varick, and Gyth will feel this loss as I once did. He will pay for taking my daughter, Vicery Beth, from me, and he will pay for her death. She was everything to me, my flesh, my blood. He took her from me, stole her and disappeared." She groaned as he tried to stand, her powers over him waning as he struggled. "I'll own you, Destroyer, and you will do as I command. You'll kill him for me. You will carve my name on his forehead so he'll know I won you."

Through clenched teeth, Varick heard himself ask, "Why would Gyth waste his time with your daughter? Why would he take her?"

Zena grabbed his chin, forcing him to look into her eyes. "Vicery was the epitome of beauty, and she had a soul. Two thousand years ago he took her. He wanted her." She smiled, her fangs gleaming. "You will avenge me. You will avenge her."

Muscles straining, Varick stood, his topaz eyes glowing casting profuse light onto her face as he towered over the goddess that looked so much like his mother. Like lightning striking, he grabbed her throat and slammed her down to the sand.

"You'll never control me. No one controls me. I am a Destroyer. I'm not your servant." Varick struggled to keep his vampire half in check, struggled to keep his grip on her throat. "I am two thousand years old, and not once have I ever fell under your compulsion. Not once have I ever given in to the incessant need to do as you would command."

A choked laugh escaped her as she smiled. "Listen to yourself, Varick."

Throwing his head back, he hissed as his fangs elongated. Black, scaled wings rippled out of his shoulder blades as his claws dug into her flesh. His topaz eyes burned, changing, swirling with fire as he forced her head to turn, revealing her beating pulse.

He caught his breath as his eyes fell to the mark under her earlobe. A small teardrop, outlined in black and filled with red, stared back at him as his other hand unconsciously went to his own mark. His mother had once told him it was their mark, a family trait.

He jerked away, falling backwards and scrambling out of her immediate vicinity. The dead vampire language rolled off his tongue. *"Miatha?" Mother?*

His mother's name was Vicery Beth. His mother had given birth to him two thousand years ago. She had had a soul and she was a vampire with incredible power. Power held in check by Grace. If she was indeed Zena's daughter, it would mean ...

"Oh, hell no!" He stood, his head pounding. "No, it cannot be!"

His wings stretched wide as he paced, deep in thought. "No! She would have told me. She would have warned me. My mother was good. She was clean and free of evil."

Zena stood, laughter washing away the sound of the ocean. "Have you gone insane, Destroyer?"

He turned. "Was your daughter pregnant when Gyth took her?"

Zena hissed, and her own wings rolled out of her shoulder blades. Varick watched as she transformed into half dragon, half female. He sucked in a harsh breath, his lungs seizing and burning. Her form was much like his own. It didn't make sense. The dragon was his Destroyer form, not his vampire.

"Was she?" Varick was unaware of the power that flowed through his voice as he roared at the goddess.

She trembled. "Of course not! She was pure; she was untouched by any!"

"Under her right earlobe, she had a mark, a small..." Varick paused.

Zena stepped back, sadness overwhelming her beauty. "A small black tear filled with red." She buried her face in her hands. "My baby. My precious daughter."

Varick took a deep breath and pulled his hair back, revealing the teardrop under his earlobe. "My mother looked a lot like you."

Zena cursed and wiped at her eyes. Turning to mist, she sped across the beach out of his sight, out of his reach. Varick watched as she grasped the ball of water that awaited for to return to the River Styx. Screaming in agony, she warped into the portal and cried as she let the river of hate take her away from her grandson.

• • •

Gyth gritted his teeth as he heard Varick roar from the Earth to the Heavens. He stepped off the cloud he had been sitting on and freefell to the ocean shore where Varick waited. He knew the time would come when Varick would call, but he wished it could have been a time of his own making, not Zena's.

The Destroyer was livid with anger. He watched for several long minutes as Varick slashed and hacked his way through the last of the vampires. His glorious black wings arched and spread with power as he displayed what he was famous for—methodical and unmerciful killing.

Gyth shimmered and appeared at Varick's side. He took in the scene that lay in front of the Destroyer. Bloody, mangled bodies of at least two-dozen vampires lay sprawled across the beach; blood splatters painted the moon lit sand.

The calm Varick was known for was evading him this night. The carnage had not been performed in the neat, precise manner he usually displayed.

Gyth shook his head. Varick's Mating Rite was at hand, and it was seriously affecting his behavior. With care, he approached the Destroyer knowing he could attack without thought or care of consequence.

"Varick, you called?"

"Why did you not tell me?" He turned on his heel and held out his palm, willing the vampires' tokens, the black orbs he collected, to appear in his hand. "When you awoke my soul, when you reanimated my body nineteen hundred years ago, why did you not tell me I am the grandson of Zena, the she-bitch of the Underworld?"

Gyth, in his usual manner of silence, nodded slowly. "Is this what is bothering you?"

"Answer me!" Sarcastically, he grunted. "Oh, great wise one, what is the answer I seek?"

"Sarcasm does not and never has suited you, Varick." Gyth clenched his fists at his sides and prepared for the Destroyer's anger. "Your mother asked me not to tell you about Zena."

Fire swirled in his topaz eyes. "And you expect me to believe that? All this time, I believed my position with you was for the safety and survival of mankind, to protect the One Race. But it wasn't, was it?" He took two steps, nose to nose with the god. "Do you get off knowing you took something from her? That her grandson kills her minions?"

Varick growled so low the rumble sounded like a cannon going off in the distance. "What sick part of you finds amusement knowing Zena didn't know, either?"

Gyth held his ground, his eyes narrowing. "I did as your mother asked of me. Don't make me regret it."

"How dare you! You took her from the Underworld, stole her like she was a possession." Icy resolve moved his tongue. "Zena had suffered these long years because of it, and yet you do not see the wrong in your actions."

"Vicery Beth," murmured Gyth as he looked into Varick's eyes. "She was the loveliest female ever born, even to this day."

"You kidnapped her. Took her from her home and left her mother in agony." Varick roared and spun away from the god before he slugged him.

"Don't play the saint with me, Varick!" Gyth demanded between clenched teeth. "Kidnapping Angelica Dark is no different than me taking Vicery Beth from that hideous place."

Varick twisted, leapt into the air, and grabbed Gyth by the shoulders, slinging him to the ground. Pushing aside the fact he had the power to blast Varick into oblivion, Gyth allowed to Varick to slug him. Gyth allowed Varick his anger as he drew back to repeat the action.

Gyth's eyes closed as Varick's fist slammed into his jaw the second time. With a roar of anger, Gyth shoved him off and jackknifed to his feet. Violence erupted in his eyes as he kneed the Destroyer in the face and sent him sprawling.

"I did as she asked me to." He grabbed Varick by the arm and swung him around to his feet so he could look him in the eyes. "She wanted you to become a Destroyer, wanted you to be able to deny the call of your queen."

Varick jerked away. "No! She killed me. She couldn't bear what her son had become."

"You were the first, Varick. You were the first Destroyer because she wanted you to be free of Zena." Gyth sidestepped, barely missing Varick's suddenly appearing swords. "She killed you to save you. She sacrificed you so you could be reborn as you are now. The Destroyers were created out of her love for you; out of her need to know she had saved your soul from Zena."

"No!" He screamed with rage, with pain, and with heartbreak.

Gyth caught his wrist as the blade sang through the air, dodging the other. "Zena kept her locked in her chambers, refused to acknowledge her to any other. A mother who chained her to her throne and made her watch the carnage that comes with the queen's lust."

Varick screamed as he twisted his wrist, gaining his freedom from Gyth's hold. "Then pray tell me, why was I raised in a camp of assassins where death was closer than any lover?"

Gyth stepped back and leaned on the same post where Varick had laid his coat. "You had to be trained. Had to be the best of the best."

He laughed. "Trained by warriors, by assassins created by Grace? Trained to be your slave?"

Gyth visibly swallowed hard. "Yes, so it would seem."

"And what did Grace get out of this? What was her role in this?" Varick swiped at the blood on his lip with the back of his hand. "And why would you take pity on a female vampire? Who was my mother to you that you would go through all this trouble?"

"Grace was the only one who had the power to cloak Vicery Beth from her mother. She hid you and your mother. But, as with all the gods and goddesses, she required a price."

"What the hell was the price?"

He held up his hand. "Enough of your questions, Varick. I did what I did because your mother asked it of me. Believe what you will." As an afterthought, Gyth whispered, "I know not what Vicery Beth offered Grace. It was her decision, one even I could not interfere with."

Before Varick could take a step or make another move, Gyth vanished. Black smoke rolled out of Varick's nostrils as rage and defiance consumed him. Scales rippled down his spine, the blood of the slain vampires taunted him, lured his inner demon. It was indeed feeding time.

Chapter 23

"Grandson. I have a grandson!" Zena roared, her claws slashing into the first servant who dared to come close enough to her.

He fell in groaning agony at her feet, a slight smile upon his face. She roared again at the injustice.

"Gyth is responsible for this. He will pay! I'll tear him apart, eat his heart."

Her chamber door, now sealed, groaned as she slammed the body of her fallen servant into it without mercy. Her set of double fangs punched out of her gums as her black wings unfurled across the chambers.

"If Varick will not come to me willingly, then I'll be forced to use other methods."

Her black eyes narrowed as she plucked a black hair from her head and pulled it into a straight line. As she twisted it, it turned into an arrow, the tip black and sharp as her fangs. She used the tip to slice into her palm, letting her blood coat the sharp point. From the folds of her robes, she withdrew a small piece of parchment she had stolen from one of Damon's many books.

She cackled as she laid the arrow on a black slab of marble and read from the parchment.

"Straight and true, this arrow I imbue." The arrow lifted and glowed with an odd, swirling, green light. "Find the one Varick holds dear." The arrow purred with menace, with awareness. "Bury deep into the flesh, so I can find you." She grinned as her voice dropped several octaves. "Go now and find the one to spear."

The arrow vibrated as she opened the portal to the River Styx. Without warning, it zipped across the room and disappeared into the gate. Zena's laughter spilled forth, and her minions slithered to the ground, rejoicing in her beautiful tyranny.

"He'll come to me one way or the other. And then he is going to help me find a way to make the great Gyth fall to his knees and beg for mercy." She patted one of her servants on the head. "Now, it's time to feed your mistress. I think I'll have need of two of you."

• • •

Trying to keep his mind on the clean-up job on the beach, Varick slipped the orbs into his pocket, turned to the last body, and growled when his cell phone rang. Alexander's ring tone chimed, and he answered, trying to keep the leave-me-the-hell-alone-I-have-problems-to-deal-with tone out of his voice.

"Go."

"Tirney Church, east side of Fether." A pause and a gunshot in the background. "Damn it! The bastards are shooting at us."

"Where's Payne?" He didn't need this right now.

"To my left and dodging bullets as we speak." Alexander laughed. "Fuckers are swarming in the churchyard, headed inside."

Varick looked across the beach and nodded. "I'll be there as soon as clean-up is done here."

Watching the last body burn to ash, Varick tuned out the hum in his head. He locked onto Alexander's location and dematerialized his body. From the sounds he heard in the background, he knew it was going to be bad.

Payne and Alexander were hunched behind an overturned Bronco as Varick appeared to their right. "How many?" He peered past the front tires at the abandoned church.

Payne grunted. "At least twenty. And the fuckers are armed. Since when do vampires arm themselves? And why the hell are they gathered inside a damn church?"

Varick rolled his eyes. "Please, those vampire myths are rubbish and you damn well know it." A bullet whizzed by his head, and he grunted. "Armed but incredibly bad shots."

The breath in his lungs hurt. Varick rubbed his chest trying to keep the calm he needed. A black scale appeared on his right hand, his beast beating at the walls in his brain.

"I say we burn the church and be rid of it. It'll save us the trouble of unearthing any who are still under ground." Alexander eyed Payne. "Why the hell are you still here, anyway? You're supposed to be in Kentucky."

Payne growled, his black hair falling across his cheek as he pulled his scimitars from their sheaths. "I told you, I'm not taking some clinging woman through her Burning. Not now, not ever."

Alexander grabbed Payne's arm. "It's an order from Gyth. You cannot disobey a direct order."

Payne jerked away. "What's he going to do to me that hasn't already been done?"

He wanted to keep the beast at bay, suddenly knew he couldn't. The stench of vampire was everywhere, drifting into his nose, making the beast's mouth water. Trying to concentrate on what Payne had been saying, he urged the beast to stay calm.

Varick fell forward, leaning his weight on his palm as pain splintered up his back. He cursed viciously as the pain spread out into his limbs, his muscles jerking and spasms twisting and violently crushing his lungs.

"Varick?" Alexander twisted around on his hunches. Payne grabbed Varick's waist before he fell onto the sword in his hand. "Stubborn son of a bitch, the Mating Rite is demanding your attention."

"Fuck. Me." Varick groaned as he swallowed hard, another wave of pain backslapping him. "I'm fine. I can control him. Let's just finish this and get the hell out of here."

Another bullet whizzed by followed by laughing taunts. "What's wrong, Destroyers? Afraid of our guns?"

The red haze of the beast returned. Blinking his eyes, Varick grabbed his head muffling out the sounds around him. Two trains collided inside his head, the deafening sound snapping through his control.

Varick's back arched, his shoulder blades ripping through the silk. "I'll kill them all!"

Payne released Varick as his body lifted. A distinct, low vibration was coming out of his chest, growing louder with each second. Payne looked at Alexander and cursed.

"He's going dragon. Get out of his way, Alexander. He'll be in a rage when he transforms completely."

Varick's eyes glowed with red rage, and he roared catching a bullet in the shoulder. Scales slashed out of his skin and rippled down his back as his wings spread. Alexander barely rolled out of his range as the spiky tips slashed through the front and back tires of the Bronco.

Giving in to the beast because he didn't have the strength to resist him, Varick slipped into the back of his consciousness. He could only watch through the dragon's eyes, hear with his ears, and pray that the beast didn't harm the other Destroyers. This was the reason he liked to fight alone, alone was safer for his friends.

The black dragon reared back and spit black fire into the night air. Bullets bounced off his scaled chest and pinged against the truck. Payne and Alexander grinned at each other and barreled out from behind the truck as a bullet hit the gas tank. The dragon hissed and climbed over the truck as it exploded into flames. His body glowed, the flames catching against his scales and running up his great neck.

Overhead, Payne and Alexander heard another cry and blinked twice as another dragon circled above them. The two dragons eyed each other, and Varick lifted from the flames, his wings carrying his weight upwards and toward the church.

"What the hell is going on?" Alexander shouted as the dragon above roared.

Payne laughed as two vampires came charging at them. "Don't you think it's getting hot out here?"

"Screw you, Payne! You knew, didn't you? You knew he was a dragon in his Destroyer form."

He met the two vampires head on as Alexander leapt on another that slithered out from behind several bushes. "Yeah, I knew."

"And"—Alexander crushed the vampire against a tree with his weight and snapped his neck like a twig—"the dragon above us? Who the hell is that one?"

Payne sliced and diced the second vampire as he crushed the head of the first one under his boot. "Don't know. But that one hangs out in the shadows everywhere Varick goes."

Alexander paused; his sword posed over the vampire's chest, as he watched the black dragon land on the church and rip the steeple off with his gigantic talons. "Damn! He's the first dragon I've ever seen."

"Fucking awesome, isn't he?" Payne turned on his heel, sheathed his scimitars, and grabbed a third vampire by the throat. "Wicked little beast."

"Yes, he is." Whirling around, he sent a dagger flying into the chest of yet another oncoming vampire, its fangs gleaming and its stench whipping about in the wind.

Varick watched as Payne buried a dagger into a vampire's throat and slammed him to the ground. The scene played out before his eyes, and he was helpless, trapped inside the dragon's mind. In one fluid motion, Payne thrust his hand into its chest and pulled out the black orb. The vampire gasped and went completely limp.

Screams ripped out, and they turned to the church. It was engulfed in flames. A horde of vampires came scrambling out of the inferno, guns raised and firing erratically as they sought safety. A bullet caught Payne's right leg, and Alexander rolled to his left as dozens of the bastards descended on him like harpies on fresh meat.

Two went down as Payne released the blades in the toes of his boots and kicked into their chests. Four more replaced them as he flipped backwards, his blades catching the first three but not penetrating deep enough. He grabbed one by the throat as two ran at him and body-slammed him to the ground. He willed his dagger to his hand and punched into the closest body. Shrieks split the air as burning pain pierced his left arm, the vampire sucking greedily through Alexander's leather jacket as his comrades grabbed at whatever limbs they could.

From out of nowhere, Kreach appeared, his vicious snarl hovering above Alexander's head and a dead vampire hanging from his hand by the throat. Black blood coated his fingers and arm. As Alexander knifed another, Kreach tossed the vampire aside and grabbed two more from behind and crushed their necks. In complete Kreach fashion, he slammed them to the ground before plunging into their chests and ripping out the black orbs.

Alexander tossed the last one aside, the orb tucked into his jacket pocket with the others he had collected in the last three minutes. Payne got busy with two more as the church fell in and flames licked up the trees. The dragon was swallowing one vampire after another and spewing black fire at the ones daring to escape its wrath.

The dragon watched as several vampires went screaming with terror back into the flames rather than be devoured by the beast blocking their escape. He snapped at three bodies huddled in the doorway. Body parts fell to ground as the dragon snapped its jaws shut and swallowed.

The Destroyers moved back as the dragon turned and inspected them. As he stepped forward, he bent to eat the remains of a dead vampire. Bones crunched and black blood splattered as he chewed. He took another step and eyed the dragon above. He roared, but his eyes came back to the Destroyers in front of him.

Payne stepped forward. "Varick. Come back to us. Control. Control the beast."

Varick tried to focus on the man before him. He knew him. His face was in his memories, his past, his present, and his future. What the hell was his name?

The dragon roared, its talons clawing at the ground, black flames pouring out of his nostrils. The stench of vampire rolled off his tongue.

"Varick, come back to us. It's me, Payne. Remember me? You and I go way back." He stepped warily. The dragon fell to his knees, his body jerking.

Varick fought against the pull of the beast, fought against the demands the beast was making. He was out and he wanted to stay out. It was his time, his Mating Rite, and he wanted it now, with her, with the woman in his chambers. He roared as her name bounced around his brain. The beast wanted Angelica, would devour her. His back arched as Varick refused the beast.

"She's mine!" The words ripped out of the beast's throat in a tidal wave of black flames and smoke. "Mine!"

Varick was losing the battle; the beast had claimed the right to be out and was refusing to give in. Like soft whispers of chaos, Payne's voice made its way inside him, beckoning, almost pleading.

"Varick, come back to me. Without you, what am I going to do? You are my mentor, my teacher, my friend." Payne dodged the dragon's tail. "You don't want to hurt me. I am your friend—come back to me. Fight the beast. Fight it, Varick."

Fight it? No one fought the Mating Rite and survived. No one except Kreach had ever fought it, but even he had almost died, had slit his own throat before he took the unwilling female. Would Angelica be unwilling? Would she deny him? Would he kill her? Could he do as Kreach had and stop himself if she did deny him?

Topaz eyes flickered as Payne stepped cautiously closer, his voice low and compelling. "Listen to my voice and hear me. Take control of the beast."

The dragon inspected Payne, saw his wounds, felt his pain. Pain? Pain was an ally. Pain was his friend—no, not pain, Payne, the Destroyer, Payne—his friend, his closest friend.

The dragon groaned and dropped his head as the scales decreased in size. His great body trembled and seized as it shrank and his wings curled and disappeared into his shoulders. Steam rose from his back as Varick fought the beast, demanded his body back. He took control of his needs, his wants. Lifting his head, he groaned and sagged forward. Payne caught him as he fell and lowered him to the ground.

Sirens blared in the background and lights flashed in the distance. "We need to leave now."

Alexander looked up as the other dragon nose-dived, spewing flames that engulfed the tree line and the road leading to the church parking lot. The Destroyers vanished, taking Varick with them, all with grim expressions on their faces.

Chapter 24

"Is he awake yet?" Gyth appeared beside of Alexander. He had hoped Varick had taken care of the Mating Rite.

"No," Payne gritted out. "Where the hell did all those vampires come from?"

Gyth pushed past him and looked down on Varick's unconscious face. "Long ago there were portals between the Underworld, Earth, and the Heavens, but they were sealed. A portal has been opened, and it seems Zena is in control of it at the moment."

He turned to face the Destroyers. "And we have a new player to add to the game."

Kreach growled as the air around them grew heavy and taxed with misery. Alexander reached for the daggers strapped to the insides of his thighs, and all three Destroyers surrounded the bed in full defense mode. No one and nothing was coming after Varick while he was unconscious.

Gyth held up his hand. "Stand down! He is here at my request."

"He who?" growled Payne as he withdrew his scimitars.

A figure wearing a long black robe and holding a scythe appeared. "I am Charon, the ferryman of River Styx."

Charon's bony fingers were wrapped around the scythe. Gyth watched Charon use his voice to fill Payne's soul with hatred and misery. "What the hell is this, Halloween?"

Gyth gave him a pointed look. "I said stand down, Payne!"

"Whatever, but if he has a beef with Varick, screw him!" He grinned. "He wants our boy, he'll have to fight us for him first."

Alexander nodded and looked at Gyth. "What the hell is going on?"

"One of the portals in the Underworld was opened, and the ferry was not paid. Charon has informed me a be-spelled arrow entered the portal and had Varick's name written all over it."

"An arrow? Arrows won't kill us." Alexander replaced his daggers. "Bespelled?"

Charon glided forward. "A spell was attached. It's not directed toward Varick but toward one he holds dear. It isn't meant to kill—it is meant to find."

Payne came forward, putting himself between Charon and the bed. "Why are you telling us? What do you gain from this information?"

Charon laughed. "Call it a mutual alliance. I have long been confined to Styx and am somewhat at a disadvantage. I have no knowledge of the world today. I need allies, and I'd prefer them to be the enemy of the one who opened the portal."

Payne growled and faced off with Charon. Toe to toe, he said, "We don't need allies! What the hell do you want from us, and what the hell aren't you telling us?"

Charon's hand shot out from the robes, and bones curled around Payne's massive neck. "The ferryman always gets paid, by blood or deed, by token or soul. I will have my payment, Payne, warrior of the One Race."

Payne grinned as his black eyes locked with red ones. "I'd prefer you to die."

With his left scimitar he sliced into the robe, and with the right he hacked at the arm attached to the hand at his throat. Charon laughed as he dissolved into black ribbons of mist and appeared at Varick's bedside, in the same place Payne had previously stood.

"I am the ferryman, the collector of the souls condemned to the abysses of the Underworld. I do not die, I do not live; I simply exist, and I will collect one way or the other."

He looked down at Varick and ran his forefinger down his cheek. "Oh, yes, he has a strong soul, full of delicious fire and smoke. Full of"—he paused—"full of heavenly blood and hell's wrath." He suddenly looked up as a growl ripped out of Gyth's throat and the god took a step forward.

Misting away from the bed, Charon reformed at the door, laughter echoing around the room in streams of agony and sorrow. "Secrets, so full of secrets."

Gyth roared and crossed the room in a blink of an eye. The chains wrapped around his waist were in his hands, and his hair was blood red, the white completely submerged. "If you ever touch him again, Styx will no longer have a ferryman."

Confusion hung in the air, the Destroyers gasping their surprise as Gyth slammed Charon against the door. "Trust me; you can die an agonizing death. I know your weakness, Charon."

"Secrets, king of the Heavens, have a way of eating at one's soul." Charon's voice dripped with venom. "Secrets of the Heavens have always found a way to bring downfall. I now know your weakness, Gyth, so we are tit for tat."

Before Gyth could make good on his word, Charon vanished in thick smoke and cruel laughter. Gyth turned and ran his hand through his hair, changing it back to its usual white tinged with red at the bottom, and took a deep breath as his Destroyers sat on the bed with worry on their brows. They knew that if Gyth had a weakness, they were as good as screwed.

Regaining his composure, Gyth spoke in an even tone, "Who is the one he holds dear?"

Alexander stood. "His angel." He looked at Gyth. "The female he is infatuated with, the one he calls Angelica."

Gyth turned on his heel. "Find her before that arrow does. If Varick falls prey to whatever Zena is planning while he is in the throes of the blasted Mating Rite, we may very well lose him."

The Destroyers nodded and Alexander spoke. "She works at Tortured Souls. Alera will know where she lives and all her closest kin."

"Go. Time is something we have very little of." Alexander and Kreach vanished as Payne turned back to Varick who was finally stirring.

"Welcome back," Payne mumbled.

Varick sat up and swung his legs over the side of the bed. "How the hell did I get here?"

"In a pumpkin, princess." Payne leaned against the bedpost as Varick stood on shaky legs. "Piece of advice—go get laid before you try to eat us all and we have to put your ass down."

"Enough, Payne." Gyth stared at Varick. "The Mating Rite is upon you."

Varick growled a few choice obscenities as he lurched toward a chair. "Where am I?"

Payne grunted. "Figure it out, my brother. Old statues of long forgotten Greek generals, several unique volumes of Aristotle's philosophies, and a desk piled to the ceiling with battle plans."

Varick looked up, a snarl on his lips. "How long have I been here?"

Payne rubbed his chest. "An hour at the most."

Gyth's eyebrows pulled together as Varick' face fell and his eyes filled with worry. He eased into Varick's thoughts, listened to the commotion and found what Varick's main thoughts centered on.

Angelica was in his chambers with no way to get out, and she was hungry. She was hungry and angry. Varick didn't know how long a human could go without food. He was worried for her welfare.

Gyth let out a soft sigh. At least Angelica was at Varick's place and safe for now. He knew he couldn't help Varick deal with the beast or the Mating Rite and he had things to attend to. Leaving in a soft flash of light, Gyth vanished, intent on finding Charon.

• • •

Every muscle in Varick's body ached. His head felt like it had been smashed between two boulders and used as a bowling pin. The soft flash of light made him squint, sent pain through his eyes. On unsteady legs, he went to Alexander's closet.

Payne followed rambling on about Charon the ferryman and Gyth. Varick really didn't know what Payne was saying. He heard something about Gyth going ballistic but couldn't process the information.

Shifting through the clothes, he managed to find a descent pair of leathers without skulls and crossbones and a black T-shirt. Awkwardly, he used one hand to steady himself on the wall and the other to pull the leather pants up and over his hips. He pulled at the crotch and wondered how the hell Alexander went commando all the time. Payne grabbed his shoulder and swung him around.

"Are you listening to me, Varick?"

"I have to go." Varick jerked back and sidestepped Payne. "Something needs to be taken care of. I screwed up, and I have to make it right."

"Damn it! Varick, this is important. Listen to me."

He turned on his heel. "What the fuck is it, Payne, that it can't fucking wait?"

Payne narrowed his eyes. "Charon, the ferryman of the River Styx, was here, and it seems Zena may be after your little beauty."

Varick stepped back. "What?"

"Oh, let me see. For the third time—bad queen of vampires wants Varick's little angel. She sent an arrow through a portal and aimed it at the one you hold dear. If she finds her—and she will—she'll suck your angel dry. And if that isn't bad enough, Charon seems to think he knows Gyth's weakness." Payne crossed his arms over his chest. "Any more questions?"

Cursing, Varick misted and vanished, leaving Payne grumbling under his breath. "Yeah, well, a simple thank you would have been nice, asshole!"

Chapter 25

Traveling faster than the speed of light, the arrow searched the world over, seeking the one Varick held dear. Deep within the Earth, in the dense forest of the Amazon, the arrow aimed true. Slicing through dirt and rock, it homed in on the female walking in the chamber below the ground.

Angelica's stomach was rumbling, and she was getting a killer headache. How long had she been here? Hours? Days? She had been pacing back and forth for an eternity. Where was he? Had he left her to starve to death, or was this some kind of sick test of wills? Pulling the black jogging pants up she had found in Varick's closet, she screamed.

The knife she had found with the gun was in her hand, her knuckles turning white. She had no clue what she was going to do with it but it made her feel a little safer. Sliding it into the waistband of the jogging pants, she readjusted them as they began sliding off her hips from the weight of the knife.

She groaned and sat down in the floor, bringing her knees to her forehead. Tears slid down her face as she cursed. She was going to kill him, beat his ass until he begged her for forgiveness. She would, if and when he came back.

She gasped as a slicing pain hit her in the back of the head, vibrating inside her skull with a violent screech—or was that her voice that made that sound? She clutched at her temples and screamed as the pain splintered into her veins and coursed through her body.

Laughter filled the room as Angelica seized, her body jerking uncontrollably, her bloodshot eyes rolling back into her head. "It does hurt, does it not?"

Minutes passed as her body calmed and her breathing returned to normal. Slowly, she sat up and turned to the voice. A woman grinned down at her, showing off a pearly white set of double fangs. She was dressed in black, fingernails painted black, lips painted black. The long hair falling over her shoulder to the floor was black, and to top it off, her eyes were black too.

The woman licked her lips and purred. "I haven't taken a human in a very long time. Your blood will be a nice little added bonus."

Angelica laughed hysterically. "I must be suffering from dementia. Yeah, I've lost my mind and my body has followed."

The woman laughed. "Afraid not, sweetling. I am Zena. And what is your name?"

Angelica sat there not knowing to laugh or to cry. "Screw you."

Zena cackled. "Well, Screwyou, I have come to offer you a deal."

She backed up and scrambled to her feet. "What kind of deal?"

Zena shrugged. "I want Varick. You will be bait, and after he has come for you and falls into my clutches, I will give you immortality."

Angelica's spine jerked, prickly sensations working at her heart. She focused on the woman's words. "Why do you want him?"

Again, she shrugged. "That makes no difference."

"It does to me. Tell me why you want him." Angelica reached around to her back and grasped the handle of the knife hidden in the waistband of Varick's jogging pants. "Oh, let me guess, it's a vampire secret."

Zena hissed, her fangs scaring the crap out of Angelica but she refused to give in. "You'll have to do better than that if you want to make a deal with me."

"He is mine, and you are nothing but a passing trinket, one he will discard after he uses you." She smiled as she edged closer. "He is a rare breed, and he will not deny me any longer."

Angelica laughed. "He is an asshole who is as insane as you are. You want him—be my guest and take him."

Zena narrowed her eyes and stalked around the female before her. "You don't care for him?"

"Why the hell should I?" Good question. "He kidnapped me! When he gets back—if he comes back—I'm going to rip his eyes out!"

Angelica startled herself with the vicious hatred she suddenly felt toward this woman who she didn't even know. "How the hell did you get in here?"

"Have you slept with him?"

What? She narrowed her eyes and spit on the floor at the woman's feet.

"The both of you are sick in the head." Angelica hadn't been aware she had that kind of fire in her. "Pah-lease! Like I'd sleep with the likes of him!"

She turned. "It doesn't matter, anyway. Like I said, I'm here to offer you a deal. I have implanted a homing beacon in your body. I want you to latch onto him and scream my name."

Angelica stepped back as the woman came forward, her eerie eyes glittering with menace. "I'll give you immortality for your assistance."

Angelica huffed and made her feet dig into the floor. "What? Turn me into a vampire? No thank you, psycho. Afraid I'll have to pass on that." She ran her tongue over her teeth. "I don't have anything in my wardrobe that would look good with fangs."

With a little prayer in the back of her mind, Angelica jumped at Zena, the knife in her hand. The knife embedded in her shoulder and Angelica staggered back expecting Zena to scream or fall. Instead of crying out in pain, Zena threw her head back and laughed. Angelica swallowed hard and took another step back. Zena pulled the knife out, brought it to her lips, and licked the blood off before throwing it to the floor.

"We shall see what you will do when Varick tires of playing with you and takes you to his bed. We shall see if you can suffer the beast that lies under his skin." Zena grabbed her chin and drug Angelica closer. "We shall see if you decide to take me up on the offer when he turns on you. I wonder if he'll force himself on you or put you under a spell before he drinks from your veins."

She released Angelica and stepped back. "Think about this very carefully, human. He is a vampire with a healthy appetite, and he will eventually sink his fangs into your flesh." Misting, she added, "My name is Zena. You only have to say my name, and I will free you from him."

Angelica sank to the floor as the woman vanished just like Varick had. Vampires. Freaking vampires. She laughed, tears spilling down both of her cheeks as she rocked back and forth. She was going to kill him. This was all his fault.

More than anything, she wanted to see her brother. Eli would make things better. He was all the family she had, and she needed him.

"Oh, for the love of the ocean, get up and stop sniveling!" Angelica looked up at the sound of the voice, accompanied by a stamping foot. "At least act like you have a backbone!"

Shimmering light illuminated an almost transparent woman wearing a black leather dress. Shades of gray and sparkles of gold cast shadows everywhere about the room.

Hysterical laughter bubbled up from Angelica's throat. "And who are you, my fairy godmother?"

The woman raised one eyebrow and replied, "No, I'm your great grandmother."

Angelica shook her head and tried to process what she was seeing. "No, I'm nuts. I'm certifiably crazy as hell, and I need a large dose of tranquilizers and a straight jacket, purple if you would."

"Get up or I will kick you in your backside and then bend you over my knee and give you twenty lashes." The woman crossed her arms over her chest. "I'm the goddess Amay, and you are my descendant. My blood runs through your veins."

"Am I supposed to be proud?" On shaky legs, Angelica stood and dried her eyes. "Gods and goddesses do not exist. I know I have to be nuts—there's no other explanation. First Varick thinks he's a vampire—hell, at this point I believe it. And then Miss Black-As-Death shows up and says she wants him, which makes perfect sense because, hey, she's a vampire too."

"Who wants him?"

Amay stepped forward. Angelica jerked back and put a chair between them, completely ignoring her question. "And now this. What's next, a werewolf somewhere in my genetics?"

Amay made a twisted face and then laughed. "No werewolves. Necromancers, but no werewolves." She shimmered to Angelica's side. "Who wants Varick?"

At this point, Angelica was getting used to people just popping in and out of thin air. "I can't say her name."

"Why not?"

Shoulders slumping, she replied grudgingly, "If I say her name, she said I would be transported somewhere. She said she would grant me immortality if I grabbed him before I said her name." She laughed and swiped at the fresh tears. "She has another thing coming if she thinks I'll willingly become a vampire like her."

"You're the descendant of a goddess. You are entering the Burning. If you survive, you will be immortal." The goddess huffed, her black eyes glowing with eerie, blue-green light. "If that bitch thinks she can use you, use someone of my blood, to get to him, then she shall regret the mistake dearly."

Angelica pointed at her. "You're a figment of my deranged mind."

Amay rolled her eyes. "You're beginning to get on my nerves."

"Well, you aren't exactly on my A list right at the moment, either, so we're even on that score."

Angelica grabbed the chair as her mother's diary appeared in the woman's hand. "Does this look like a figment of your imagination?"

After careful consideration, Angelica slid around the chair and sat down. "I…you…I can't believe this. I'm not even sure I believe in God." She looked up at Amay, studied her face, and frowned. "You remind me of someone. Someone I just recently met." Pausing, she took a deep breath. "Alexander."

Amay closed her eyes. She stood there in silence for a few seconds before she opened her eyes and pointed her finger at Angelica. "You have a problem. You've entered the Burning and you need a Destroyer to take you through it. Varick is the best choice for a lot of reasons. I suggest you jump his bones as soon as possible."

Chapter 26

Varick materialized inside his chambers and set the brown sacks down on the night stand, which was oddly out of place. Giving it little thought, he took a deep breath and let her scent wash over him. Ocean storms and musk.

Slowly, Varick turned and met her gaze. Not an ounce of terror lay in their depths, but something darker and far more potent was inked into those glittering pools. Feral instincts were written all over her, submerged in her stance, and glistening in the tight line her lips held. She was pissed. The knife in her hand should have been his first clue.

But his gaze lingered on her lips before dropping to the rest of her. Her nipples were hard enough to slice his icy heart, and she was wearing his favorite black T-shirt. He groaned in silent appreciation. She should have been born a goddess.

She was leaning against the bedpost, his jogging pants slipping down her hips, showing tanned skin and a glorious curve. His Smith & Wesson 952 was in her other hand, hanging by her side. And she was not wearing her underwear.

His throat went dry, his tongue suddenly needing moisture, her moisture. Damn, she was smoking hot in his clothes holding weapons he had used to kill.

He took a step toward her, his gaze full of all the exciting and delicious things he wanted to do to her. She raised the 952 and snarled. He stopped, a mischievous grin lifting his lips.

"If you so much as come one step closer, I'll blow your head off."

He pointed to the brown sacks on the night stand. "Eat."

She stood unblinking and still as he pulled the black shirt from his chest. He heard her sudden intake of air and gave her a smug grin as he unbuttoned Alexander's leather pants. She swallowed as her eyes went to his hands. As he peeled the pants down to his ankles, she groaned.

"I…" She groaned again as he turned and gave her a full view of his backside. "I will not be a willing captive."

"Eat." He walked toward the bathroom, all too aware that her hands were shaking, her breathing was labored, and the scent of her arousal was heavy and erotic. "I'm taking a shower, and I fully expect the food to be gone when I return." Her mouthwatering, typhoon scent rained havoc on his growing appetite.

• • •

Angelica wilted onto the bed as the door closed off her view. All she had to do to gain her freedom was say her name. Just one word, one little bitty word that started with Z and ended with A. It was simple…but not.

Her options, at best, were either to have probably mind-blowing sex with a…She was not going to say that word—with a whatever the hell he was, or take Miss-I-Want-Him's offer. She stared at the ceiling and cursed. Or she could believe Amay and literally jump his bones, have mind-blowing sex, and gain immortality.

She stood as the sound of the shower invaded her thoughts. Before she knew where she was going, she was at the door and leaning her forehead against it. Oh, she could just see him in all his naked, well-hung glory. His hands were soaping his ripped chest, his strong, well-toned arms, his long, delicious backside, his tapered, sinewy legs, and that wonderfully chiseled butt.

She whimpered; she so wanted to be that bar of soap! Damn him and his long white hair that she wanted to wrap around her fingers and never let go. And those amazing eyes that seemed to reach deep into her soul were utterly breathtaking in their beauty.

For the life of her, she couldn't figure it out. What was it about this man that made her internal temperature reach critical meltdown? Well, other than the fact that he held first, second, and third-place titles in perfection. And he strutted about with enough raw sexual magnetism that it was a wonder women didn't fall at his feet or swoon just looking at him.

Lost in hot fantasies of his flesh wrapping around hers, she gasped as the door swung open and she fell into his arms. Instantly, every carnal piece of knowledge she possessed swam straight to the forefront of her brain, and she latched onto his shoulders and sealed her fate with a heated kiss. Fingers tangling in his hair, she kissed him like she was possessed with the god of lust.

Never in her entire life had she wanted a man like this; never in all her thirty years had she done such a thing. But damn, it was good—hot and good, like honey in tea, like powdered sugar on donuts. He tasted like heaven, like hell, like every sinful fantasy she had ever had, and she wanted more.

His tongue met hers and she melted against him. His hand drifted down her back, slid under the loose jogging pants, and stilled over her bottom. His touch was electrifying, a glorious narcotic to her blood.

When his head lifted and his lips made a blazing trail to her ear, she slid her hands down his shoulders, relaxing into the tight hardness of his big body. She gasped as he nipped her earlobe, laved a path down her neck, and suckled her skin. His rumble of a groan speared her chest and tightened her stomach muscles, and a wet heat drenched her core.

She had no doubt he was going to eat her alive, and damn if she didn't want him to. "Heaven help me."

His short bark of laughter sizzled in her ears. "Will you come for me, Angelica?"

Oh, hell yes, and if she didn't know any better, she already had. Her mind was screaming out every possible warning, blaring sirens were going off in her ears, but she wanted this, her body demanded this.

Sweeping her off her feet and into his arms, he carried her to the bed and slowly deposited her in the middle. He grabbed the waistband of her jogging pants and tugged as she lifted her hips and groaned. She bit her bottom lip as she watched him throw them over his shoulder and rip the towel from his hips. The sight of him opened every floodgate in her body, and she arched instinctively as he slid over her and settled his knee between her aching thighs.

She arched as his erection rubbed against the inside of her thigh. His mouth trailed along her throat, and he planted his hands on each side of her head.

"Forgive me," he said as his erection penetrated her.

She screamed out in bliss as he slammed deep inside her.

"Look at me, Angelica," he whispered.

Angelica slowly opened her eyes and stared at his mouth. Her eyes widened as she saw the pointed fangs hanging down against his lower lip. She twisted and tried to squirm away.

"Twelve hours, and you're free to go!" His eyes darkened, regret heavy in his heart. "But I must warn you what lies ahead."

Angelica arched under him. She didn't want to talk, she wanted him to finish. "Warn me?"

"I'm going to bite you more than once. And I am going to make love to you more than once. I'm sorry if at any time I hurt you." His words were softly spoken, a hint of pain in his rough timbre.

"Get off me!" She was whimpering, but she didn't care. Her body betrayed her words and she arched under him sending his erection even deeper.

He tried to hide his grin, but it slid across his lips as he kissed her nose. "Oh, no, I haven't even gotten started yet. I was merely"—he paused as he nipped at her lips—"giving you time to adjust to my size."

He moved slightly, rocking slowly against her, and groaned as she gasped, "Varick!"

"You're so beautiful—truly an angel." He groaned as she grabbed his shoulders and arched under him. "My perfect angel, my raven-haired beauty."

She looked up and gasped as his fangs gleamed. He was devastating, but good grief; he had fangs, for crying out loud. She just couldn't get past the damn fangs.

She smiled as he groaned and his head sagged forward. She ran her hands down his back and then traveled up his arms. His skin was hot and hard, and she wanted to touch him everywhere. Fangs or not, she wanted him.

He rocked against her slowly and held his breath as her hands roamed his body. His strokes became faster and faster. She arched higher, and he slammed harder into her. She met each thrust with sheer ecstasy and screamed his name. He bared his teeth, and she pulled his head to her neck.

Angelica didn't know what the hell she was doing, but somehow she knew he needed her neck. She smiled as his tongue touched her skin, and then he sucked hard. Her eyes flew open as he growled and bit into her. She winced but was lost as he rocked faster inside her and took her to the brink of insanity.

He collapsed on top of her, licked the bite marks, and rose up on one elbow. She simply stared at him; the expression on his face was utter satisfaction, like he had won some great battle. Her heart was thundering in her ears.

"Are you hurt?"

Angelica stared into his eyes, and a tear escaped her eye. He quickly wiped it away as he asked again, "Are you hurt?"

She slowly shook her head but winced when he ran his hand down her stomach and between her legs. He frowned and rolled to his side. She raised her hand to her neck and grimaced as she ran her fingers across the puncture wounds. He rubbed her arm and pulled her to his chest.

"I'm sorry I hurt you."

Angelica tensed. Her thighs pounded, and her skin burned as if it had been rubbed raw. She looked up, and tried to smile as her fingers ran across the bite marks again.

"I'm a fucking bastard! Go ahead and curse me, hit me, or whatever the hell you want to do to me. Fuck, I'll hit myself if it will make you feel any better." He took a ragged breath. "I'm a sick bastard. I'll give you my dagger, and you can cut me into tiny pieces."

Angelica smiled and forced her laughter down. "I don't want to do any of those things. It's just that you have fangs. I can't get past the fangs."

Softly, he asked, "Does it terrify you that I'm part vampire?"

"No, not really." She sat up and ran her hand down his arm. "Not now. I'm kind of getting used to that part. It's the fangs, yeah definitely the fangs."

Varick groaned and lay back against the pillows. "I should have been careful with you."

Angelica twisted away and swung her legs off the bed. "I don't think I would have wanted careful."

Varick grinned and raised an eyebrow. He was hot, sexy hot, and she wanted more.

"Is it hot in here?" Angelica took a deep breath. Sweat beaded her upper lip. "I think I'm having a heat flash."

Angelica stood, grabbed the chair, and fell to one knee as a blast of internal heat took her breath. Sweat beaded her forehead, dripped into her eyes. Before she could pull herself up, Varick was hovering over her and pulling her to her feet.

"I need to go to the bathroom." She leaned into him and groaned as pain raced up her back. "I think I've had too much excitement for one day."

He lifted her into his arms and carried her to bathroom's entrance. He set her down in front of the sink and stepped back.

She gritted her teeth and turned to the tub. "I'm just going to take a bath. I'm sure I'll feel better after."

Varick turned and grabbed a towel from the little linen closet and then reached for the faucet. She grunted and jerked the towel out of his hand.

"I can do it by myself. I'm not dead. I'm just a little sore and overheated!"

Varick jerked upright and grinned. "Call me if you need anything."

"Just get the hell out of here."

• • •

Varick turned and left Angelica filling the tub, needing to escape for a private moment so he could think. But he couldn't help but feel like he'd won some great prize. His grin turned into a full-blown smile as she slammed the door in his face. She was by far the most passionate woman he had ever bedded. And he couldn't wait to go at it a second time.

He turned to the bed and sat down. Her sultry scent was all over him, and he liked it. He stripped the sheets from the bed and tucked them neatly into a hamper inside his large closet. He pulled two fresh ones from the shelf and fought with them, trying to make the bed. His thoughts kept going to the woman in the tub as he continued to smell her on his skin.

His shaft hardened, and he went to the door. He could hear her breathing; her heartbeat thumped in a steady rhythm as water ran down her arms. He envisioned her naked in his tub as she shampooed her long, silky hair.

Varick leaned his head against the door, and his fangs extended to their full length. He wanted her to be his and his alone. He wanted her body like he had never wanted any other before. And her sweet, deep, rich blood was a bonus he was all too aware of. He'd kill any other for touching her. It was his right; after all, had he not put his mark upon her neck?

With a growl of possession, he roared, "Mine!"

Varick jerked his head up.

What the hell am I saying? It's just the Mating Rite talking. After I am done with her, she will just be a damn memory. Hell, she'll probably never speak to me again. She might not survive the beast.

The thought stopped his heart in its tracks.

Chapter 27

When Angelica came out of the bathroom, Varick was standing in front of the fireplace in a pair of black silk boxers and boy, did he look edible. He turned and smiled as she reached for her clothes. He walked across the room and took her clothes from her hands. She couldn't help but notice he was drenched in sweat, but then again so was she.

"It's time."

"Time for what?" She slapped Varick's hand as he reached for the towel wrapped around her body.

"The Mating Rite."

Angelica shook her head and sat down in the chair. "Look. I know we just had sex and it was great and all, but I don't know about this rite of yours. What exactly are you asking me to do?"

"Mate with me."

"Didn't we just do that?"

"Mating is a little more complicated," Varick offered as he ran his hands through her hair. "Mating with me will be an unexplainable journey."

Her face reddened, and he grinned at her embarrassment. "More of the unexplainable? Don't know if I'm ready for that."

"Just trust me," he whispered as he caught her chin, knelt, and forced her to look at him. "Do you feel this?" He took her hand and placed it on his chest.

She felt the hammering of his heart, and the heat from his skin was so hot it almost burned to touch him. "Yes."

"I have a beast inside me. It's part of me. In essence, it is my soul. I am a Destroyer, and every once in a while it demands to be released. Now is his time. If I don't release him, it will drive me insane." He sucked in a harsh breath. "One of my friends will have to hunt me down and destroy me."

Angelica's face paled as she felt his skin crawl underneath her fingers. She looked up and groaned as his eyes turned red. She was either having a nightmare or she had lost her mind. She pulled away and took the towel from her hair and rubbed at it as she tried to calm her nerves.

This is not happening…I have gone completely insane. His eyes were not red, and his skin didn't just…it didn't just…Oh, shit! I'm committable, crazy, nuts…whacked!

"I know you're scared, and you should be, but I'll hold him back as long as I possibly can and try to make it as quick as possible."

Angelica opened her mouth to make a rude comment but was silenced as Varick's face filled with pain. She went to him and ran her hand along his jaw. He was burning up—not like a fever, but more like a fire was inside of him.

"I'm hurting inside, Angelica, and I need your help." His voice dripped with pain.

She took his hands and grimaced as he sagged into her body. "What do you want me to do?"

Varick kissed her neck, trapped both of her hands into one of his, and whispered, "Love me."

"But I don't really even know you," she whispered back as he led her to the bed.

"My name is Varick Ta Farg. I was born to a clan of assassins, and I lived by their creed faithfully for the remainder of my first life. When I was thirty, I died at the hands of my mother. Gyth took my soul and offered me immortality in return for my servitude." He paused as a dark expression crossed his face. "My mother was the daughter of the queen of the vampires. Gyth took her, and I was bred to be a killer. I am his Destroyer. I kill for him."

Angelica sat down on the bed as Varick took her face in his hands. "I have killed thousands of people, and not once have I shown any remorse for my deeds. I have brutally tortured, maimed, and gutted more humans in my life as an assassin than any other in the history of the world. As a Destroyer, those skills have come into use on a daily basis but each day that passes is torture to my soul. The things I have done were unforgivable, and my mother took pity on my soul the night she stabbed me in the black pit of my heart."

She slid back onto the bed as Varick grabbed the towel and tore it from her body. "The Mating Rite refuses to be denied any longer. I don't want to be driven insane by my beast, nor do I want to hurt you."

"I don't understand any of this. Why me, Varick?"

"I need you to understand." He gritted his teeth. "I was raised to be a killer. Throughout history, it was I, or one of my kind, who assassinated people of power. So many names, so many times, so very many…" He paused as a deep regret filled his face. "They were strangled, poisoned, and tortured to death by my hands all for the sake of the goddess that commanded us. These hands, Angelica, these hands are the hands of a cold-blooded killer. And not once under her rule did I question my orders, not once did I take a stand and defend any of those I killed. Not once."

"But?"

"There are no buts. Even after the clan of assassins was slain by my hand at the order of that goddess, I continued to be an assassin. For two years I continued to be an assassin because it's all I knew."

"You said it yourself; you were raised as an assassin and lived by a goddess's rules. Why do you beat yourself up about it? You were taking orders."

"I was…" Varick looked the other way turning from Angelica. "Then one night, witches kidnapped my mother and used her against me. I had to do as they commanded, or they would have killed her."

Angelica ran her hand up his chest, and she whispered. "You were afraid, weren't you?"

"Not for myself. Never for myself."

"Your mother?" Tears streaked her cheeks.

"One of my last assignments before they took her was for a coven of witches. Damon, the king of the Underworld, wanted a group of men assassinated that worked for one of the church missions in Belgium. I took the job and killed them all. When I went to collect, the witches had my mother and knew she was my only weakness."

"Your mother—how did she die?" Angelica ran her fingers up the glorious length of his arms, catching her breath as heat flooded her loins.

"I did as I was told in fear for her life. The witches came for her after she killed me. My soul was there, still suspended above my body. Damon hand-delivered her to a rogue band of vampires and watched as they sliced her to pieces." His voice quivered. "I couldn't do anything; I was trapped in a purgatory because Gyth had captured my soul before the queen of the vampires, my grandmother, Zena, could call my soul to the Underworld."

Zena was his grandmother?

"They used her to keep you as an assassin." Angelica gritted her teeth, wanting to take away the pain that scorched Varick's heart. "Gyth made you watch."

Varick's expression darkened, and his nostrils flared. "Gyth offered me immortality, power, and the ability to see vengeance come full circle to all those involved."

Angelica's eyes widened. "Revenge? You wanted to come back to take revenge for your mother and for yourself?"

"I kill, one at a delicious time. I take great pleasure torturing vampires, mutilating them, desecrating their bodies, and claiming their black hearts because it's the only thing I know how to do."

"All because some of them killed your mother?" Angelica tried to understand. "And Damon?"

"Gyth cast him to the Underworld, imprisoned him there." Varick dropped his head.

Angelica tried to soothe him, ran her hand up his arms. He pulled back, his golden eyes full of tears.

"My heart is a black void of hate, diseased with the disgusting animal instincts that were beaten into me. I am a…" He swallowed as he looked into her eyes. "I am…"

Angelica threw her arms around his neck and clung to him as she whispered, "You are Varick Ta Farg, and your past isn't important. What matters is the future. My heart is breaking for you."

Varick pulled away, took three steps, and turned to face her. "There isn't going to be a future. I can't allow you to do this. I won't let my beast hurt you."

Angelica's insides snapped, popped, and her stomach flipped. She clutched at her stomach as pain hammered through her. Falling forward, he reached out to take her hand. She backed up until the backs of her legs hit the bed. A scream ripped from her lips as her body seized.

Angelica fell backwards onto the pillows as she clutched at her heart. Pain shot up her neck and down her spine as Varick slid over her body. Sweat beaded her forehead, and her vision blurred.

She twisted underneath him. "What the hell are you doing to me?"

Varick whispered, "I'm not doing this to you. The Burning has claimed you."

Chapter 28

Varick growled as he caught the odor of the Burning. The beast inside his mind roared, pain splintering in his skull. He couldn't go through with this, couldn't take the risk of hurting her. But the Burning could kill her even if the beast didn't.

Maybe he could hold the beast off until after the Burning was over. Maybe he could spare her. She cried out as Varick trembled and closed his eyes. Flames shot out from his shoulders and crept down his spine.

This could not be happening. There was no precedent for the Burning and the Mating Rite to take place at the same time. It could not be. He feared he was not strong enough to deal with both at the same time; either she would die or he would. Or they both would.

Why did it always have to be the hard way—why did things go from bad to worse every time a situation arose, and for the love of all the misbegotten gods, why had he chosen her?

Mine!

"Your human blood is pooling inside your stomach. I'm going to take that blood and release the human impurities from it. And then you are going to take that blood back and become who you truly are."

Angelica screamed out in intense pain as sharp needles of lightning pricked at her insides. She kicked and twisted in agony as Varick held her to the bed. He felt her anger swell inside her, and she pushed with all her might at his chest. He strained to hold her still as his knee landed between her legs.

"Not me! This is not happening! Get off me! I'm not like you." She twisted and jerked as a spasm of pain hit her in the pit of her stomach and radiated out through her limbs. "Alera and Amay. They warned me about this."

"Your father was a Destroyer like me, and your mother was descended from a goddess. You are an immortal female by blood right, by birthright."

Her back arched as needle pains splintered up her backbone. "It hurts!"

"It's the Burning. Your thirtieth birthday marks the day your body begins releasing your human half and accepts the true powers of the One Race. The signs should have started. Dizziness. Confusion. Your body temperature getting hotter than normal. Muscles pains."

Varick watched her body transform. Her eyes began to glow as she arched again. He released his hold as she sat up and stretched her arms out. Tiny droplets of blood hung in the air as her skin released the being inside of her.

Long, black wings emerged from her shoulder blades, dripping in blood. Instead of feathers, long strands of black, silky hair fell from their length. Her fingernails grew and blackened. Her skin paled, and black daggers appeared down both her arms and across her collarbone. He watched as the daggers danced down between her breasts and down her stomach. They appeared along both her legs as little black horns emerged from her temples.

The black daggers were just like the ones in his dream.

He caught his breath as he stared at her. She was glorious and beautiful.

"I'm not hurting anymore. My stomach…ohhh…I'm sick to my stomach." She glanced at her wings and laughed hysterically. "I have wings!"

"I have to take your blood now." The words were spoken as he lengthened his incisors.

"Oh, hell no, you are not going to stick those fuckers into me again!"

She scrambled to her knees and groaned. Her body ached. She looked down, and her eyes widened in disbelief at the black daggers dancing on her skin as if they had a life of their own. Varick took advantage of her moment of hesitation and slammed her down onto the bed.

She laughed as his eyes rolled back into his head. "What's wrong, Varick? Not feeling up to the job?"

Varick grunted as he showed her his fangs, and his back splintered open. Black flames leapt from his back as a set of black-and-gold wings emerged. Horns ripped out of his shoulders and forehead—long, sharp, black horns twisted with gold. His long, scaled tail forced itself from his body and twirled around his head before coming to rest alongside Angelica on the bed. He felt her stiffen as black flames engulfed him. Her thoughts poured into him, fear building inside her.

I'm going to burn to death underneath him!

"Angelica, don't be afraid."

She turned her head and pulled him closer. Varick groaned as he sank his teeth into her flesh. As her blood filled his mouth, he could taste her passion, her being, and her soul. She was innocent to evil, and her soul was as pure as a newborn babe. He could feel the protection she had been placed under, he could feel Amay's possessive shroud hovering around her, and he could feel her completely putting her trust in him.

And he could sense another power, one so much like her father's. In her blood, her very DNA twisted, melted, and recalibrated itself, allowing that power to sense her, to home in on her. And that being was a Destroyer. Like her brother Eli, she would awake not only as a member of the One Race but also as the first female Destroyer.

In that second, more than he had ever wanted anything, he wanted her to love him. His heart lodged in his throat, tears filled his eyes. He had never wanted or needed anyone's love. Fisting his hands in her hair, a blood red tear fell from his eye. He wanted and needed her, like fire needed oxygen.

He pulled from her neck and licked the wounds. He watched as she looked up at him and gently wiped her blood from his lips. Then, of all things, she smiled and kissed his chin as her eyes fluttered closed.

His insides burned as her blood settled inside him. Her memories were filled with the love of her brother, her protector. She'd had a wonderful childhood and knew only their love and commitment to her. When she had left home her heart had broken and had been breaking every day since. Her love of Eli ran through his soul and forced its way into his heart; that black orb of hate and disgust opened and burst under the pressure of her unconditional love.

Only one thing plagued her—the death of her parents and the secrets that surrounded her brother. She had wanted to know her mother, and she often cried when she tried to envision her. She wanted a mother's love, a gentle hand to caress away her fears, to soothe her heart.

Varick fell to his elbows and turned her to face his neck. He cut into his skin with his fingernails and brought her lips to the gash. Awakened from her slumber, she licked the wound he had made. The hot liquid was delectable, and her teeth sank into his skin. She sucked as if her very life depended on it.

When she released him, a primal lust filled him. The beast clawed through his defenses, screaming Angelica's name. He wanted her as bad as Varick did.

She grabbed his arms and arched under him as he sagged against her. Her nipples hardened as they rubbed against his chest, and she groaned as he slid into position. She arched again and whispered his name.

"Angelica, this is where I have to release him. Please forgive me."

Huskily, she begged, "Now! Do it now!"

Varick closed his eyes and released the beast. His flames leapt to the ceiling, and his wings expanded to their full length. His body arched, and his tail whipped through the air like a lethal sword. Half man and half dragon, Varick and the beast stared down at her. When he slammed into her, she screamed his name for the whole world to hear. His fingernails dug into the mattress as her hand flew to his chest and her fingernails buried themselves deep into the skin above his heart.

He watched as her fingernails turned, twisted, and went across his skin. Deep within his heart, in his very soul something snapped, popped, and lodged itself in his throat. Under her fingers, her name was written. She had marked him and he had never felt such a wonderful sense of belonging.

Moving against her, he reeled in the pleasure they were both feeling.

Angelica went wild with pleasure. She arched again and again to meet his hot, burning need. Her wings braced on the floor as he pounded into her. When his hand captured her breast, she clawed her fingernails down his chest.

She hissed in ecstasy as his tongue flicked out and ran across her nipple. She pulled him down and brought his face to hers. The kiss was blinding as his tongue encircled hers. She moaned in his mouth as his hands went to her hips. He could feel her fingernails digging into his skin, but he refused to acknowledge the pain. Every second he was inside of her, he could feel his heartbeat, and it was total chaos to his senses.

Varick was lost in her. Harder and faster and deeper he went as she met each of his thrusts. His body surged with hers and accepted her delicious ecstasy.

His tail whipped around her body and brought her into a sitting position around his thighs. The tiny horns on his tail dug into her skin and crushed her as close to him as possible. Her hands flew around his neck, and she rocked against his shaft as his wings encircled them both. Tiny, sharp scales on his wings turned sideways as they hovered above the bed. They dug into her wings as he thrust one last, hard time deep within her.

Her eyes burned bright as his tongue came out and caught a drop of blood that had slid down her wing and dripped onto her neck. His fangs sank into her shoulder as he found his release.

Varick had other plans; he groaned as his hands went to her arms. His black flames licked her arms and jumped onto her skin as she dug deeper into his shoulders. He grinned as he pulled his fangs from her shoulder and watched as the steam and the smell of scorched flesh filled his nostrils. The flame etched into her skin around her wrists, leaving behind his mark.

His satisfied growl echoed hers as the black flame seared itself into place. The mark, his mark, was wrapped around her wrists. Delicate intertwining black vines for the whole world to see.

His! "Mine!"

He laid her back against the pillows and pulled from her body. She let out a soft moan as he inspected her wounds. When he touched her soft stomach, she arched and caught his hand. His eyes met hers, and he growled as he witnessed her desire for him. She wanted him again, and she reached for his chest.

The beast roared in delight as he claimed his female in her true form. His! She belonged to him and him alone. No other would ever touch her; no other would take her as he did. No other would ever feel his soul and accept him as he really was, and for that he fell deeply and madly in love with her as he released his past to her heart.

"*Xsp thix rane drine*," he breathed into her ear. "Mine for all time!"

"Mine!" he roared as the walls trembled and the bed shook violently.

Chapter 29

Night settled over the city of Fether, and a low, thick fog filtered around the dark shadowed walls of buildings groaning with the onslaught of the midnight hour. Deep down inside the club, Tortured Souls, in the thirteenth level of the Destroyer sanctuary, eleven Destroyers gathered around a square table.

Not a soul at the table had not heard Varick's mental roar as the Mating Rite took place the night before, and not one had not taken a deep breath of ease as it had passed. All Destroyers were linked on a mental level; a necessary precaution that warned all of them when a Destroyer was at his weakest or, worse, captured and tortured.

Alexander grinned at Varick. "You seem to be in fine spirits."

Varick grunted but couldn't keep the smile from his lips. "You may be the only one here who is pleased I made it out alive."

"I still wish to have that discussion with you," Payne growled as he looked at Varick, "and when the business at hand is taken care of, I expect us to settle our disagreement. Of course, if you fear me and do not show, I will understand."

Varick leaned up onto his elbows and gave Payne a blinding smile. "Seems I no longer have the urge to kick your ass, my friend."

Payne rolled his eyes and turned to Alexander. "Why did you call us tonight?"

Alexander frowned as he looked around the table. "Before we get down to business, there is some serious shit here that needs to be taken care of."

Varick looked to Eli Dark. He knew the secrets that he had been harboring needed to be out in the open. If necessary, he would wrench it from his mouth by force. And he didn't hide that fact as he looked him directly in the eyes.

Eli sat in silence as he looked around the table at the other Destroyers. Slowly, he worked his fingers through his spiky black hair.

"I won't have any more secrets getting in the way of our duty." Alexander gave Eli and Varick a determined look. "I don't care which one of you spills your guts first, but you're both going to "

Eli glared at Alexander as Varick opened his palm and looked at the black orb that held Eli's mother's soul. "Tell your boy that if he doesn't release my mother's soul, I'll rip his throat out."

Eli stood, leaned over the table, and turned his glare to Varick. "She has suffered long enough."

Alexander jumped to his feet to shove Eli back in his seat, but Varick held out his hand. The black orb pulsed, and Alexander sat down as Varick brought his hand to the tabletop. Varick closed his hand over the orb and felt the pulse, a deep agonizing beat screaming for peace.

"Go, Varick." Alexander gave Eli a hard look, one that dared him to open his fanged mouth. "We can wait until you return to finish this."

Varick grinned half-heartedly. "No. I want to share with all of you what I go through every time I release a soul. Perhaps then each of you, my friends, my brothers, will understand why I do it in private."

Alexander nodded. For a brief moment Varick saw the look of confusion in Alexander's eyes. The Destroyers all assumed Varick didn't care what anyone thought or felt. But they were wrong. He had always felt a friendship with each of the Destroyers, a bond. He cared about them, each and every one of them. Perhaps there was reason beyond the insanity. Or insanity behind the reason.

Everyone at the table watched in silence as Varick placed the orb in his mouth and swallowed. His eyes blazed as the orb slipped down inside his stomach. Varick's knuckles turned white as he clutched the table's edge. His head flew back, and the flames inside him burst from his skin. As the flame inside his body consumed the vampire's heart, his back arched against the pain and misery of the trapped soul buried deep within the black orb.

Multitudes of hot, pulsing streaks of pain reached out to the other Destroyers, and Varick's agony gripped their hearts as the soul of Antonia screamed inside their minds. The brothers closed their eyes as Varick's nose bled and his eyes rolled back into his head. He fell forward and groaned as Antonia's soul misted out of his mouth and swirled around the room.

Varick gripped the table and stood. His guts twisted and lurched as the orb was forced from his body. He coughed and gagged as the orb came up his throat. His stomach flipped, and he puked; black blood and the now-white orb spewed out onto the table. The Destroyers sighed as the pain disappeared from their minds.

Antonia's soul whipped around Eli, a transparent hand hovering over his heart. "Mom. I'm sorry it took me so long."

Gyth appeared, his form shimmering next to Varick. In his hand, a round glass container glowed softly. Antonia's soul swirled around Gyth, taking shape and settling between him and Varick. She held her hand out over the container and turned to Varick.

"Thank you, Destroyer." Her words were the barest whisper of sound.

Her form misted, slowly swirling as she slipped inside the container. Gyth held his hand out, closed his eyes. The container vanished.

Eli spoke, his voice cracking. "What now? What happens to her soul?"

Gyth answered, "She will be taken to Illusion Fields where she will wait for Feverand's soul to be released. She is at peace now."

Varick took a handkerchief from his pocket and wiped his mouth and nose as he slowly sat down and took a deep breath. His insides trembled. Nausea followed. But then it always did. Breathing through the nausea, he met Eli's eyes.

Eli's head dropped. "When I find the vampire holding my father's soul, I will bring the orb to you."

Varick nodded and looked up at Gyth as the god laid his hand on his shoulder. He met his eyes. An odd sensation ran down his spine as Gyth continued to stare at him.

When Gyth spoke, Varick looked around the table. None of the others seemed to be able to hear the words. "Do you see the importance of the power inside you? Do you understand why the beast is necessary?"

"The beast is a curse."

Gyth shook his head. "It's a blessing."

Varick shrugged out of his grasp. A quick retort was on his tongue. If he could piss the god off enough, maybe he would disintegrate the beast along with himself. But then, there was Angelica and he wanted to see her again, feel her again.

Alexander spoke bringing Varick out of his thoughts. "Eli, just where the hell have you been for the last thirty years?"

All heads snapped to Varick's face as he answered. "He was raising his sister as he searched for the vampires that took his mother and father's souls."

"How the fuck did you know that?" Eli demanded as he gave Gyth a wary look.

Gyth's lip twitched. His eyes narrowed. The red ends of his hair fanned out slightly as if a light breeze had swirled through the room. Varick knew the god well enough to know Eli had crossed him. And there would be repercussions.

Varick spoke softly, "Angelica is here."

Apoc, Kreach, Alexander, and Payne leaned back in their seats and groaned. Only one question needed to be asked, and not one of the four was about to ask it.

"Where the hell is she?" Eli asked. "And why the fuck is she here?"

Alexander held his breath as Varick smiled and answered, "She is in my bed at the moment."

Eli jumped to his feet with and blood in his eyes. "You fucking half-breed vampire bastard! She deserves better than you."

Varick slowly stood. "She has gone through the Burning and has taken me through my Mating Rite."

Payne groaned as Varick unbuttoned his shirt. The shirt fell to the table as Varick showed his chest. Several curses erupted. Eli slammed back down into the chair with a curse. They all stared at the mark on his chest. It was deep, scabbed. Angelica's name was etched into his flesh above his right nipple, the letter *l* shaped like a dagger.

"I should kill you where you stand." Eli pulled his Glock 45s out of the holster hidden under his trench coat and laid them on the table. "She is my sister and deserves better than a half-breed."

Payne stood pulling his swords from the sheath on his back. "You'll die before you fire the first shot."

Bloodshot topaz eyes met black ones. "He's not stupid enough to attack me now, my brother. If he does he'll have to deal with his sister, and she is one even I don't want to quarrel with."

"If anyone is going to kill you, it's going to me." Payne replaced his swords.

Varick laughed. "Don't worry yourself. If anyone can, which I doubt, it would most certainly be you."

Alexander cleared his throat. "Payne?"

Payne grumbled under his breath, "What?"

"You have an assignment. You're going either of two ways." Alexander rubbed his temple.

Payne slammed his fist down on the table, looked at Gyth. "And what are my choices?"

"You have two choices." Gyth's lip twitched again. "Your own methods or mine."

The power in his voice was undeniable, but Payne was Payne. "Screw you!"

Gyth grunted, the red-tinged ends of his hair flaring out before settling once again down his spine, and snapped his fingers. Payne vanished in a cloud of sulfuric smoke. "My way, then."

Varick snarled, hatred seething and simmering in his eyes. "Where did you send him?"

Gyth slammed his fist down on the table, splintering it down the middle. "Silence! I am lord and king, I am your master!"

The low vibration that rumbled out of Varick's chest sent all the chairs scraping backwards and brought the other Destroyers to their feet. Several gasps escaped as black wings unfurled through two slits on Varick's back. His mouth opened and his fangs extended past his bottom lip as he glared at the god before him.

"Where. Is. Payne?" The Destroyer in Varick roared, the vampire hissed, and the friend in him screamed. "Tell me or destroy me! I won't follow a god who places himself above those who have followed him without question, without pause."

Gyth's eyes were molten red, his hair fanning out again, his fingernails extending. "Stand down, Varick Ta Farg, or suffer my wraith!"

Alexander leapt across the table. Eli caught Apoc around the waist, taking him to the floor as Alexander slammed Varick into the wall. Kreach stood, stepped past Eli and Apoc, and reached for Gyth.

Gyth roared and slammed his palm into his chest. Kreach flew backwards, his head bouncing off the steel wall and blood splattering. He fell to his knees with a thud. A low and menacingly evil sound vibrated from the center of his being and rippled across the room. Winds danced around his body, lifting him from his knees to his feet. His body was bent, his shoulders shaking with rage and violent intentions.

Varick caught Alexander with an upper cut and used his shoulder to shove him away just enough to sidestep and rush Gyth. Kreach was two steps ahead of him as Varick went for Kreach's legs. Gyth snarled and brought his hand back, his palm filled with electrical sparks. Kreach opened his mouth as Varick wrapped both arms around his legs and brought him down.

The floor and Kreach's chest crushed together, the floor groaning and dust swirling upwards around him and Varick. He caught his breath as Varick rolled him over and got in his face.

"Look at me." Varick wrapped his fingers around Kreach's skull, forcing him to look Varick in the eyes. "Stop, Kreach. Don't fight my battles. Don't look death in the face and growl at it, my brother, no matter how bad you want it. Not today, not for me."

Kreach's emerald eyes focused slowly on the brother on top of him. His anger diminished, his soul clawing at his skin but calming. Varick's deep baritone invaded his mental barriers.

Not for me, Kreach, don't die because of me, not for me.

Kreach was stunned, shocked to say the least. *Varick?*

Don't give him the satisfaction of fighting him.

Kreach grunted and shoved Varick aside as he stood, gathering his composure and running his clawed fingertips over his shaved skull. Varick knew Kreach would have gone postal and there would have been no turning back. Turning on his heel, Kreach vanished, leaving his guttural growl behind him to echo around the room.

Gyth uttered in disgust. "I'm going to have to put that beast down if he does not learn how to control himself." He turned to look at Varick. "And you—you will stand down and take orders. You're out of your element, be it due to the Mating Rite or letting Angelica Dark mark you, but because of it, you're taken off patrol for at least a month."

Varick shoved Alexander out of his path as he headed for the door. "Is that a fucking order?"

As Varick slammed the door behind him, he fell to his knees, clutching his head. Gyth's voice bounced around inside him, vibrating his bones.

You bet your less than sweet ass it is, Destroyer! Enjoy your mate, Varick, for time is not on your side.

Despite the excruciating pain, Varick laughed. "Says the god who gave me immortality? Time has always been on my side."

Prepare yourself, warrior. Soon, a diverged road will appear before you. Choose carefully—your destiny is at stake.

Struggling to get to his feet, Varick took a deep breath as Gyth's presence left his senses. "In Payne's words, screw you."

Chapter 30

"Your mother is speaking about her pregnancy in this section." Varick brought Angelica's fingers to his lips and pressed a small kiss on her knuckles. "And the next one is how Feverand talks to Eli inside the womb."

Angelica cuddled closer to Varick as he read from the diary. "'I'm in my late third trimester. Eli is a kicker; my ribs stay sore. I still have a hard time believing I'm finally having a child. Feverand is excited, but I have my worries as all mothers would, I suppose. Eli is going to be Destroyer, born into it, unlike his father. Gyth has told us he will go through the Burning but he will not have to suffer the Mating Rite.'"

Angelica abruptly sat up. "Oh, my God."

"What is it, Angelica?" Varick closed the book and gently laid it aside.

"I just realized my brother isn't as young as he looks, is he? I mean, that diary is old—really, really old."

He chuckled. "I remember the day he was born."

Turning, she gave him an exasperated look. "Just now thinking about telling me that little bit of information? Don't you think that would have been pertinent info before you started reading the diary? Just how old is he, Mr. Keep-It-to-Myself?"

He chuckled again as he slid his hands behind his head, giving her an ample view of his splendid chest. "He's eight hundred years old."

His grin turned into a full-blown smile when her mouth dropped open. "Eight hundred?" She closed her gaping mouth and narrowed her eyes as she leaned across his chest and propped her head in her hands. "And just how old are you?"

"Much too old for you, my angel."

"Yeah, well I knew that by all that white hair of yours." She grinned as she slipped her hands up his chest and worked her fingers into the silky strands. "How old?"

He took a deep breath, filling his lungs with her stormy fragrance. "I was the first of the Destroyers."

A mischievous grin spread across her face as she worked her way up his chest, pressing feather-light kisses along her path. "Oh, I see."

He groaned as her pink tongue flicked out onto his skin. "You see what, exactly?"

She paused at his collar, nipping gently as his hands found her waist and then her hips. "I see you have robbed the cradle."

He laughed as her teeth grazed his skin. "For someone as innocent as you claim to be, you sure do know how to set my blood on fire."

Straddling his hips, she sat up and raked her nails down his chest. "You know that old saying isn't true."

His white brows bunched. "What old saying is that?"

Taking his hands and placing them on her breasts, she whispered, "You can teach an old dog new tricks."

He arched as she slid down onto his erection. As she rocked against him, he groaned with pleasure. "Then by all means, teach this old dog."

She smiled. "As you wish."

• • •

Angelica watched Varick as he slept. He was the most beautiful man she had ever seen—so very perfect. Running her finger down his cheek, she smiled as his lip twitched. Her finger followed her gaze to his lips, and she giggled as he latched on to her fingertip and sucked playfully.

"Did you have something particular in mind, or do you like your fingers in my mouth?" He rolled onto his side and wrapped his arm around her protectively. "Or should I show you far better uses for my mouth?"

She grinned. "Far better uses?"

He nodded and slid his hand down her back, over her hip, and between her thighs. Her legs parted, allowing him free access to her core. When his fingers slid over her heat, she groaned. When they slid into that heat, she gasped with pleasure.

"Should my mouth follow my fingers?" In and out they worked at her, making her forget how to talk. "Or"—he brought his fingers to his lips—"Should I taste you like this?"

Her eyes widened in shock as he licked the moisture from his fingers. "I want to lick you, Angel. I want to feast between your legs until you come in my mouth, until you beg me for mercy."

"I…" She swallowed hard. "I don't beg."

He grinned as he raised himself onto his elbow and rolled her onto her back. "Oh, but darling angel of mine, you will. Trust me, you will."

He slid down her body, kissing a path straight to her core. Arching under him, she met his tongue and fisted her hands in his hair as he laved her without mercy or a moment's pause.

"Varick!"

He laughed. "Are you begging yet?"

"No!" she screamed as he used his fangs and his tongue to torment her.

He felt her building toward a climax as he nibbled at her flesh, her sweet, stormy taste running down the back of his throat and making his appetite grow hard and strong. She bucked under him, screamed his name, and tried to pull him up her body.

He caught her hands and brought them between her legs as he sucked on her fingertips. "Come for me, Angelica. Right now."

He pressed her hand on her core and slid his tongue between her fingers, tasting her, making her entire body spasm with pleasure. "Come for me."

"Yes," she breathed as he removed her hand and slid his finger deep inside her slick heat. "Make me come for you."

He growled as he forced her legs farther apart and licked her as he slid two fingers into her. She arched, her body burning hot as the coals in hell. He threw his head back and roared as she climaxed.

Dragging himself up her trembling body, he settled between her legs and pushed his aching erection deep, her heat scalding him, covering him. He gasped as her nails raked down his chest and her legs wrapped around his hips. Every feral instinct he had overrode his meticulously planned-out lovemaking, and he slammed down hard—so hard the bed jerked and banged violently against the wall.

Her hips arched upward, meeting his demand, needing his complete attention. He gave it all, drilled into her with force and need. His fangs elongated as she turned her head and bared her neck.

"Bite me, Varick. Suck on me," she begged. "Please, Varick, please finish me now."

Roaring, he struck, piercing her skin with precision. He pumped into her body as he drank from her throat. Her precious blood fed his pleasure, spiking his every emotion and filling every void he had ever had. Her body clenched, tightened around his flesh, causing his release to explode from him in tidal waves. She dug into his shoulders as her own release met and matched his.

Collapsing on top of her, he chuckled. "Thought you said you don't beg."

She shrugged breathlessly as she kissed his shoulder. "Changed..." She panted. "Changed my mind, Vamp-boy." She tried not to laugh but couldn't keep from it. "I think I actually like it when you bite me."

He lifted his head and rolled to his side as he pulled her into his arms. "Then I shall bite you often, and in places you'll be dreaming about."

She hissed as his hand cupped her breast and his mouth sucked hard on her nipple. "Varick, let me catch my breath."

He licked and teased her with his fangs. "I think I like it when you beg." He bit down playfully on the curve of her breast as his hand splayed across her hip. She grinned as her hand slid between their bodies and cupped his already growing erection. He groaned and caught her head with his hands.

"Now," she whispered, "I think I shall hear you do some begging."

Her fingers wrapped around him and gently pulled, gently glided up and down. Pushing his shoulder with her other hand, she had him on his back, his massive erection still in the palm of her hand. He hissed, his neck straining with tension and pleasure.

She straddled his legs and watched his face as she used both hands to work him over. He arched under her, his hands fisting in the sheets, his claws ripping through the fabric and piercing his own skin.

He looked up, met her eyes as she started lowering herself to him. He released the sheet and grabbed her face with both hands, stopping her progress, stopping her from going down on him.

She smiled, removed his hands, and arched a brow. "Beg me, Varick. Beg me to do to you what you did to me."

"No," he whispered as she placed his hands on her breast. "I've never begged."

Bending, she placed a kiss on the tender flesh of his netherhead. He roared, his back arching as the back of his head slammed into the pillows. When she took him into her sultry mouth, he swallowed the scream of pleasure.

"Angelica." His guttural cry fell on her ears but she chose to ignore it.

She sucked hard, nipped at him until he looked up and opened his mouth. She sucked harder.

"Angelica, you're killing me."

Licking him from base to tip, she used her hands to assist in his pleasure. "Do you not like this?"

He groaned as his hand caught her chin and forced her to look into his eyes. "Yes, I like it very much."

His eyes glowed, topaz to red in a flash, as she went down on him hard and without mercy. "Angelica, plea…"

She rubbed the smooth skin beneath his erection, felt the tension building in that tender area. "I love the way you taste. I love the way you react to my touch."

He jerked violently. "Please, Angelica, oh gods above and below, please finish me."

Beaming, she did as he begged of her.

Chapter 31

Half awake, half dreaming, Angelica watched Varick climb back into the bed. Two days had passed, and she had not left the bed for more than the time it took to shower or eat. Two days of blissful lovemaking and talking. It could not have been more perfect except for his occasional popping in and out.

She took a deep, relaxing breath as he slid next to her and kissed her forehead. "Hi there."

He grinned, his white hair sliding down her cheek as he kissed her lips. "Hi. Sleepy?"

She nodded as she closed her eyes and melted to his chest. "There's something I need to ask you."

Wrapping his arm around her shoulders, he arched a brow. "Ask."

She wasn't really sure how to go about asking without saying Zena's name. One breath and then two, she pondered for a moment before asking.

"Who is the woman who came here looking for you? I thought it was your grandmother but you said your grandmother was the queen of vampires, that she was confined in the Underworld."

He stilled, his fingernails softly grazing her skin. "What woman?" Fire glinted in his eyes.

Angelica huffed. "It's not likely you or any other guy could forget her. She's darkly beautiful, sexy as hell, and has these really long, black, sharp fangs."

Varick sat up and turned her to look at him. "What was her name?"

She watched and bit her lip as fury lit up his eyes. "I can't tell you that."

"Angelica, tell me her name!" He ran his hands over her, looked at her questioningly. "Did she do anything to you?"

Angelica shook her head, sheepishly murmuring, "Not exactly."

Varick's lip twitched, his jaw tightening. "Did she threaten you?"

Angelica yawned. "Not exactly."

He stood, his naked male body tempting her even in her sleepy state. "Could you stop saying that? How can you not exactly know? What did she want of me?"

She shrugged and turned away so he could not see the anger lighting her face on fire. "I'm not sure. Well, not exactly, but I have my own theories on that one. She said she wanted you, and offered me a deal she apparently thought I would not refuse."

She could hear his heels hitting the floor in a pacing motion, back and forth. "What offer?"

"Immortality." Angelica shivered as ice hit her blood veins. "She wants you, and wanted to use me as bait to get you."

Another wave of cold dread hit her in the chest as Varick asked another series of questions; at least, she thought he had. Her head pounded, her temples rippling with pain and tension. She grimaced as Varick grabbed her arms and twisted her around to meet his stare. She watched his lips move, his fangs flashing, and knew he was angry about something, but she couldn't hear him, could barely feel his hands upon her shoulders.

She opened her mouth and gasped as all the air left her lungs. Nothing but a burning in her chest remained. She clutched at his arms, fear surfacing in her eyes. He was still ranting about whatever it was he was angry about as she tried to pull away and stand. He was in her face, and his hands caught at her shoulders as she slid backwards from the bed and landed in a heap on the floor.

"Varick." Her throat grew tighter with each breath. "Help… me."

Hot tears burned a trail down her face as another wave of ice pelted through her veins. He was in front of her, picking her up when Zena's voice filled her ears, filled her mind. Clutching her head, she tried to scream out, tried to breathe.

"Foolish girl! He is mine! And I will have him, all of him!"

Looking wildly around his shoulder, she clutched at her throat, focused on her lungs, forced herself to take a breath. "Varick, she is here."

Varick dropped her to the bed and turned, his stance protective, his roar loud and laced with warning. "Where is she?"

"Reach out and grab him! Say my name! Bring him to me!"

Angelica shook her head. "No!"

Varick turned and reached for her. Scrambling away, she held out her hand and shook her head. "Don't touch me!"

"How can I fight what I cannot see, Angelica?" His deep voice vibrated, bounced around the room with menace. "Tell me where she is!"

She pointed to her head, shoved her hand in front of him, and stepped back as he came forward. "No!"

"You pathetic little idiot! He will tire of you; he will use you for your blood. Take my offer. Grab him now!"

She stared into his eyes, knowing she would never allow Zena the pleasure of taking Varick from her. She dodged his hands and shook her head as he reached for her.

Varick bared his fangs. "Angelica! Tell me who she is!"

Wrapping the sheet around her, she bent to retrieve her clothing. "I can't say her name! But I think she's your grandmother and she isn't trapped in the Underworld." Digging in her pocket, she grasped the pendant Alera had given her and held it up by its golden chain for Varick to look at. "What is this to you?"

He narrowed his eyes. "Drop that pendant now! It belongs to the goddess Grace."

Angelica gasped as pain shot down her spine. "I need to tell you. Your grandmother…"

Varick stepped closer as she closed her eyes and tried to continue. "She came here and wanted me to bring you to her." She fell as another wave of pain hit her in the chest. "She wants me to bring you to the Underworld."

Varick reached for her, and she scrambled backwards. "No. I will go, but not with you. I won't let her have you; I won't let her take you from me."

Angelica pulled herself to her feet and twisted out of Varick's reach as she clutched the pendant to her chest. "Don't touch me."

Time slowed, the hands of destiny and fate carving out two distinct paths before Varick. His future was his to choose. Charon appeared cloaked and unseen at Angelica's right as she slipped the chain around her neck.

Whispering Charon leaned down to Angelica's ear and forced his compelling voice into her mind. *"Say her name. For his sake, say her name!"*

Gasping as time released its hold, Angelica screamed, "Zena!"

• • •

Varick leapt as Angelica vanished, his hands clutching at the mist before him. "No, no!"

He turned as Gyth, Alexander, and Apoc appeared. "No!"

Charon laughed as he made his black-robed presence known. "Yes, Varick, she is gone."

At a snap of his fingers, leather covered Varick's body, and there was a thunk of metal as his weapons followed. Rage burned brightly in his heart and glowed forth from his eyes as he turned to Gyth and roared, "Open a portal to the Underworld now!"

Charon waved his hand and time once again stood still, leaving Varick and himself unaffected. "Gyth cannot open a portal."

Varick spun around, grasped Charon by the throat, and tore the hood away. "Gyth is the king of the Heavens; he can do anything he wants."

Charon laughed. "Gyth cannot open the portals I control. He is unwilling to pay the ferryman. Unwilling to give me what I want."

Snarling, Varick let his sword appear and pressed the burning tip to Charon's throat. "Then what price must I pay?"

Smiling, Charon pulled back from Varick' hold. "What's Angelica's life worth to you?"

"What do you want?" Varick's eyes glowed red as the beast surfaced under his skin. "Why would I believe you? You're just an old misbegotten god from times long past and forgotten."

Hissing with unrestrained anger, Charon moved so fast Varick couldn't track him. Varick gasped when Charon slammed his hands into Varick' chest. "I want…" He paused as Varick punched into the wall and the painting above the fireplace fell, the glass shattering. "I want the set of books that are sisters to the *Book of Creation*. I want the set that are brothers to the book. And I want the *Book of Destruction*."

Varick licked his lip as blood trickled down his chin. "I don't know anything about these books. I want her back. I want her safe."

"A bargain between us, then? For her safe return?" Charon watched as Varick staggered forward. "You will do as I say."

He grunted. "Is that all?"

Charon waved his hand, and Varick stepped back as a small ball of water appeared between them. "Not exactly."

Before Varick could blink, the god had taken the ball and grabbed his wrist. The air bubbled and swooshed as he felt himself sucked into a vortex of purples and blues. And then blackness consumed his sight. All Varick could hear was the deep baritone of the River Styx and the whispers the river fed through him.

Chapter 32

The witch stood limply before Grace in Grace's white-walled chambers. The look on her face was slack, and her blue eyes were quite empty. The goddess gritted her teeth. This was the way Damon liked his followers—mindless and obedient. Obedience she could understand, but this slack-jawed emptiness was repulsive.

Swallowing, Grace spoke. "Damon, it is Grace. We need to talk before Gyth figures out I have one of your witches in my chambers."

The witch swayed, her mouth dropping open. Grace grimaced as the star on the witch's forehead glowed, sizzled, and smoked as the flesh charred.

Damon's voice was warped, yet as seductive as ever as it fell from the witch's tongue. "Grace? What could you, Gyth's little pet, possibly want to talk to me, the stuff of nightmares and perversions, about?"

"Funny you should mention Gyth's name." Grace forced a smile.

"Funny you mentioned him first." He laughed, the sound much like that of a well-fed jackal. "Tell me what is so dire you are willing to cross your master."

She calmly said, "He is not my master."

"Perhaps you want to come to my side of things." Again his laughter echoed around her. "I could show you things that would set your blood on fire, make your heart race with need and want."

"Make my skin crawl?" Grace turned on her heel, knowing he watched her with wariness.

"Better yet, I could make your skin fall from your bones as I enjoy watching you scream in pain."

"In your dreams, Damon, in your dreams." Turning back, she decided to get it over with. "Zena and I had a bargain. I told her about Charon's portals. She has been using them to convince Varick Ta Farg to kill Gyth. I suspect she has taken drastic action in her desire for this Destroyer."

"What do you mean, drastic actions?"

"She has found a portal, and it has been opened." She knew she had him right where she wanted him. "I now see Zena is a weak link. I would like to make new allies, and you're the perfect candidate."

"Why do you need allies?" She heard the change in his voice, heard his anger reaching a volatile level.

"I have grown weary of Gyth's foolishness. The heavenly gods and goddesses need a new king, and I must admit I'm not his equal. That's why I need you. You're as strong if not stronger than he."

She waited as the witch before her gasped and clutched at her hair, tearing wads of the long red strands out of her scalp.

"Brand the humans in your control with my mark, and I will return to you as needed." Damon's menace and vile nature reached her through his voice. "And the next time we speak, I would have you wear black, not that disgusting white you think makes you look virtuous."

Grace gasped as the witch before her exploded into flames and her scream ripped through the white-walled chambers. With shaking hands, she covered her mouth, and tears flowed from her eyes. The witch's death had been quick but painful and brutally disgusting. Charred flesh and burnt blood fell into a heap of broken bones and rancid mush. With a wave of her hand, the mess vanished.

"That bastard better make this worth my while."

•••

Stumbling, Angelica grabbed the chain around her neck and gasped as something hard and cold sliced into her thigh. Reaching down, she ran her fingertips over the jagged rock sticking out of the wall.

Note to self: Stay away from the walls.

The pain was bearable, but it stung. She turned in the blackness as an eerie green light pulsed in the center of the room. It pulled at her senses, almost begging her to come.

A dark shadow twisted and snaked through the room. The dark cloud settled between the green light and Angel. Pulling herself together, Angelica watched wearily as the shadow's black and yellow eyes sparkled with menace.

"Welcome to hell, child. How was the ride here?"

"If this is hell, why is it so damn cold?" She hissed as Zena's shadowy fingers reached out toward the cut on her thigh.

"What is that smell?" Zena cocked her head to one side and sniffed the air. "You're no longer human."

Angelica jerked the chain, shattering the link attached to the collar, and smiled rather smugly. "How very astute of you, vampire queen."

Zena materialized in her human form. "What are you?"

Angelica shrugged, taking two deliberately slow steps toward the dark goddess. "A variety of things, I suppose, but mostly I'm just pissed off that my entire world was turned upside down and inside out."

Curling her fingers, Angelica grinned as she felt a trickle of archaic power flow into her palm. It was an unnatural rush, a thing of beauty and dark menace. She watched Zena carefully; completely aware she had absolutely no idea how to use this newfound power.

"You know, two weeks ago, I lived a fairly normal life." Angelica paused as she ran her fingers over a root shooting down from the ceiling. "If you had approached me then, I would have probably run screaming for the closest exit or died of fright."

"Stupid child! I am a goddess and you should fear me." Crossing her arms, she huffed, "Fall to your knees and worship me, and I might take pity on you even though you did not bring Varick to me!"

Angelica looked up through hooded eyes. "I don't think so."

Screeching, Zena threw her black-clawed hands outward. "Then die!"

A dozen black-hilted daggers appeared suspended in midair before Zena as she laughed. Angelica lurched backwards and dropped to her knees, rolling out of their path as they sang sweet death. One grazed her shoulder, and another embedded itself in her thigh. Gritting her teeth, she jackknifed to her feet, grimaced, and called on her new power.

Holding out her hands, she opened her palms and fell to her knees as a black flame shot outward and nailed Zena in the chest. The goddess bounced off the wall and fell to the floor, hissing and spluttering in outrage. Stumbling, Zena stood as wings of black velvet sliced out of her back and her double set of fangs elongated.

Angelica swallowed hard as Zena leapt upward with a shrill cry, bringing a thousand red eyes popping open. Suspended in the air, black wings flapping silently, Zena threw her head back and laughed as her vampires crawled and slithered out of the darkness, kneeling before their queen.

This is not good.

Before Angelica could react, the chamber door splintered open, and a tall, snake-covered man with an ashen, sunken face entered the room. Zena turned, her laughter abruptly dying in her throat, her already pale features turning green.

"Damon," she whispered as she went to her knees. "Forgive me, my king."

At a wave of his hand, the snakes melted into his body, his thin frame filling out with hard muscle and strength. The deadly arrogance that hung around him shrouded his shoulders with power and refined anger. Angelica tried to stand as he closed the distance between them.

"Who…or just what do we have here?" Damon's deep voice jerked her head up, and her mouth fell slightly open as a menacingly slow smile appeared on his perfect lips.

Angelica was stunned. Without the snakes, Damon was the epitome of dark seduction, evil enshrouded in perfected beauty. Her eyes scoured his body regardless of how much she did not want them to. She took him in, his height, his perfectly honed muscles and tight, black-and-red leather pants. She instantly longed to reach out and run her fingers through his straight, floor-length, jet-black hair.

Almost as instantly as his looks took her off guard, his dark empty eyes sent fear racing through her. It embraced her and shattered her resolve. This was evil incarnate—this was the devil people had nightmares about.

Standing over her, he hissed, his serpent tongue tasting the air around him. "One Race and a touch of something else…"

Turning, he went to the center of the room and jerked the black veil away from the green light. He roared, his head snapping around and his eyes pinning Zena with a hate-and anger-filled stare. He raised both hands and a wave of black miasma filled the chamber, sending her minions sprawling on the floor in agony. Zena's eyes widened and a cry escaped her as she watched them wither and die.

"You are a treacherous little bitch, vampire queen!" Damon roared, his tongue flicking in and out of his mouth. "How dare you make such a futile effort to hide the portal? How dare you bring"—his long finger pointed at Angelica—"the likes of that one to my domain, to my kingdom?"

Zena blinked, and his fingers curled around her throat, lifting her off the floor. "You're a fool to have trusted Grace. She was your undoing. Have you not learned enemies are not to be trusted?"

Fury opened her mouth as his tongue ran up her cheek and tasted her tears. "No! We had a deal. She cannot go back on her word."

His laughter stilled her tongue. "You'll pay for this deceit with blood and bone. Your hallowed cries will pacify my anger, so please do scream loud and long."

Terror ran across Zena's face. Damon released her and laughed as she vanished. "You can run, Zena but you can't hide for long." He raised a dark, arched brow and smiled, his sharp fangs gleaming intently in the green light. "Zena has done me a favor."

He raised one hand and held out his palm casually. "Come, let us talk."

"Not a chance in hell!" she screamed as she sent a nasty ball of black flames hurtling toward him.

Damon staggered back, grunting with the force of the blow, and growled at her. "You're no match for me. I am Damon, lord and king of the Underworld, the most powerful of all demons and their like. I was created a god among gods. You're nothing compared to me!"

Angelica huffed and blew at a stray strand of hair. "Yeah, Mr. I-am-Big-Bad-Scary that's just great and all, but you suck. Are you trying to win the award for scariest demon?"

He gritted his teeth. "Such a nasty little mouth on such a beautiful potential consort."

Angelica stiffened. "Like hell! Consort, my ass."

Back-flipping, she launched herself up the side of the wall and somersaulted over his head, placing a well-aimed kick to the back of his head. She landed squarely on her feet in a perfect jiu-jitsu pose and grinned lopsidedly as Damon turned with a hiss.

"What's the matter, snake-man from hell, little girl go and kick you in the head?"

Unhurriedly he stalked around her. "I can smell Destroyer on you, in you. Do you know who your father was?"

Angelica watched him carefully, turning as he walked around her. Her fists were up, like a pro-boxer ready for the big fight.

Damon held out his hand, snakes slithering from his fingertips. They edged toward her, striking at her ankles. Willing the power back to her hands, she blasted them one at a time. They disintegrated instantly, leaving a poisonous odor behind.

"Feverand Dark's daughter." Damon threw his head back and sniffed the air. "You're a Destroyer. One of Gyth's little toys."

Angelica stepped back as he came toward. "Jealous?"

He held his hand out again. "Take my hand little Destroyer. I can make your stay here pleasing or full of pain. Your choice."

Searching the dark cavern, she tried to find an escape route. "You know, snakes give me the creeps. I think I would rather cozy up to a werewolf than touch the likes of you."

Ripping his cloak from his shoulders, he released his serpents. Dozens of them came pouring out of his mouth as Angelica shrieked and turned to run with her tail neatly tucked between her legs. Shooting forward, they took her to the ground in a spread eagle position, wrapping tightly around her wrists and ankles. A small one covered her mouth and hissed in her ear.

She tried to kick, but the serpents tightened their hold, shutting off the blood supply to her feet. Damon chuckled as he crawled up her arm and stared into her eyes. His hair draped over her like death's veil, and he slowly pushed the serpent off her mouth.

"I remember your father. He was fearless, such a fighting machine. Then he met your mother. He became weak and afraid." Angelica bucked hard under him. "Varick Ta Farg will do the same but I'm not going to kill you. I'm going to convert you. I'll watch him fall apart as he loses you as your father did when I had your mother slaughtered."

Lifting her chin, she spat in his face. "Leave my parents out of this, you fatherless, motherless, second-rate Satan!"

Damon roared, his fangs scraping her cheek as he grabbed her hair and jerked her toward his chest. She shivered as his cold skin contacted hers. Running his fingers down her shoulders, he slipped off the sheet that was tied there and laughed.

"Varick will kick your ass!"

Cold, bitter hatred filtered out of his eyes. "This is my domain. Mine! He'll not save you from me. Destroyer or not, you will suffer all that I am in every possible way. Your suffering will be so long and loud Gyth will hear it in the Heavens."

His fingers trailed down her stomach and farther down to her thigh. She screamed as his black-clawed hand wrapped around the dagger and unmercifully jerked it out. He brought it to his lips and watched with pleasure as she arched her back and tried to break free of his serpents.

Licking the blade, he lifted her into his arms and stood her on her feet, bringing her flush with his body. She cursed him as he cupped her bottom and kissed her temple. She blocked out his whispers of possible outcomes as she tried to paint a vivid picture of Varick in her mind. His fingers dug into her flesh, and she felt a trickle of blood flow down the back of her leg.

"Blood of Amay, seed of a Destroyer, and mate to Varick." Damon released her and stepped back with a slow laugh. "Well, it seems I have in my possession a unique little pawn."

Angelica forced herself not to think about what he was going to do to her. So, yeah, saying Zena's name had been the stupidest idea she had ever had. Her powers could have come ages ago, but no— they had to wait until she would have no time to learn to use them.

She gasped as the serpents flipped her around, and she dropped like a wet cloth to the floor on her face. Her bare butt must have caught Damon's attention because she felt his bony hand swat her. The place burned and hatred welled in her heart.

"I'm going to enjoy converting you, little Destroyer. I promise by the time I am done with you, you will have forgotten all about Varick." His laughter sickened her as the serpents dragged her across the floor to the broken door. She grabbed the doorframe and twisted around to throw a venomous look at Damon.

She caught her breath as he bent down and lifted one of the vampire carcasses from the floor and ripped its head from its body. Black blood spurted across his chest and splattered across his cheek. His tongue darted out and licked at the blood. Her stomach flipped as he turned and grinned, sinking his fangs into the vampire's skull. The crunch of bone thundered in her ears as she let go of the doorframe.

As she was dragged down a long, winding hallway of gravel and mud, she felt the pendant around her neck grow warm, then hot. Her eyes flashed. Alera had told her she would know when and how to use the blasted thing. Well, no time like the present, right?

But there was one small problem. How was she going to get her hands free?

Chapter 33

Three long strides were all it took before Varick's control snapped. He turned on his heel in the stark, white walled hallway he and Charon had just entered. He roared with full intent to do bodily harm to the bones under the black and silver robe.

Charon grunted, his scythe stopping Varick in his tracks. "Patience is a virtue of the highest and most honorable order. I strongly suggest you put it to use before you find your ass on the floor."

Undaunted by his words, Varick insisted. "Every second she remains in the Underworld is a second that she could die there!"

"Time is on our side at the moment—time has always been with you." Charon nodded toward four tall, black doors, each adorned with gold symbols. "You must choose wisely, for your destiny has grown weary of waiting."

Twenty feet tall and looming like perpetual dead-ends, the doors stared back at Varick as he studied the symbols on each one. The first door was covered in stars and planets, vast universes reaching out across space. A dragon danced among the stars, its wings touching two of the planets, which oddly enough resembled Earth and Venus.

The second displayed eight symbols inside the pattern of infinity, simple yet strong in their meaning. The equal sign was at the top, a times sign at the bottom. A right-facing crescent moon was on the left of the top loop, a left-facing one on the right. On the left side of the bottom loop was a full moon, on the right a sun. The last two signs, a plus and a minus, were embedded between each of the other symbols.

The third door had one symbol, one he had been well acquainted with since his birth. He looked down at his bare ankle at one of his birthmarks; a purple circle with a crescent moon attached to each side. Inside the circle were six dots. His mother had often told him it was the mark of his father's race, whatever the hell that meant.

He looked up. After all these decades, why was he being confronted with his father's mark? Why now? And why was it important, anyway? But it was important; this he knew beyond reason, felt it in his bones.

He didn't have a clue who his father was or why he had not been around when Varick had been growing up in a camp of wingless dragon assassins. He only had his mother's answers—answers she had all too often kept vague and misleading. He had assumed she did not speak of him because he was human and she was vampire and things had not worked out. Once, as a small child, he had even asked her if she had fed from him, and if he had died.

Had his mother loved his father? Had he loved her?

Love? Was there indeed such a thing? Thoughts of Angelica slid into his heart, her smiling face looking up into his. Even now, he longed for the fire in her eyes, the soft touch of her fingertips, and the gentle havoc her voice created within his cold heart. He suddenly knew he did not want to exist without her. Not even death would keep him from her, not now, not ever. Was this how love felt?

A growl erupted from his throat as he looked at the last door. It was covered with demons, all crawling out of the bowels of all nine hells in the Underworld. The clouds above them had opened; the sun's light blocked by a shield that a one-eyed demon carried. This was destruction; the future with hell overrunning humanity and the Heavens losing control.

For the first time in his life as a Destroyer, he turned away from the demons of the Underworld and looked elsewhere for answers, for purpose. Reaching forward, he turned the doorknob on the third door and paused as he heard a soft sigh escape Charon's throat.

The door pulled open, the knob slipping out of his grasp. A vortex of purple and blue swamped his senses. The doorway was a portal. As an assassin, he had traveled through vortexes more often than he could remember; the faces of his assassinations all blurred together, their names long ago forgotten.

"Step forward, Varick Ta Farg. Your destiny awaits on the other side."

Varick stepped through and sucked in a harsh breath as he peered down a steep, rocky mountainside, barren of life. The sky above was ominous, and dark clouds rumbled as lighting flashed in a blaze of glory. The four winds howled furiously as he heard the unique pop and crackle of the vortex behind him closing.

This was the mountain from his dream. Glancing at the horizon, he turned and stared at Charon. In the dream he had been alone and uncaring. Somehow, for reasons he couldn't pinpoint, this day did not seem like a good day to die.

But it was not fear that made him think this.

Charon nodded, the black hood bobbing up and down slowly. "As with all awakenings, one must be reborn. Don't think of it as death. For you, death has come in degrees, each one bringing you a step closer to your true destiny." He pointed at the horizon. "Prepare yourself, this is going to hurt."

Snarling, Varick narrowed his eyes as Charon vanished into thin air. The hair on the back of his neck tingled as the sun began to rise. He had an achingly bad feeling things were going to go from bad to worse in the next couple of seconds. The teardrop under his ear began to burn, the mark smoking with warning.

Facing the horizon, he held out his arms and closed his eyes as a single ray of light descended, streaking downward relentlessly. His back arched, his fangs cutting into his bottom lip. Blistering heat enveloped him, his flesh melting and dripping from his bones. And yet he refused to scream; he refused to fall.

His wings unfurled from the muscles on his back, their black feathers flaming and ashes blowing into the winds. Bleached-white bones laced with streaks of titanium and steel stood embraced by light and held together by charred and useless tendons. Varick's soul glittered and hummed in the skeleton's chest.

The clouds parted, the rocky mountainside swamped with harsh bright light. A lone figure, white robes flowing around his feet, appeared at the base of the mountain and began his trek upward. Slowly, he made his way to Varick, humming as he went. As he grew closer, his features softened and his shoulders relaxed.

With a quick wave of his hand, Varick's wing bones broke and fell to the ground. A black and silver robe appeared, draping over Varick's shoulders, and shimmered as it flowed to his feet. The male stepped back and started to hum again.

Varick's soul hummed in rhythm, his bones swaying with the sound.

Placing his hand on the skull before him, the figure sang out, loud and long. Electricity filled the sky, bounced around the rocks, and arched from one mountaintop to the next. Life flowed back into the skeleton, knowledge and power forming inside Varick's soul. Blood veins raced anew as tendons and muscles rippled across bone. New flesh grew, merging and pulling his features together. His hair grew longer and whiter than before. A thick strand of red formed at his temple, running down to his waist, braiding itself as it grew.

Placing his other hand over Varick's chest, the figure leaned in close and blew new breath into his body as he sent an electrical surge into his heart. "I am Isten, and I welcome you to the Isle of the Blessed and the Condemned."

He stepped back and waited.

Varick's mind switched back on, the floodgates to his memories, his thoughts, and his feelings ripping open and rushing through his system, eradicating any hope of remaining calm. Grabbing his head, he screamed as he took his first ragged breath. His heart thundered as he staggered and fell to one knee.

His back arched as electrical sparks popped and sparked, arching along his skin. His muscles jerked and twitched with each spark. Lighting flashed; the form of a great dragon appeared as dark clouds dampened the sky, its shadow creeping along the ground circling Isten.

Looking up, Isten smiled. "Stand, Varick."

He groaned, the weight of his pain shaking his legs as he clutched his chest. Through his blurred vision, he focused on the barely contained, commanding voice.

"The choice has been made. Hold out your hands, palms up, and accept your destiny. As ordained at the moment of your birth, you have chosen as it was meant to be."

Desperately trying to clear his head, Varick looked up and watched the dragon, Terror Sky, gracefully land at Isten's side. Terror Sky arched his back and transformed into a man. Varick grunted; he still looked the same as he had all those years ago. He wore the same armor, the same sword hanging at his side, and the same red braid hanging from his temple.

Terror Sky spoke. "Accept your destiny, boy!"

"No," Varick's voice gritted out, the sound of gravel on metal. "To hell with your destiny! I must save her."

Stepping forward, Terror Sky grinned menacingly and willed Varick's hands upward. "She can save herself. That one doesn't need a hero."

Isten rolled his eyes and smirked. "What was I thinking when I granted all life the right to be stubborn?"

"Free will was indeed one of your less than memorable decisions. Now, if I had been in your oversized shoes, I would have granted them the inability to argue with me."

Isten laughed. "Yes, well, most life would be most thankful you were not around at the time of Creation."

Varick wanted to scream. What the hell was going on?

"What about my free will?" Looking down at his hands, he tried to move them and found he could not break free of Terror Sky's hold.

The two males before him continued their conversation as his anger grew. "Excuse me? Destroyer speaking! What the hell about my free will? Don't I get a say in whatever the hell you're doing to me?"

Both gods cast him a disapproving look.

Isten spoke. "You're no longer a Destroyer. As a matter of fact, you never were meant to be a Destroyer. And before you accidentally stumble upon another small fact, I'll inform you now. You're a god." Isten took a deep breath. "You are descended from me, the father of this world. Your DNA had been rewritten, but now you are as you were meant to be."

Placing his hands over Varick' palms, he chuckled. "And by the way, it was free will that led you here."

When their palms made contact, Varick felt time and space rip through his very being, felt his blood boiling inside his veins and his bones bending under the onslaught of power. His body and soul warped and twisted in pain so excruciating he forgot how to use his vocal cords. He wanted to scream, and he wanted to cry.

Death by degrees had been too vague a term, and he was forced to silently curse Charon.

Casually, Terror Sky walked around Varick as Isten released his palms. Terror Sky turned to Isten. "Is all the pain necessary?"

Isten shrugged nonchalantly. "Pain always comes with pleasure, and it is the balance of all things. Yin and yang. Tit for tat." He sat on a nearby boulder and watched Varick writhe. "And in Varick's own words, pain is an ally. It assists one in bringing the evidence of life into focus."

Terror Sky nodded, running his fingers down the red braid at his temple. "Makes one appreciate the simple pleasures."

Isten laughed. "Might want to stand clear—he is about to go postman on us."

"Postal," Terror Sky corrected as he stepped back and leaned on the boulder beside Isten. "He is about to go postal on us."

"I can never get that one right."

Varick slung his arms outward, his muscles bulging as sparks arched over his back. His golden eyes glowed intensely as his voice returned, and a scream ripped from his throat and echoed around the mountain. Straining, he stepped back, refusing to go to his knees.

"What. Have. You. Done. To me?" His voice was hard.

Terror Sky answered slowly, "Today you have been reborn from your ashes. The Destroyer you once were no longer exists, and in his stead now stands a god."

"I thought I had already told him that." He nudged Terror Sky's shoulder. "You sure this one is as intelligent as you thought?"

"I don't feel like a god," Varick roared as thunder bounced around inside his skull and needles scoured his flesh. "I don't want to be a god!"

Isten nodded. "It does take some getting used to."

Varick ripped the robe from his chest and cursed as the mark on his ankle appeared in the flesh just below his six pack. The circle was around his navel and the six dots appeared to the left of it. Colors seeped in, the moon glowing white as the crescent turned as red as blood. Clouds and lightning formed behind it, Varick feeling it as if an unseen tattoo gun were working at his flesh.

"That is the mark of my legacy, my descendants. It only appears on those of my descendants who are worthy enough to be a god or goddess of Creation. You have been found worthy."

"What the hell is that supposed to mean?" Varick staggered, uncontrolled power racing through his body. "I am not worthy of this. I was an assassin. I killed without mercy, without pause. I wallowed in my own ignorance and called it bliss."

"And what regret lies in your heart? What sorrow has these actions caused?" Isten shook his head. "One cannot truly know justice or fairness unless they have experienced the exact opposite. One cannot find the path to retribution unless one meets their regret and accepts it for what it is."

"Like it or not, you are a god now. So stop sniveling and go to it." Terror Sky grunted. "Don't make me regret saving your sorry ass time after time."

"Screw you!"

Terror Sky turned to Isten with a smug smile. "Told you he would be a handful."

Isten nodded in agreement. "True this."

"This is true," Terror Sky corrected. "When are you ever going to figure out these sayings?"

"When pork chops fly." Isten chuckled as Terror Sky slapped himself in the forehead. "Or maybe when toads stop bumping their backsides on the ground when they hop."

Grumbling, Terror Sky replied, "It's when pigs fly and frogs bumping their asses on the ground when they jump."

Varick stepped back. They were cracked. Both the gods were nut jobs! And he thought he had problems.

"Terror Sky and I have been waiting for your arrival for many, many centuries. And since I cannot leave this Isle, I had Terror Sky watch over you since your birth."

"You're out of your mind." Varick took another step back. "Both of you."

"Maybe." Isten eyed Varick. "There are many things you must do. Many lives hang on the edge, lives you must save."

"How do I get to the Underworld?"

"You're a god now—figure it out." Isten growled low. "I did not waste my time creating the perfect bloodline for you to be ignorant."

Terror Sky laughed. "You contain the power in your blood, Varick. All you have to do is find a way to manifest it."

Shaking his head, Varick slowly sat down on a small boulder. "None of this makes sense. How can I have anything to do with the powers that be?"

"Fate. Destiny. Whatever you want to call it." Isten grinned. "I planned your birth. You are blood of my blood."

"Who is my father?" The question hung in the silence that followed.

"Is that not obvious? Who has constantly been a thorn in your backside since he turned you into a Destroyer?" Terror Sky asked. "Who has taken great pains so you would and could deny Zena's call?"

"No." Varick stood and willed every ounce of power he had to dematerialize. "That miserable leech can't be my father!"

Chapter 34

Varick Ta Farg roared to the Heavens as he materialized inside the hall at Tortured Souls. Sparks of energy jumped from his back and sizzled through the air as he turned to the empty table and splintered it with his mind. He heard the Destroyers coming, heard their heartbeats getting closer as he unleashed his power and the entire building rumbled. The sound grew louder, and the ceiling groaned, threatening to come down on his head as he morphed into dragon.

Varick raged down the hall as his dragon breathed flames and crashed its head through the walls. Several of the Destroyers were thrown into walls and through doors as he rampaged through the corridor.

Gyth appeared to his left, and the words fell from his lips like a signature on a death warrant. "No! What have they done to you?"

Forcing the dragon back, Varick transformed into man. He flung himself at Gyth's throat as rage filled his soul. Noticing that Gyth allowed him to attack only added to his anger. Gyth's head snapped backwards as Varick's fist slammed into his chin.

The hall filled with Destroyers. Apoc pounced and grabbed Varick' arms trying to pull him away from Gyth. Eli flung himself across Varick's chest. Varick screamed and flung his brothers to the floor as he grabbed Gyth's neck. Eli cursed as he slid into a chair and it splintered under his weight.

"I will kill you! Let me save her!"

Gyth raised his hand to the approaching Destroyers, stopping them in their tracks, and stared deep into his son's eyes. Varick fell forward as tears ran down his cheeks. Unable to control his own limbs, he melted into Gyth's arms.

"I love her…I love her…" Varick's words echoed around his mind. His beast roared. He had never loved anyone except his mother. Every fiber of his being knew she had become his entire world. Without her, he didn't want to continue, didn't want to walk the path before him.

"I know, my son. I know."

From out of the corner of his eye, Varick saw Charon appear. Black robes swirled around his feet as he grabbed his arms and pulled him to a standing position a few feet away from Gyth. Varick winced at the strength pouring from his fingertips and had the uncanny feeling the devil was latching onto his soul.

"There's another way," Charon stated. "There is another way to get to the Underworld if you don't want to use my portals."

"Varick, you must not use that power," Gyth whispered intensely. "Damon will know you are coming, and I cannot protect you from him in his domain."

"What power? You've been to the Underworld so why can't you go now?" Varick turned and faced Charon. "What power do I have?"

Apoc stepped forward to glare at Gyth. "What difference does it make? Damon will know the second any of us set foot in the Underworld, anyway."

Charon laid his hand on Varick's shoulder, his voice flowing through his mind. *The power of Isten flows through your veins. The universe is his domain and now it's yours as well.*

Gyth spoke, calmly. "I order you to stand down, Varick. Going to the Underworld is too much of a risk. Damon is more powerful than you."

Varick looked at Gyth over his shoulder. "Regardless of your orders or this two thousand year old war you have with Damon, I will save her."

Charon stepped back and bowled slightly to Gyth. "This war wasn't part of the greater plan."

Gyth closed his eyes as he spoke. "Damon broke the laws of the Heavens. I did what I had to do." His eyes opened, a soft white glow illuminating Gyth's face. "If you fail to return to this realm, all will be lost. The future of this world depends on all of you.'

Alexander and Apoc stepped beside Varick. "Let's do this. If she means enough to you that you'll defy Gyth and face Damon, we're going to help."

Charon stepped in front of Varick and placed his hand on his shoulder. "Manifest the power in your veins; urge it to your thoughts. Create a path from this realm to the Underworld."

Concentrating on Charon's words, Varick let the power in him collect together, and centered his every thought on the Underworld. Once the Underworld was a clear image in his mind, he imagined a road.

"When you see the path, focus the power and let it wrap around you." Charon's voice was a whisper in his ear. "Let it take you where you want to go."

Varick's body tingled. Looking at his hands, he saw the same shimmer as he had seen on Gyth a thousand times before. He felt the power; saw his destination and the path clearly in his mind. Charon nodded and vanished in a wisp of smoke.

The Destroyers gathered around him. He held his hands out. Apoc, Alexander, and Kreach grabbed his hands. In the second before the group disappeared, Eli stepped forward and latched his mighty hand onto Varick's arm.

Deep within the bowels of hell, the warp opened and the five warriors stepped through. Each looked to the other without uttering a word and drew out their weapons as the sound of pounding feet—or was it paws—echoed in the halls. Battle ready, hearts pounding, and fangs flashing, they stepped forward to face the legions of hell that came barreling down the black maze with red eyes blazing.

Never before had such an undeniable strength set foot in hell. The walls shuddered in their presence as they formed a single line of defense. Eager smiles and deadly intentions filled the hall as the enemy screeched their arrival.

"Prepare yourselves, my brothers, for hell is coming to devour us!" Apoc scoffed.

"Only if we don't devour it first!" Varick screamed as he leapt forward with blades dancing through the foul-smelling air.

• • •

Damon snapped his fingers, and Angelica's unconscious body appeared spread out on his massive bed. As he slithered closer, she slowly opened her eyes, somewhat conscious of her predicament. Her eyes widened in fear as the serpent at her shoulder latched onto her wrist and entwined itself up her arm. Her body jerked as the serpent sucked hard on her wrist.

Damon's head fell backwards as a moan escaped his lips. "Such sweet blood."

Frightened, devastated that her whole life had been reduced to crumbling ashes, Angelica leapt from the bed like a lioness defending her cubs. It had happened—it was not a dream or some vivid daytime nightmare her subconscious had conjured up.

She was in hell. And she was going to die, right here, right now.

There was no frigging way she was about to let that happen. At least she hoped not. She had so much going for her, truly she did. She was the descendent of a goddess and she had finally met a guy that made her heart go pitter-pat.

Oh, for the love of God, she had just found the guy she had fallen hopelessly in love with, and there was not a chance in hell she was going to let him slip through her fingers. She wanted her life with him, and she'd fight the devil himself to keep him.

Prying the snake from her wrist, she turned to the demon god before her and tried not to vomit. Saying a quick prayer to whatever god might be listening, she braced her feet and flung the serpent across the dimly lit room.

"Little Destroyer, the more you fight, the better I like it," Damon urged. "Come on; show me that power that lurks under your skin."

A cloaked figure appeared behind Damon, a large scythe in his hand. "For a small price, I will aid you, Angelica Dark."

Damon advanced, and she scurried across the bed, staying out his arm's reach. The figure leaned against the dark wall and watched silently as she edged around the bed.

"What price?"

Damon let several of his serpents slither out of his fingertips. "What do you speak of? There is no price except your blood!"

Apparently Damon either couldn't hear the other guy or see him. What's the odds of that? Who really cared? Now was not the time to kick a gift horse in the mouth.

"I want your mother's diary! Give it to me of your own free will, and I shall tell you how to pull out your powers."

"That's it?" Angelica asked as she jumped back, avoiding the serpents. "And if I refuse?"

Damon laughed. "You will not refuse!"

"I will take my leave, and you can fend for yourself, hoping you figure out how to use those newfound powers. And we can hope that, for Varick's sake, you're still alive when he makes it here."

With a deep breath, she stood still. "Okay, it's yours." What other option did she have?

Damon grinned, his tongue flickering out into the air. "Come to me."

"Close your eyes, listen to your soul. Let your blood flow through your veins and harness the energy inside. Once you harness it, let your blood carry it to your fingertips."

As Damon slithered closer, Angelica closed her eyes. Digging deep within herself, she found the energy and channeled it, and quietly thanked the mysterious robed being.

Damon stood before her, his tongue slithering out of his mouth inches away from her throat. He watched her eyes flicker slowly open. He stared mutely, awed by what he saw.

She knew what Damon was seeing. She could feel power swirling in her eyes as she stepped forward and grabbed his serpent tongue with a small grin on her face.

"Let the blood carry the power to your fingertips and release it!"

Blue-white lightning shot out of her hands and across Damon's chest, sending him sprawling backwards. His roar of anger bounced around the room as Angelica raced toward what she hoped was a door. Her heart pounded in her ears as she pushed it open and came to a skidding halt. Outside the door, dozens of demonic creatures lay broken and crushed.

Dozens more poured into the tunnel as she turned and ran down the path, which was littered with bodies. She heard Damon as she ran harder. His roar split through her skull as she rounded a corner and ran face first into a hairy creature.

Stumbling backwards and falling hard onto her backside, she screamed as a werewolf reared back on its hind legs and howled. Without thought, she raised her hands and sent the blue lightning at the creature. It groaned, stumbled, and fell to the side as she scrambled back to her feet and peered over her shoulder. Damon's eyes were glowing red as he raised his arms and dozens of serpents came out of his fingertips.

• • •

Zena crept along the walls as the fighting continued until she caught side of Varick. She watched him hack and dice his way through the hordes of minions hell-bent on finding Angelica. Her heart raced, and then suddenly it stopped. This was her grandchild.

Looking back, she realized the girl was just a corner away facing Damon's wrath. She turned back around, her heart lodged in her throat. Varick and Angelica loved each other. He had come to save her, and she was fighting to get back to him. How odd these feelings were.

A ruby-red tear shimmered in her eye as Varick came completely in view. He was so much like his mother, so very much. And he loved Angelica. A pang of guilt ripped through her soul as she turned and misted down the corridor, taking the corner where she knew Angelica was.

"Damon." She growled the name as his serpents brought Angelica to him. "Let her go!"

He laughed. "Go back to your caves, vampire queen, and wait your turn!"

"Let her go!" Zena misted and reappeared behind him before he had time to calculate her move.

Manifesting two daggers, she stabbed him in the back of the head. He fell to one knee, his serpents releasing Angelica and slithering back to their master's fingertips.

"Run!" she screamed at Angelica as she grabbed the handles again. "Varick is just around the corner!"

Angelica jumped to her feet and spun around on her heel. Racing down the corridor, she pulled the pendant from her neck and rubbed the thing so hard she felt the skin pulling from her thumb. As she rounded the corner, Varick swung his blades, slicing through a vampire, and skidded to a halt in front of her.

"Angelica." He breathed her name, relief washing over his face.

"Don't stop now." Angelica grabbed his arm and pulled. "Mr. Ugly-as-Sin is coming right behind me!"

The pendant glowed and grew hot in her hand as a vortex of power appeared behind the Destroyers. Gripping their swords and knives, the Destroyers prepared themselves as Damon came barreling around the corner, a horde of minions on his heels. Pulling hard on Varick's arm, Angelica turned to the vortex and prayed with everything she had.

"Come on!" she screamed as the Destroyers faced the horde. "Go through the purple hole thing!"

"Need a hand?" Terror Sky asked as he stepped from the vortex. "Or shall I leave you to your own devices?"

Varick stepped back, shoved Angelica through the portal, and shouldered Kreach toward its opening. "Not today, Kreach. Not today."

With some disgruntled curses, the Destroyers entered the portal and reappeared in Tortured Souls. Terror Sky calmly took the pendant from Angelica's hand and laughed.

"A well-placed helping hand," he muttered as he vanished.

Chapter 35

Gyth glared at Charon and Terror Sky from the throne in the Heavens. "As long as I sit on this throne, you will do as I command."

Grace and Amay sat to the left of the throne in cathedral chairs denoting their positions in the Heavens. They were Gyth's advisors. Mostly, anyway.

"It will be done as the *Book of Creation* commands it to be," Charon stated with mild irritation. "The next time you or one of your council interferes, your precious throne will crumble at your feet. The laws are not to be broken."

Grace swallowed hard as Charon's eyes sent a blaze of goose bumps along her spine. Turning her attention to Gyth, she hoped the god had a backbone and stood up to the creepy, black-robed male. Really, who did he think he was?

It did not have anything to do with the fact she was afraid—very afraid—of the male standing before Gyth as if he could care less about pissing him off.

"Interferes? With what, Charon? The words of a dead god? The laws of a dead legacy?" Gyth leaned forward. "You may be the hands of Isten but he no longer rules this universe."

Charon's eyes glowed from under his hood. "The vampire god's future has been realigned."

Gyth stood, his white hair streaking with red as he spoke. "Varick is mine. His future is what I make of it."

Charon laughed, dead leaves appearing and swirling around his robes. "His future is already set in stone, and try as you might, what will be, will be!"

Terror Sky stepped forward, his eyes flashing. "Jaiden's books, if they're not returned to the Isle..." He paused as he looked at Grace. "They will be the Heavens' downfall."

"His books are missing and have been since he was slaughtered." Gyth roared as he took a step down from the throne. "Go back to your Isle and protect the only remaining book, Charon. That is your duty."

Grace's heart stopped in its tracks. No one was taking her books. She stood, her skin feeling tight around her bones. "My lord?"

"What?" Gyth asked without taking his eyes from Charon.

"You are our king. What right do these"—she wrinkled her nose as she looked at Charon and Terror Sky—"peasants have to demand anything?"

Charon's dead voice filtered around the throne room, the misery of death in its wake. "So many secrets in the Heavens. So many hands in the proverbial pot of gold."

Amay and Grace shifted, looking at each other hesitantly. If Gyth found out what they had conspired, they would be cast out of the Heavens for treason. Or worse. It could always be worse where Gyth was concerned.

Grinning, Gyth replied. "They have no right. You, Charon, are from times long past, and your presence is no longer required in the Heavens."

Laughter rang out as Terror Sky spoke. "There sits upon the throne a father blinded by his heart. He who doesn't see his enemy is forsaken. Doom shall befall the throne, and new gods will arise." An eerie feeling slid up Grace's spine as Terror Sky paused. "Past acquaintances will not be forgotten, and neither will the need for revenge."

Reaching upward, Gyth called the godbolts and flung them at Charon and Terror Sky. Grace watched intently as Charon vanished leaving a trail of smoke in his wake. Terror Sky jumped back, the bolts splintering the floor.

"Make no mistakes from this moment on, Gyth. Charon and I may be from times past but you'll do well to remember who your enemies are and who they aren't." Terror sky's voice echoed around the room as he shimmered and vanished. "Don't start another war that you won't win because I won't assist you again."

Terror Sky was not going to be a problem, but Charon was another matter. There was a presence that loomed around him like a dark shadow. Grace knew the presence. She recognized the gloom filled essence that weaved its way throughout time and space. It was the same presence that loomed around the books. Her books.

A small grin formed on her lips as Gyth left the throne room. No matter. The Heavens were his to rule and would be until he saw fit to give the throne to another. Or lost it. And he most certainly had no intention of doing that, at least not that he was aware of. All Grace had to do was bide her time and with the help of Jaiden's books, his downfall would come soon enough.

• • •

"I don't give a hairy rat's ass if he is busy! You open this damn door or I will break it down!"

A moment went by and the Destroyer standing outside the door stuck his head in and glanced at Varick. "She's insisting that she see you right now."

Varick didn't have a chance to answer as the door swung open and Angelica pushed the guard out of her way. The fierce look on her face was pointed straight at Varick's head.

"Don't you dare leave me like that again! The next time I awake to find you gone, your head will roll!"

Varick grinned. "Do you not wish to speak to your brother?"

"Don't you dare try to change the subject." She turned to Eli and smiled. "I've missed you, but we can catch up later."

Eli chuckled as she grabbed Varick's hand and pulled him to the door. He went obediently to the hallway pulling her into his arms as she turned to face him. A soft smile filled her face as he bent to kiss her.

"Mine!"

"I have questions and I want answers!"

"I want you, and I mean to have you after we are finished with our meeting," he whispered as he ran his fingers up her back.

"Questions first, then answers, and then you can have me," she answered as she slid her tongue across his lips. "And the meeting can wait. It's not like you don't have all the time in the world."

"*Et ou ghin*," he returned.

"What is that language? What did you say?"

Varick sucked on her lip and bit down on her tongue before releasing her from his grasp. "It's my mother's language. And I said, 'As you wish.'"

"Get a room!" Apoc was standing in the doorway. He winked at Angelica, whistled, and batted his eyelashes at Varick. "We can reschedule the meeting, loverboy. Payne's not here anyway."

Angelica smiled sweetly at Apoc. With her right foot, she shut the door in his face. She chuckled as Apoc's muffled curse.

"It's the strangest thing but…"

"Something's bothering you."

Varick tilted her head back. She could feel him searching her face.

She ran her fingertips across his shoulders. "I keep getting this weird feeling in the pit of my stomach. I don't think Damon is going to leave well enough alone."

Varick grabbed her waist, and they shimmered. She held to him tightly shutting her eyes. Seconds later, they reappeared in his bedroom.

"This isn't over, is it?" she asked.

"No." Varick nuzzled her neck. "The fight with Damon is of Gyth's making. Gyth condemned him to the Underworld two millenniums ago. Damon retaliates by using witches, vampires, and werewolves to kill members of the One Race and humans."

Angelica rubbed her temples. "Why did he condemn him?"

"For breaking the laws of the Heavens." Varick shrugged. "The past is the past. The reasons don't really matter. The important thing is that we protect all the innocent lives that Damon threatens."

She nodded. "And I'm a Destroyer now? Like Eli?"

Varick's jaw flexed, his eyes growing dark. "Yes. But I won't have you fighting."

Angelica smiled and pulled his lips to hers. She ran her tongue over his lips and reached for his pants. He growled as her hand slipped behind his zipper, grasping his erection.

"Tell me you won't fight. Promise me."

Angelica purred. "I want to taste you. I want to suck on your skin. I want to sink my teeth into you. I want to make slow, lasting love to the vampire inside you, and then I want the god in you to take me places my body has never been."

He stepped back, his eyes swirling with the golden fire she loved. "Promise me, Angelica. Swear you won't put yourself in harm's way."

She sighed. "Do you really expect me to sit around and do nothing knowing I can help people, knowing I have this power inside of me?"

He stood there, silent for a minute. His shoulders relaxed and he brought her back into his arms. His head went to her neck, his lips hovering over her pulse. "Then promise me you'll always be careful. Never let your guard down."

Smiling, she nodded. "Promise."

"If you do, I might never forgive you." His fangs grazed her neck. "I'll always protect you no matter what. I'm a god, whether I wanted it or not. I am what I am. Easy as that."

Angelica wrapped her arms around his neck. "I don't care if you're a god. I don't care if you're a vampire or a Destroyer. I wouldn't care if you were human or an ogre. I love you, Varick." She pointed to his heart. "I love what's right here."

She gasped as he shimmered and they reappeared on his bed, her clothes vanishing. His blinding smile made her heart melt.

When he spoke, his voice twisted, gravel turning into silk. "Gyth said my beast was a blessing but he isn't. He is a part of me that I was unwilling to accept. You, Angelica Dark, you are the blessing and because of you, I welcome the part of me that is a beast."

Angelica listened to the voice that could make angels weep, demons fall to their knees, and diamonds fall from the clouds of heaven. She watched as her mate with his eyes glowing white, and fangs flashing, roared his love for her as he embraced the power of the gods and the fire within his soul.

A Sneak Peek from Crimson Romance

(From *The Other Side of Heaven: Book 1 in the Italian Time Travel Series* by Morgan O'Neill)

A.D. 951, Castle Garda, Italy

Willa of Tuscany trembled before the witch-basin awaiting the sign she feared would never come. "I beseech you," she chanted, "I beseech you, I beseech you."

She clutched dirt in her hand, the bits of earth warm and elemental to her touch. Sprinkling it over the water in the basin, she took a breath and blew across the surface. A tongue of blue flame burst forth, showering the air with silver stars.

"Send who is needed!" She lifted her gaze skyward. "Answer me!"

A distant thunder rumbled beneath the night sky and the stars whispered, *He is found.*

Clouds parted and the moon smiled, *He is found, he is found.*

Willa stared down at the water, now quieted and mirror-smooth, and pondered the virile image of a man. Emerald light filled his eyes, his hair spun gold, glittering. And his face! Perfect as a statue of old, a chiseled wonder: the brow noble, the chin square, his smile wide and sensuous.

Here was the one to father her child, the daughter who would carry on the family legacy, the otherworldly gifts.

She shook herself free, to action, and cried out, "Come to me!"

As she plunged her fingers in, breaking the water's surface, the basin pitched and roiled. Willa staggered and fought to keep her balance, the ground quaking with dark purpose. She felt demon-cold ice arise and she screamed, battling pain and terror, reaching, grasping, and holding on. Green and gold whirled and exploded in a shower of crystals, yet she knew she had touched him, a bare instant of contact.

It was enough.

Breathing hard, Willa nursed a hand bleeding and numb, and then looked into the witch-basin once more. The vision had vanished; only shards of ice remained.

Sharp and cold as her heart.